The Community

by

Daniel Austin

Huntsville, Alabama

This is a work of fiction. All of the characters, organizations, and events portrayed in this novel are either products of the author's imagination or are used fictitiously.

THE COMMUNITY

ISBN-13: 978-1-956834-06-2

Published by Up Past Dawn. Find us at:
https://www.facebook.com/DanielAustinAuthor

Dedication

For Dad,
who taught me work ethic
and introduced me to so many great books
that inspired me to become a writer

Chapter 1

Brice woke to a baby crying. An angry baby, desperate for something it could not express. His head ached. He didn't want to open his eyes. Instead, he listened, waiting for a mother's soothing words.

The cries escalated. Brice tried to locate the baby and figure out why it was unattended, but his eyelids wouldn't budge. Nor would his head rise. It was like a nightmare in which he was conscious, but unable to control his body. He pushed with his forearms to raise himself onto his elbows, without success.

The baby took it up a notch.

Was he responsible for the baby? Was it crying for him?

Beneath the baby's bawling, he detected repetitive, steady beeps. A timer?

The bed vanished. He was suddenly standing on his own feet despite not moving. A wall of white blocked his view, as if someone had covered his eyes with a tube, restricting his vision to a narrow tunnel of fog. A chill filled his entire body, but it was dry, unlike what he'd expect in a fog. And he had the distinct sensation that he was indoors. Where had the fog come from?

The baby's bawling hadn't waned. He wanted to find the baby.

Her.

He wasn't sure why he thought she was a girl, but it fit somehow.

No matter which direction he swung his head, the same narrow tunnel of white moved with his eyes. Taking steps forward didn't help him.

Voices shouted all around him, urgent but in a foreign language. He looked for them, but saw no one.

"Can someone take care of the baby?" he asked.

Whoever was speaking sounded Japanese. Or perhaps Chinese. More words, in the same foreign language, seemed to issue from an intercom. The speakers surrounded him, close enough to touch, but no more visible than the baby.

Her wails turned to whimpers, as if she was overcome with exhaustion, or had simply given up.

"Please, will one of you get the baby?" He struggled to find her himself, but failed to even pinpoint the direction of the cries. He almost wished she would start wailing again to guide him to her.

One voice dominated the rest, bellowing orders like a general.

Hands latched onto his arms. He tried to pull away, but the grips tightened. Moments later, straps secured his arms to something cold and hard, like metal poles.

"Let me go!" His heart raced. He still couldn't see anyone.

Then he was sinking into the core of his body, which blocked everything else out.

Chapter 2

Nate looked up from the Deadpool comic he was reading to Brice, thinking he'd heard his friend make a noise. He studied him for a few minutes. Brice lay unconscious in the hospital bed, the cardiac monitor above his head droning on like a residential fire alarm whose battery was dying. He must've been mistaken.

It was difficult to see the boy—Nate still thought of him as a boy, though Brice was a full-grown thirty-two-year-old man—with his head covered in scabs and bruises, the physical signs of the injuries that had led to his ten-day coma.

Could Mary have really bludgeoned Brice into a coma in some sort of domestic dispute? It didn't seem possible. Mary was a good eight inches shorter and at least seventy-five pounds smaller than Brice. Not to mention that in the fourteen years Brice had worked for Nate as a mechanic, the boy had never lost his temper or raised his voice with anyone, much less shown aggression.

Nate had spent most of the past ten days wondering what had happened between the couple to trigger such violence. On the day after Christmas, no less. By the time the police had arrived at Brice's home the night of the attack, Mary had fled.

Whatever had happened that evening, Brice didn't deserve to be lying here in an ICU room, the electrodes from a cardiac monitor attached to his chest, breathing supported by a ventilator. He was a good kid. Not that Nate wanted to believe ill of Mary either. None of this made sense.

Nate fished for his phone, deciding that's what he had first heard. Perhaps Jaxon checking in. Brice's older brother had come home for the first few days, but as the coma dragged on, he'd had to return to Chicago and work. That left Nate to spend his evenings here, praying that Brice would wake up.

To pass the time, Nate had brought comics and read to Brice. A shared passion from their childhoods, though nearly thirty years apart. The first five days he'd read classics: Superman, Captain America, X-Men, the ones he'd read as a boy. But as the coma had persisted, and Nate had begun to fear it was permanent, he'd switched to Deadpool, Brice's favorite.

The boy loved the humor, but Nate suspected he identified with Wade Wilson because of his disfigurements. As with many children who suffer a significant childhood injury and are picked on by their peers as a result, Brice had perceived his physical deformities as worse than reality. The bottom of his right ear looked cut off. The tip of his nose was a little misshapen, with nostrils a tad wider than normal. At present, the feeding tubes inserted through his nose covered that up.

They were nothing compared to the scars he'd have now. Besides his injuries, he'd have a scar from the tracheostomy the doctors had performed to insert a breathing tube in his neck. His hair would grow back where they'd shaved it to drill a hole in his skull and insert an intracranial pressure monitor.

Nate hoped Brice would get the chance to learn to live with these new scars. Better the scars than the alternative.

Brice's finger, the one with the pulse oximeter attached to it, twitched. Nate sat up, breath catching in his throat. He studied the finger, then Brice's hands, which were also covered in scars from his childhood accident. There were no further movements.

Had he been mistaken? The lights in the room were dim. He must've imagined it. Was he so desperate to see Brice awake that he was hallucinating?

Brice shivered once. Nate half rose from his chair, wondering if this was reason enough to get a nurse. They kept the room cool, so Nate had brought a coat, despite it being unseasonably warm this Alabama winter. Was the shiver an unconscious reaction to the temperature? Would someone in a coma have an unconscious reaction to temperature?

When Brice shook his head as if disturbed, Nate almost whooped. That had to mean something. Three separate movements. A pattern, right? There had been nothing for the past week.

He ran to the door to look for Nurse Ashley or Gina. The former stood at the nurse's station, reading from a binder. She was young.

She couldn't have graduated from college more than a year or two ago, but she took great care with Brice.

"Nurse Ashley!" Nate shouted.

Her head popped up; eyebrows raised with concern. She started toward him.

"He moved. He's moving." Excitement bubbled up in Nate. He chastised himself not to make assumptions. It could be nothing. But it was his first sign of hope and he couldn't squash it.

Alarms rang behind him and he turned back. Brice had started thrashing, in the process knocking the IV out of his right arm.

"Move aside," Nurse Ashley demanded as she ran past him, jostling him with greater force than he'd expect for her size. She shouted for help.

Nate stood frozen, hope swallowed by fear. Other nurses and a doctor swarmed in.

"Help me control his arms," Nurse Ashley demanded as she attempted to restrain his right arm to the bedrail. A second nurse grabbed Brice's left arm while a third attempted to secure the arm. Brice's head jerked left and right.

The doctor shouted orders, but Nate failed to process anything she said. He watched as Brice struggled, as if fighting off captors. Nate took a step forward, thinking he should try to reassure the boy. Maybe a familiar voice would calm him.

A nurse grabbed both his arms and shoved him toward the door. "You need to wait outside."

He resisted. "I need to be here for Brice."

She stuck a thick finger in his face. "Let us do our jobs." Her tone brooked no argument. "There's nothing you can do. We'll take care of him."

For a moment she clenched her fists, a bouncer bracing for a fight. She needn't have bothered. There was no fight in him. He stared over her head while Ashley shouted instructions, before nodding and turning away.

He walked away from the room, pulling his cell phone from his pocket. His right hand shook as he attempted to dial the office. Twice he hit the wrong number before getting it right.

To his surprise, Lisa answered on the first ring. The shop had closed an hour ago.

"Day's Mobile Mechanic, how may I help you?" she asked.

"Lisa, it's me," Nate said.

"Nate, are you all right?" There was alarm in her voice.

"Yes, yes. I...." He was jittery, as if someone had injected fireflies into his veins. "Brice, he's moving. He might wake up." Tears blurred his vision. He couldn't decide if they were tears of joy or fear, or simply stress.

"Oh, thank Jesus," Lisa shouted. He knew she'd been praying and worrying for Brice ever since they'd learned about the attack.

Nate lacked her faith, but he had thrown in a few prayers of his own because what else was he going to do? He was powerless and figured it was better than doing nothing.

"What's happening?" she asked. He heard the clang of tools over the phone. Lisa shouted, "Warren, keep it down. Nate, what did the doctors say?"

"I don't know," he admitted. He recounted what he'd seen, the doctor and nurses charging in to take care of Brice and kicking him out.

"That's right, you let them do their jobs," she scolded, as if he were a child that needed reminding to stay out of the grownups' way.

He almost laughed. She had been bossing him, Warren, and Brice around ever since he'd hired her as office manager five years ago to handle all the paperwork, bookkeeping, and appointments. She knew little about cars beyond checking fluid levels, but viewed it as her duty to keep them in line and on schedule. And to be honest, he wasn't sure how he had ever managed the business before he'd hired her. Sheer dumb luck, he guessed.

"Should we come up there?" Warren hollered loud enough for Nate to hear. Lisa repeated the question.

Nate shook his head. "Not tonight. Even if he's waking up, he won't be in any condition for visitors. I'll call you if anything changes."

"You better," she said.

"Yes, ma'am. I'm staying here tonight and tomorrow morning. I want to be here for him."

"Don't worry about us," Lisa said. "Warren and I have things in order. Take care of our boy."

"Will do." Nate hung up.

He turned to check Brice's room. The noise and commotion level had died down and the alarms quieted, but the nurse who had kicked him out still guarded the door. He debated asking for an update, but the set of her jaw told him it was best to give them space for the present. Brice was in expert hands.

Nate's stomach rumbled, so he headed to the cafeteria for something to eat. Once he'd gotten some food in him, hopefully things would have calmed enough that they'd let him back in to see the boy.

And, with a little luck, to talk to him soon.

Chapter 3

Brice's adrenaline spiked when he awoke. His eyes popped wide, taking in everything around him. White walls. Equipment surrounded him, some attached to him as if he was a lab experiment. He tried to lift his arms to his swollen, aching head, but restraints secured them to the bed rails. Was he a prisoner?

Even with a blanket covering much of him, he shivered from the cold. Exhaustion weighted his brain, an unnaturally powerful pull, as if some force attempted to make him sleep. Had someone drugged him?

A man sat slumped in a nearby chair, chin on his chest, asleep. A comic book lay splayed open in his lap.

Dismissing the sleeping man for the moment, Brice tried to make sense of where he was. The equipment around him, with tubes leading to a needle in one arm and to patches on both, he guessed was medical. A tube pressed into his nose, giving him a cool, fresh flow of oxygen.

The place resembled a hospital room. Why was he here? What had happened to him?

A plausible answer escaped him. Then he remembered a crying baby that nobody had soothed. Doctors talking in a foreign language. Was he in a hospital in Japan?

The man sleeping in the chair was older, with graying hair but for a few remaining streaks of brown. He wasn't dressed as a doctor or nurse, but Brice didn't recognize him either.

A dull pain dug into Brice's left temple. He reached for his head, only to rediscover his arm restraints. The movement shifted the needle in his right arm. He sucked in air, bobbing his head in a way that made fresh pain flare through it, too. His vision swam. He tensed against the pain. The restraints dug further into his wrists, cutting off circulation and eliciting a cry from him. He forced himself to relax, and things eased.

He yearned to sink down through the bed, even the floor, to escape it all. Why was he here?

Tears flowed to the edges of his eyelids as he struggled with confusion. The pain and the restraints, combined with his inability to remember how he'd gotten here, frightened him.

At that moment, the stranger jerked, his head popping up. He took one look at Brice and a broad smile lit up his face.

"You're awake." The man straightened and slid to the edge of his chair.

Brice tensed, wanting to pull away, but regretted the movement as pain flared up through his arms and wrists once more. He was at a disadvantage, and powerless to do anything about it.

"How do you feel?" the man asked.

Brice stared at him, unsure how to answer. And why should he? The man should answer his questions. What had happened to him? Where was he? Why was there an assortment of flowers and boxes of Red Hots candy on the nearby table?

"Can I get you anything? Should I get the nurse?" The man rose, eyes flickering to the door, then back to him, as if asking Brice what he wanted.

Brice pivoted his head toward the doorway, half expecting to find a nurse there, but it was empty. Had he been in an accident? He tried to ask, but only a weak moan escaped his lips.

The desire to sleep tugged at him, but he struggled to shake it off. He didn't want to sleep without knowing what was going on, or if he was safe.

"Yeah, I'll get someone." The man strode to the door, poking his head out and calling someone named Ashley. He remained there a few minutes until he moved aside to let a nurse bustle past him.

Brice half-expected a Japanese nurse, but she had curly blonde hair. She almost looked too young to be a nurse. She strode right up to the side of his bed.

"Hello, Mr. Dunn. I'm Nurse Ashley." She gave him a brief smile before turning to study something over his head.

He tilted his head back to find a monitor. Another lance of pain shot through his skull. His stomach turned. He groaned.

"Try to stay relaxed." She placed a gloved hand on his right arm. She probably intended to comfort him, but only the threat of pain from the needle kept him from yanking his arm away from her.

He wasn't a child in need of comfort. He wanted answers.

"You've been in a coma," she continued, which made him tense again. His heart skipped a beat. A couple beats. She reached for his head, picking at a bandage. "You've suffered some pretty serious brain injuries, but the good news is you're recovering."

His eyes darted to the stranger, who had returned to the foot of the bed. The man nodded to confirm the nurse's story.

"Dr. Windstetter is on her way. She can provide more details. Are you hurting?" She looked him over as she spoke before meeting his gaze.

He was, but his most pressing concern was his wrists. "Why am... my wrists?" He eyed the restraints.

"Oh, forgive me." She removed the one from his right wrist. "During the night, you started thrashing and ripped the needle right out of your arm. The restraints were to keep you from causing greater damage to yourself."

Brice sighed, comforted that he at least had a little more control over his arms. And that the restraints had been for his safety.

"Be careful with your right arm," she warned. "You still have the IV in for the moment."

His arms were stiff and slow to respond. He reached up and gingerly touched his head. He wanted to see himself, to process the injuries he'd suffered, but there was no mirror. Touch was all he had.

His face felt uneven from swelling in a few places. A scab covered a part of his lower lip. His head had been shaved, and he found stitches at the top of his skull that made his skin crawl.

"Is there anything I can get you?"

"Water," he managed in a raspy voice. His dry mouth and throat felt as though someone had soaked up every drop of moisture.

"Sure, I'll be right back." She gave him a gentle squeeze on his forearm before departing, leaving him with the stranger once more. At least the man didn't touch him.

"It's so good to see you awake," the stranger said. "We've been worried. Didn't know if you'd pull through."

They knew each other. Why couldn't he remember the man?

The effort of voicing his thoughts was too much. He blinked, his eyelids fighting to remain shut. He forced them open, uncomfortable with sleeping with this stranger standing over him.

"I'll call your brother in a bit. I'm sure he'll be on a flight right back."

That was the first bit of news that gave Brice comfort. A ray of hope. If his brother was coming, things would be okay. He'd make sense of everything.

But why wasn't his brother already here? The nurse said he'd been in a coma for days. Couldn't he have arrived by now?

A doctor entered the room. She looked to be in her early forties, with long red hair and a runner's physique. After giving the stranger a brief nod, she focused on Brice.

"Good afternoon, Mr. Dunn," the doctor greeted. "I'm Dr. Katarina Windstetter. How are you feeling?"

Before Brice had time to do more than croak, Nurse Ashley returned with a Styrofoam cup of water with a straw in it.

"Excuse me," the nurse said to the doctor, slipping past her. She held the cup close to his face and bent the straw close to his mouth. All he had to do was lean forward to sip the water.

It was cold and welcome. He took a second sip, enjoying the spread of it across his tongue and down his throat. The relief of it made him think of a wilted flower standing up, its petals expanding after the rain.

After a couple of more sips, he leaned back against the pillow. The nurse set the cup on a tray to the right of his bed, then stepped back out of the way.

"What's your pain level right now?" Dr. Windstetter asked. "On a scale of one to ten."

He considered this for a minute. His head pulsed in rhythm with his heart. He was sore, but not in agony. As long as he didn't sit up or move too much.

"Six?" It came out like a question.

The doctor nodded. "Mr. Dunn, I need to run a few tests to gauge your condition. They're simple and won't tax you too much. I'm sure you're tired. Would that be okay?"

He nodded. It wasn't, but he felt he couldn't say no.

"First off, what do you remember? Do you recall what happened to you?"

He shook his head, worried that she didn't seem to know. He'd expected they'd tell him.

"That's not unusual," she said, as if this was all routine. "People who experience severe injuries like you did often can't remember the events that led to their trauma. Can you tell me the last thing you remember?"

He stared down at the electrodes on his chest. Nothing violent or scary floated to the surface. Instead, there were mundane details. Eating peanut butter toast with coffee. Working on a maroon Miata in a shop. Driving a beat-up old Corolla. He couldn't put a timeframe on them. They might've occurred days, weeks, or months ago for all he knew. And none of it explained how he'd ended up here.

He shook his head. "I'm not sure."

The doctor gestured to the stranger. "What about him? Do you recognize him?"

The question caught Brice off guard. He examined the stranger once more. The man possessed a wrinkled forehead and emerald eyes. He looked strong, but with a bit of a gut. Was there a hint of familiarity to the man?

Once more Brice shook his head.

The stranger's smile fell at this. His lips pursed, and the concern in his eyes made Brice uneasy. He willed himself to remember, but that only made his head hurt worse.

"Are you sure?" the doctor prompted.

Again, he was reluctant to say no. He shook his head. "I don't. I'm not... sure."

"What about you?" the doctor asked. "Do you know who you are?"

He nodded.

"What's your name?"

"Brice Dunn," he said without hesitation.

"What about family?" she asked. "Can you tell me about them?"

"My brother," Brice began. "I have a brother."

"His name?"

The name hovered at the edges of his memory. He knew it but couldn't quite recall. He saw his brother's face. Had he forgotten his name? The thought stressed him. The beeping on the monitor behind him increased, as if alarmed at his inability to recall the name.

Then his brain released the answer. "Jaxon." Remembering felt like a victory.

"That's good," she said. "Anyone else?"

"My mother. She passed."

"Father?"

"Left. I was a child."

"That's good," the doctor encouraged. "You're doing great. Can you tell me what you do for a living? Your job?"

The memory of working on the Miata resurfaced. In a shop. He pictured the place, familiar as his own home. Not too big. An old brick building. He worked on many other vehicles there. Something else tugged at his memory, just out of reach, same as his brother's name had been.

"A mechanic," he responded.

The stranger smiled at this, nodding. "That's right."

At his response, the stranger appeared in Brice's vision of the shop. He belonged there. Brice knew him. Co-worker? Friend?

A name floated to the surface. "Nate?"

"That's me," the man said, beaming. He brushed away tears from his eyes.

Nate was both friend and boss. They had worked together for years. How had he forgotten Nate?

"Very good," the doctor said. "Okay, now I'd like to test out a couple of other things. Then you need to rest. First, I'd like you to follow my finger without moving your head."

She held up a finger at eye level, about a foot in front of his face. She moved it past the left side of his head, pausing for a moment, then back in the other direction, past the right side. He tracked the finger with his eyes without issue, though they ached a little from the effort.

"Good."

The doctor pulled back the blanket covering him. The cold air made the hairs on his arms and legs stand up. He shivered. She tapped two fingers on his right leg below the kneecap, causing an involuntary kick. She followed suit with the left leg. He recalled the test from doctors' visits as a child.

"What?" he began, but couldn't quite voice his thoughts.

"What happened?" the doctor asked.

He nodded.

"I can't speak to what happened to you," she said, gesturing toward Nate. "I'm sure your friend can help. As far as your injuries, you suffered a skull fracture. There was damage to different parts of your brain. You had a subarachnoid hemorrhage. The trauma caused your brain to swell. We had to drill a hole in your skull and insert an ICP—an intracranial pressure monitor. It's been removed."

The kaleidoscope of medical terms scared him.

She must've seen the anxiety on his face, because she smiled soothingly. "Don't worry. The worst is past. You're stable. Awake. I won't say you have an easy recovery ahead of you, but none of your injuries are life threatening. The most important thing is you need to rest. For now, the more rest you get, the better.

"I'll be back to check on you in a few hours. In the meantime, let Nurse Ashley know if you need anything."

"Thanks," Brice managed.

Doctor Windstetter nodded once and hurried from the room. Nurse Ashley stepped forward, retrieving his cup of water.

"Would you like some more?" she asked.

"Yes."

After giving him a few more sips, she gave him instructions to call her if he needed anything. He didn't process any of it, but she promised to check on him regularly.

Once Nurse Ashley had departed, Nate cleared his throat. He looked uncertain. "I'm sure you have questions about what happened to you." He flushed.

Brice had questions, lots of them, but the tug of sleep pulled harder at him. And remembering Nate, as well as the bit of information the doctor had provided, had eliminated the immediate threat he'd felt upon awakening. The specific details about how he'd ended up here seemed less pressing for the moment. Or maybe he lacked the energy to fight sleep any longer.

He found it hard to keep his eyes open. Consciousness was drifting again. "Later."

As he closed his eyes, he thought he heard Nate respond, but he didn't catch it.

Chapter 4

A knock woke Brice.

An officer in uniform stood in the doorway of his hospital room. The officer gave Nate an uncertain look. "I'd heard he's awake. Can he talk?"

"He was asleep." Sitting up in his chair, Nate gave Brice a questioning glance. "How're you feeling? Need anything?"

The officer, an older man with graying temples, stood in the doorframe, waiting, though his posture suggested this was a courtesy. He intended to come in.

What did he want?

Brice blinked his eyes. He had a headache and felt like he still operated on minimal rest. Plus, his dry mouth had returned. He glanced over at the Styrofoam cup on the stand beside the bed.

Nate hurried around and grabbed the cup. He offered the water to Brice. After a few swallows, Brice thanked Nate. Beside the water were a few packages of saltine crackers. Nate pointed to them. "Hungry?"

Brice shook his head. He was, but needed to know what the officer wanted first. Nor did he want the intrusion to last longer than needed.

When Brice's attention turned to the officer, he approached. He was tall and thin, gray eyes weary, but earnest. He held an aluminum storage clipboard.

Nate returned to his chair, nodding at the officer as he passed.

"I'm Investigator Ben Wright with the Huntsville PD." The officer stopped at the foot of Brice's bed, pulling out a pen to take notes. "I'd like to discuss what happened to you, if you're up for it?"

Brice wished to say no. Though he couldn't say why, he was hesitant to talk to the investigator, this stranger, about what had happened. Especially while he lay here in a hospital bed. At the same time, he couldn't tell him that he didn't want to do it right then.

Taking his silence as acceptance, the investigator spoke. "Can you tell me what happened?"

"I… uh…" Brice didn't know how to answer. He'd expected the investigator to tell him what had happened, whether he was here because of a terrible wreck or an accident at work. Or something worse.

"He doesn't remember," Nate interjected.

The investigator glanced at Nate, teeth clenching, before arching an eyebrow at Brice.

"The doctor tested his memory when he first woke up," Nate persisted. "He doesn't remember anything."

Brice swallowed warm saliva, half-afraid the investigator would accuse him of hiding something.

"Is this true?" Investigator Wright asked him.

Brice nodded.

The investigator took a few notes on his clipboard, before resuming. "Ten days ago, officers reported to your residence on a domestic call. Witnesses reported shouting between a man and a woman. When officers arrived, you were alone in the house, unconscious on the floor, with severe bruises and lacerations to your head and torso. An ambulance was called to transport you here to Huntsville Hospital."

Brice gaped. He'd expected that whatever happened to him had been bad. He wouldn't be here, ten days in a coma, otherwise. The details were still shocking. The last thing he'd expected was the investigator to tell him he'd been in a fight with a woman. Who was she?

The steady beep from the monitor beside his bed quickened.

"You don't recall any of this?" Investigator Wright studied him.

Brice felt the investigator was gauging whether he was lying. "No."

"The woman, a Miss Mary Smith, left the residence in a beige Toyota Corolla. A witness reported that Miss Smith is your girlfriend and lives with you. Is that correct?"

Brice felt his face reddening. What must the investigator think of him?

And if this woman was his girlfriend, why couldn't he remember her? Had he known her long? Or had the witness been mistaken?

Again, he turned to Nate, this time hoping for an explanation that didn't make him a bad guy.

"Mary is his girlfriend and does live with him," Nate confirmed, his expression uneasy.

Brice's stomach dropped through him and the bed to the floor. He hadn't wanted to talk about this right now. After Nate's confirmation, he'd have preferred to never discuss it.

The investigator looked from Brice to Nate then back to him. "You don't recall this woman?"

Unable to meet the man's gaze, Brice glanced at the flowers already wilting on the table by the window. Nothing he said would make this any better. "I… I can't remember. I don't know…"

"He didn't remember me when he first woke," Nate explained. "I've been his boss for near fifteen years."

Investigator Wright added this to his notes, brow furrowed. "Witnesses also reported that Miss Smith was well into a pregnancy?"

This bit was a punch to the gut. Brice darted a glance at Nate, who fidgeted in his chair.

"That is true," Nate confirmed. "We were expecting the call any day."

"And was the child yours, Mr. Dunn?"

Brice stared at the officer, no idea how to respond. Was he… was he going to be a father?

"Yes," Nate answered. "At least, that's what they told us. Ms. Smith had been living with Brice for roughly ten months."

He was having a baby? Despite his injuries, he should remember a baby on the way. And the mother of his child. Yet there was nothing. What kind of monster would forget them?

The investigator continued to take notes. "Can you speculate why you and Miss Smith argued?"

Brice wanted to laugh and cry. How could he possibly guess? And what was the officer recording? Did he believe any of this?

"Mr. Dunn?"

"No. I don't."

"When the officers arrived at your residence, they reported you smelled heavily of alcohol."

"That's impossible!" Nate jumped to his feet, face flushed. "Brice doesn't drink. He's never drank."

"Mr. Day, perhaps you should wait outside. I'd like to gather more details about what Mr. Dunn knows, as little as that seems to be." Did the investigator emphasize that last part?

"No, sir," Nate crossed his arms. "I don't like where these questions are leading. Brice is the victim here. He was the one beaten and in a coma for the last ten days. I'm staying here or I'm getting a lawyer before we answer any more questions."

Investigator Wright held up his free hand. "That's unnecessary, Mr. Day. Mr. Dunn isn't a suspect in anything. I'm trying to confirm what happened and obtain any additional details Mr. Dunn can provide."

"He doesn't drink," Nate said, unmollified. "His mother never allowed alcohol under her roof, the residence you've mentioned. That was her and Brice's home until her death several years ago. But even after her death, Brice never picked up drinking."

"The officers reported finding an empty bourbon bottle on the floor beside Mr. Dunn."

Nate's jaw clenched and his face turned from red to purple.

"His BAC test came back clear though," Investigator Wright noted with a frown.

"BAC?" Nate asked.

"Blood alcohol level," the investigator answered. "Since Mr. Dunn smelled of whiskey, the doctors here had to run tests to find out what was in his system before treating his injuries. Results came back negative. He wasn't intoxicated. Just smelled like it."

"What does this mean?" Brice asked, latching on to the first bit of decent news like it was a lifeline to steady him.

"Right now, we don't know," the investigator admitted. "We put out an APB on the Toyota Corolla. Found it two days back, abandoned on I-65. Miss Smith appears to have fled. We were hoping you might know where she's gone."

Brice didn't want to say no again. Would his memories of her return like they had with Nate?

"We knew little about her past." Nate grimaced and glanced down at his hands. "Brice told us she wouldn't talk about it. He sensed that something bad had happened to her before they met, but wouldn't press her on it. He figured she'd tell him in time."

"Well, right now Miss Smith is our prime suspect in your attack. No one else was seen at the residence that day or in the days leading up to it. We pulled prints from the Corolla, found some we believe are hers. Ran them, but no matches."

Brice gripped his blankets with both hands, unsure how to respond. He kind of wished he hadn't woken up from the coma.

"What's next?" Nate asked.

"We'll keep looking for her," the investigator replied.

"I'm sorry," Brice replied.

The officer shrugged, then removed a business card from his clipboard. "If your memories return, give me a call."

Nate accepted the card for him and Investigator Wright shifted toward the door to leave.

"Investigator," Nate said.

The investigator paused and turned back.

"Despite what Brice's neighbor told you, I've never seen Brice yell or lose his temper with anyone."

"I've heard that line many times before," the investigator said drily.

Nate grimaced as he nodded. "Well, I've known him for a long time. He's worked for me at my repair shop since he was sixteen. Over the years, we've had our share of customers that didn't like what we had to tell them about repairs to their vehicles or how much it'd cost. There have been plenty who have taken out that anger on Brice and he's always kept his cool, even been apologetic in the face of outrage. More than a few times I've had to step in to defend him."

The investigator turned his attention back to Brice. "When you remember something, call me." Then he left.

Chapter 5

With Investigator Wright gone, Brice slumped into his pillow. He wanted nothing more than to sleep again, but too many new questions had emerged from his conversation with the investigator. Waking out of a coma with severe injuries and amnesia had scared him. Learning of a girlfriend and baby that he didn't remember only worsened his anxiety.

Nate dropped into the chair as if drained as well. "I'm sorry, Brice. This wasn't the time for that. You should've had more time to rest and recover, but he showed up without warning. And I didn't know what he was going to ask."

"Can you tell me… who is she?" Brice asked.

Nate frowned. "Huh?"

"Mary. My girlfriend." It felt weird to call a woman he didn't know his girlfriend. Made him feel like a creepy stalker. That he *had* known her didn't help.

Exhaling, Nate stared at the footboard for a minute before responding. "To be honest, I didn't know her well. Only saw her a handful of times. Once when I hosted a BBQ for you, Lisa, and Warren. A couple times at the office."

At the mention of Lisa and Warren, memories of them appeared beside Nate in the shop, filling two holes in the puzzle. Brice took no solace from these memories.

"She's a few years younger than you. Short, reddish blonde hair. Seemed sweet. You loved to talk about her. Said she's smart but reserved. Didn't talk much about her past, but you had so many dreams for the future. You were thrilled about the baby."

"Are we having a boy or girl?" Or was it 'were we'? She had gone, the baby with her.

"You were waiting until birth. Wanted it to be a surprise." Nate smiled, as if recalling a fond memory.

Brice closed his eyes, willing himself to remember as he'd managed with Nate and his co-workers. He thought about home, imagining a woman there with him. Instead, he recalled hearing a crying baby. He'd been searching for her while still in a coma. Had she been a product of his mind clinging to his memories of the baby? More like dreams since she hadn't been born yet. In fact, he didn't even know the baby was a girl. Nevertheless, he felt she was a girl, with a certainty he couldn't explain. He'd heard of a mother's intuition. Did fathers have intuition as well?

"I can't believe… a baby. Me. A dad."

Nate hesitated, his smile dissipating.

"What?" Brice asked.

"You believed the baby was yours, but the timing was very close." Nate looked away. "Mary moved in with you almost immediately after you met and was pregnant not long after. We hope the baby is yours, but there was some question."

Soreness expanded up the inside of Brice's right arm. He shook it a little, trying to ease the tension. The needle from the IV dug in his vein. He froze, grimacing.

"I don't mean to ruin your enthusiasm," Nate backtracked.

"It's not that." Brice shuddered. "My arm... I need a pillow."

"Oh." Nate leapt to his feet and retrieved a pillow from a closet, which he eased under Brice's right arm for extra cushion. "How's that?"

The pain from the needle relaxed, allowing him to breathe easier. "Better."

The fuss with the pillow gave him time to consider the question Nate had raised. A woman he had lived with carried a child that might or might not be his. His mind kept going back to the image of a crying baby. A perfect little girl who needed someone to take care of her. That she received love and care mattered more than who she belonged to.

"Why did she do this?" Brice pointed at the bandages on his head. "Why did she leave?"

"I don't know." There was genuine confusion on Nate's face. "There were a lot of unknowns about her, but this…."

"Do you think it was because of me?" Brice asked, feeling tears rise to his eyes. He blinked them back. "The witnesses said we fought. Do you think she… need… protected herself? Protected the baby?"

Nate shook his head, eyes turning fierce. "No. No way. I know you. When the police find her and we get answers, it won't be that."

Brice turned his head away from Nate, wishing he shared his boss's confidence.

"None of this makes sense," Nate said. "Not with what I know of you and Mary. Eventually we'll get answers, but this wasn't because you hurt or threatened her."

Brice hoped Nate was right, that whatever had happened that day hadn't given her a need to defend herself, or the baby, from him.

Chapter 6

Beulah dumped the leftover scrambled eggs in the trash before filling up the skillet with water and leaving it in the sink to soak. She needed to straighten up the kitchen before Patty woke and wanted to nurse. They were supposed to leave the Community travel house that afternoon and Garrett would be furious if she delayed them because she needed to finish cleaning.

She limped to the table to gather the dishes. Cramping in her lower abdomen elicited a groan from her lips and she rubbed it to ease the ache. She'd known birthing a baby would be hard, but a week out from delivery, she'd expected to be further along in recovery. Not that caring for a newborn, combined with cooking and cleaning up after two men, left much time for rest. She existed in a constant state of exhaustion.

Combining the leftover bits of egg and toast from the plates on the table, she carried the stack of dishes to the sink. She scraped the food from the top plate into the trash.

On her return to the table for the coffee mugs, she detoured to the fridge and pulled out a half-empty bottle of beer. She removed the cap and took a couple quick pulls. At that moment, she just wanted to sit with her beer and zone out for a bit. To not be needed for even a few minutes.

"Beulah!" Spencer shouted from his bedroom.

Beulah hated her given name. She preferred Mary, which she'd taken not long before she went to live with Brice, but she knew better than to correct a *man* from the Community.

She put the cap back on the beer and stuck it in the fridge before heading to his room. He sat on the end of his bed, wrapped in a towel, fresh from the shower. Steam billowed out of the bathroom.

In his mid-fifties, Spencer was a gangly man with too much hair on his body and too little on his head. He was always complaining. Food not seasoned enough. Coffee too weak. Beer gone stale. His room too cold. Bathroom smelled like mold. She didn't bother pointing out that the damp towels he left lying on the floor caused the moldy smell. He'd retort that she needed to clean them up faster.

"What?" she asked from the doorway, but the bulge in the towel wrapped around his waist made it clear what he wanted. He didn't care about the midwife's orders to leave her alone for six weeks.

For a response he leaned back on his arms and widened his legs. Not enough to unwrap the towel. He wanted her to do that.

She stepped forward as he leered at her breasts, which were plump with milk. With any luck he'd be quick, so she could get back to the dishes.

A cry from the other bedroom halted her midstride. Her breasts ached at Patty's cries. No rest before lunch.

Anger flashed across Spencer's face. He pointed at his crotch. "Come on."

Before she took a step, Garrett hollered from the living room. "Shut that baby up. I'm trying to read."

She gave Spencer a questioning look. They both knew Garrett's command took priority, but she wanted Spencer to admit that. If she left without his dismissal, he'd take it out on her later. Probably would anyway, but with less force if he dismissed her.

Spencer ground his teeth, almost snarling. "Oh, go on." He waved her away. "But hurry back. I want a good one." He leered at her breasts again. "A slow one."

Silent, she exited, heading into Garrett's room where Patty slept in the middle of the queen bed wedged between two pillows to prevent her from rolling onto her stomach. She lay swaddled in a gray blanket, face red from crying. She didn't quiet as Beulah picked her up, just kept on bawling. Her little hands—peeking through the tops of the swaddle—shook in anger.

She kept right on until Beulah bared her right breast and placed her up to the nipple. Eyes closed, Patty widened her mouth, rooting around until she clamped on to feed. Beulah inhaled sharply when the baby latched on, then relaxed as the initial pain eased.

She closed her eyes, zoning out while the baby drained her. One more person taking what they wanted from her. At least the effort was minimal. She didn't have to think.

Just be present.

The same would be true with Spencer when she finished feeding and changing Patty. He took more effort, but she could go through the motions. She'd done it so many times it didn't require thought. She could let her mind wander. Or in this case stop. Do nothing. Function just enough for muscle memory to do its part.

Patty unlatched and started bawling again, still hungry. Beulah swapped her over to the other breast, wishing the baby would take a little longer with this one. Spencer and Garrett wouldn't interrupt her while nursing. They wouldn't risk the baby becoming malnourished. Not with them headed straight back to the Community. Accusations that they'd deprived the baby would land the men in huge trouble. The Community didn't tolerate any harm to the next generation. For the time being, it gave Beulah momentary bits of power.

It also served as a chain dragging her back. She'd spent the last year away, living under the name Mary Smith, and had enjoyed every minute of freedom.

Now she had to return with the baby. There would be a ritual. And she'd have to stay with Patty for a time in the Community. As soon as she could, she planned to make a new deal with Arden. Get set up somewhere else. She was a better asset to the Community outside its walls.

The inside was for others. Like her mother.

Chapter 7

Brice's nerves vibrated like a twanged guitar string as Jaxon pulled the gray RAV4 rental into the driveway and raised the garage door, revealing stacks of boxes filling most of it.

From the back seat, Brice took in the one-story brick rancher. His home since not long after his twelfth birthday. Jaxon's as well, until he'd turned eighteen and enlisted in the Army.

Crumbling brown leaves from the ten maple trees covered much of the lawn. As a teenager, Brice had carved his initials into each tree trunk; he couldn't remember why.

From a thick branch on the nearest tree hung two ropes, one attached to a flat board that had served as a swing when he was thirteen, but which now hung a couple of feet off the ground. The second, frayed rope had completed the swing for a couple of weeks before snapping. At the time, Jaxon hadn't noticed the frayed point in the rope when he'd shimmied up the tree and tied it to a branch, but it had been Brice in full swing when the rope snapped, leading to a broken arm that ruined the rest of his summer.

Jaxon exited the driver seat and hurried to open the rear door to help Brice climb out. Nate retrieved Brice's bag and a walker from the trunk.

A cold wind chilled Brice's spine as he leaned on his brother. They hobbled around the rental. He should theoretically be able to stand on his own. All his injuries during the attack had been to his head and upper body, but they'd impaired his sense of balance. He'd learned that the first time he had attempted to use the bathroom in the hospital, not making it two steps before toppling over.

"Here's your walker." Nate set it before him.

Brice shook his head. "It's a short walk. Jaxon can help me inside." He hated the idea of using a walker. It made him feel like an old man.

As they passed the garage, filled to overflowing so that there was no room to walk, Brice noticed a stack of boxes marked *Comics*. He'd always kept those in the house to prevent the high summer humidity or winter chills from damaging them. Some were quite valuable.

"Why did you… my comics… there?" he demanded, furious that his brother had moved them outside, and with himself for needing his brother's support to walk past them.

"What are you talking about?" Jaxon asked, glancing at the boxes as he led Brice toward the front walkway. "I didn't put those there. You did."

"I wouldn't… outside…" he began to protest, but the words struggled to come. "Put them outside. Damage them."

"I don't know what to tell you," Jaxon replied as he fished his keys out of his jacket pocket and tossed them to Nate. "I haven't touched anything in the garage."

As Nate hurried up the porch to unlock the front door, Brice reached out and grabbed the porch rail, shifting his weight from his brother to it. Jaxon gripped his torso and pulled him back.

"Give me a minute." Brice shifted to the porch rail once more.

"Are you okay? Tired?" Jaxon asked, voice edged with concern.

Brice didn't answer. He didn't want to admit how much this short trek had taken out of him.

But that wasn't what gave him pause. It was entering the house. The place had been his home for close to twenty years, but the attack had marred the comfort it once gave him. He imagined his dried blood on the floor inside and perhaps other signs of damage. For a moment, he debated asking Jaxon to take him to a hotel so he wouldn't have to face it. But this was his home. He had to go on living here. Would it ever feel safe again?

Both Jaxon and Nate stood watching him, expressions concerned. He shook his head and took a deep breath, before reaching for his brother, slipping one arm over his shoulder, and gritting his teeth against the indignity. And his dread.

The living room was spotless, just the way his mother had always kept it—and he had tried to maintain that after her death. The blue couch against the back wall with fading pillows propped against either arm. The beige chair that belonged to Jaxon until he moved out. Afterward, Brice had taken it over. In his teenage mind it had represented his becoming man of the house, though he wouldn't have admitted that. Between the couch and chair stood an end table with a lamp and a New King James Bible. In a corner was a wood stove, accompanied by a wood bin filled with cut logs.

Pictures of Jaxon and Brice adorned the pale green walls. Commemorations of childhood baptisms, Jaxon's freshman football season and high school graduation, junior homecoming for Brice, his first morning at Day's auto body shop, one of Jaxon in military uniform, and Jaxon graduating Quantico before assignment in the Chicago field office. A flat screen television, wall mounted between two windows, was the only addition Brice had made after their mother's death.

There were no signs of the attack. Had it occurred in the kitchen? His room?

"Once local police finished gathering evidence, I hired someone to clean up," Jaxon said.

Brice stared at the dark brown wood floors, relieved not to see the damage. Yet without it… it was as if the attack had never happened. He had the injuries, but no memory of the events. A part of his life was just gone. Ten days in a coma plus countless more from the memories he'd lost.

Nate entered the living room from the hallway. He jerked a thumb back over his shoulder. "I put your bag on your bed in your room."

"Thanks," Brice said, not even having realized Nate had left.

"Do you want to sit down?" Jaxon asked.

Brice shook his head. "No." He didn't want to spend another moment in here right now. Instead, he mumbled a desire for food and they headed back to the kitchen.

Jaxon helped him to the dining room table—a dark chocolate ironwood piece passed down from their great grandmother to their grandmother to their mother and now to him.

"Whatcha want?" Jaxon asked as he marched to the fridge and opened the freezer door. "I picked up frozen pizzas and tv dinners. I can warm something up for you. Otherwise, we'll have to order in." He'd never been one to cook.

"Pizza's fine," Brice said. Anything was better than hospital food.

Jaxon turned on the oven and slipped two pizzas inside.

"Lisa's making a casserole," Nate said as he took a seat across from Brice. "I'll bring it by tomorrow. She didn't want you to worry about a decent meal while you're recovering. And Amy plans to cook something for me to bring later in the week."

"Thanks." Brice wished one of them would turn on a football game or something and stop talking about all the things they were doing for him. Not that he was ungrateful, but each offer was a reminder of everything he couldn't do for himself.

Jaxon balanced three glasses with ice in one hand and a stack of three cokes in the other as he returned to the table. He poured for each of them. Nate accepted his without comment. Brice thought it might be the first time he'd seen his boss drink anything but beer or coffee.

As he took a seat at the end of the table, Jaxon sipped at his soda, seeming to gather his thoughts. "I can stay two more days. Then I have to return to Chicago."

Brice nodded, feeling he needed to apologize that his brother had used up so much time and money on his account.

Jaxon drank more of his coke, taking his time. He had some sort of information he expected Brice wouldn't like. Brice waited him out.

"I've hired a retired nurse to stay with you for a little while. To help with your physical therapy, but also to handle the house."

Brice stiffened, but he remained silent.

Jaxon looked at the soda can as if talking to it. "Just for a few weeks, a month or two, while you recover. She can help you get about and ensure you don't have any setbacks, keep track of medications, give doctors feedback on your progress, and do some cooking."

Brice kept his expression neutral. "How much?"

Jaxon waved before taking another swallow, still not looking at him. "I've got it covered."

"How much?" Brice repeated.

He was honestly relieved. He couldn't stay home alone yet, not when he couldn't manage much of anything by himself right now. But he didn't want to be a burden on his brother. Or Nate.

"It's the least I can do," Jaxon answered. "Since I can't be here."

"I can…" Brice squeezed his cup between both hands, the rest of what he wanted to say not coming to the surface at first. "Pay."

"No, you can't," Jaxon argued. "It'll be awhile before you're recovered enough to work. Thankfully, Mom paid this place off before she died."

"I paid it," Brice corrected.

Nate shifted in his seat.

"Only a couple..." Brice grimaced, frustrated that his thoughts seemed a jumble beyond his control. "A little while. Then I'll be fine... to work. Pay you back."

"No," Jaxon pushed back, his jaw tightening. "You won't be able to work in a few weeks."

Brice leaned back in his chair, a spark igniting inside him.

Jaxon shook his head. "You may not be ready in a few months. And Nate's not letting you return until you're cleared by a doctor. You can't just push through this."

The spark increased to a burning red that popped like stars in Brice's vision. He smacked at his glass, sending it flying past his brother. It sprayed him with soda before shattering against the back door.

Jaxon and Nate both jumped to their feet, their eyes wide.

A stream of thoughts flickered through Brice's head, too fast for him to articulate. He tried to reach for them, to verbalize his anger, but all he managed was to pound both fists on the table once.

"Brice, please." Jaxon's tone softened and he raised his hands in a placating gesture.

The timer on the oven went off. The pizzas were ready.

No one moved. Jaxon and Nate stood there, waiting on him.

His anger dissipated, as if the timer had uncorked it to diffuse, leaving behind exhaustion. He needed to lie down.

"I'm sorry," Brice murmured. "I think... I'm tired."

"Maybe it was too soon to bring you home," Nate said. "Maybe you needed a longer recovery at the hospital."

"He'll be fine." Jaxon headed to the kitchen. "I'll get the pizza. You should eat first, then we'll get you to your room so you can lie down."

Jaxon grabbed the roll of paper towels and tossed them to Nate. While Jaxon grabbed the pizzas from the oven and sliced them up, Nate cleaned up the coke and broken glass.

Brice wanted to tell Nate to stop and let him clean up the mess, but at present he doubted his ability to stand without both of their help, unless he used the walker which Nate had set against the wall. He certainly couldn't bend down to clean up the soda and broken glass.

How long would things be like this? How long would he need someone to care for him? How long would they keep him away from his job?

How long before someone found out where Mary and the baby had gone?

Chapter 8

Brice woke to a creak from another room. He lay frozen in bed, straining to listen for other noises. Had someone broken in?

He reached for his phone on the nightstand, but knocked it off. It hit the floor with a thud. He stopped breathing, hoping he hadn't given himself away if there was an intruder.

Seconds later a toilet flushed, followed by running water in the sink. His mind whirled, trying to figure out who breaks into a house to use the bathroom. Then he exhaled as he remembered.

Mrs. Drew.

"Idiot." He'd been home for almost two weeks, ten days of which Mrs. Drew had been here working with him on his rehabilitation exercises. When he rested, which remained often, she cleaned, cooked, or read cozy mysteries. She kept a stack of them on the dresser in her room.

The clock on his nightstand displayed 12:03 a.m. Mrs. Drew shuffled down the hallway, the thuds of her footsteps leading toward her room. The door shut.

Brice closed his eyes, taking deep breaths. His mouth tasted foul. He reached for his water, but it wasn't on the nightstand.

Frowning, he turned on the light. Only the lamp, the clock, and a Sudoku book were on the nightstand; Mrs. Drew pushed him to do a Sudoku or a crossword puzzle several times a day. The mental exercises stimulated his brain, helping with recovery.

He swore he'd brought water with him to bed. Glancing around the room, he spotted the greenish-hued glass on his dresser beyond the foot of his bed. He groaned, remembering he'd set it there to undress before going to sleep.

The walker stood along the wall by the opposite side of his bed, but he refused to use it. He debated calling Mrs. Drew to come help, but she wouldn't bring the water to him. She would help him walk and maintain his balance, but she'd insist he'd only improve by working at it.

He decided to go it alone. Swinging his legs out of bed, he eased to his feet. The room pitched, then steadied. His cell lay at his feet, but he wasn't about to bend down for it. Instead, he gave himself a few heartbeats to feel comfortable on his feet, then turned and wobbled along the bed, leaning into it for support.

At the base of the bed he hesitated, staring at the glass of water. It was only a couple of feet away, but the distance suddenly seemed farther.

He closed his eyes, visualizing taking steps to reach the dresser. Something he'd once done without thought.

Spreading his arms wide for balance, he slid his left leg forward, the carpet brushing the sole of his foot. He eased his weight forward before sliding his right foot in a half step. The effort caused him to teeter. He froze to steady himself. Taking several deep breaths, he worked up the courage to proceed with a second step. It would be harder to turn around than to proceed.

He shuffled a third step. This time, he pushed too far and tipped forward too much to pull back. He braced for collision right before he hit the dresser. He fell to his knees, leaning against the dresser and gasping for breath.

"Crippled fool. Can't even walk two feet without help."

His head ached. Had he banged it on the dresser during the fall? He breathed through the pain until he had the strength to push himself to his feet. With the dresser for support, he grabbed the water and took a big drink.

Celebrate the victory, he heard Mrs. Drew tell him in his thoughts.

What victory? Collapsing like a toddler taking his first steps?

You've a long road ahead. Recognize each accomplishment. They are little steps toward regaining independence. It was a mantra she said every time they did his exercises.

But he didn't want encouragements. They were nothing but lies to himself. The reality was that doing the most basic things on his own—dressing himself, going to the bathroom, going anywhere—was beyond his abilities. He was helpless. Feeble.

A second large gulp of water relieved his thirst. He set aside the glass. He glanced back at the bed, debating whether to go back to sleep, but he felt energetic despite his fall.

His stomach rumbled. There was leftover spinach lasagna in the fridge. Mrs. Drew had cooked it from scratch. It was her one exception to the rule that he needed to do things for himself. Eating well—no freezer meals or takeout—was more important than him risking injury to do it himself. She cooked from his mother's old recipe books, so he'd have familiar, comforting dishes, but she mixed in her own recipes as well.

The kitchen was too far. He was too weak to get there. His office? It was adjacent to his bedroom. He could get on the computer and check out news sites. Investigator Wright still had no leads on Mary and the baby's whereabouts. The trail seemed cold. All he could do was keep checking the news, hoping a story might pop up about her.

******

Brice dropped into his black office chair and tensed from the cold leather on his bare back. It had taken him over twenty minutes to make his way along the wall to his door, back up a few steps to open it, which had been the most difficult of all—he'd almost fallen twice retreating—then edge around the corner into the office. At first he'd gone to the left to flip on the light switch, before shifting weight from one doorframe to the other and following the door to the desk and his chair.

The short trek left him drained, his shoulders and arms weak.

Celebrate the victory.

It felt more like proof of his feebleness. To keep from dwelling on it, he fired up the computer and waited as the Windows icon displayed on his monitor for ten seconds before the log-in booted up.

Once he'd logged in, he pulled up a news site and also fired up Outlook out of habit. He scrolled past news stories on the latest Presidential debates and conflicts in the Middle East before glancing at the dozens of new emails in his inbox. Most were spam, but one warned that his cloud backup was almost full and prompted him to buy more storage space.

He had two hundred gigabytes of storage. How had he filled that much up?

Frowning, he pulled up the cloud site in his browser, rather than trusting the link in the email, as Jaxon had taught him to do several years ago. The site prompted him for a log-in. He tried his computer log-in, which didn't work. For a moment he stared at the username and password boxes, trying to recall them. Where did he keep his passwords?

He checked the desk drawers. The top two lacked papers. The bottom had a large stack of papers that he fished through until he came across a sheet with log-ins. His username was his email address. The password combined his street address and his hometown before his childhood accident—Detroit.

Involuntarily, he fingered his right earlobe where the outer skin had been stripped away, leaving it red, as if inflamed: the result of frostbite from his childhood fall through the ice.

He logged in, clicked on "manage storage," and browsed the files. To his surprise, he found video files sorted into two categories—front and back porch security cameras.

He had cameras on the front and back of the house? Since when? He didn't remember seeing any, not that he'd been out back since returning home.

Had Jaxon added them to protect him? Why hadn't he said anything?

But the timestamps went back nine months. The last videos were dated the day of the attack, then they halted.

Had Mary taken them? Or the police during their search of the house? Investigator Wright hadn't mentioned videos.

He brought up the last file for the front porch camera. The file began with a timestamp of twelve a.m. For several minutes he watched, but there wasn't much to see. An armadillo dug for insects in the front yard at one point.

Fast forwarding, he saw himself leave for work not long after sunrise. Other cars drove past the house from time to time. He hoped Mary would come out so that he could see her. Thus far a police sketch of her face was all he'd seen, which wasn't the same. If he'd taken any pictures of her with his phone, someone had deleted all of them.

If only his memories would return, the way they had with Nate, Warren, and Lisa.

Nothing else of interest occurred until he pulled into the driveway around six fifteen, not long before the attack. He wanted to yell at himself to turn around. To not enter the house.

He slowed the footage down to normal speed and watched. The camera was video only. He had no audio of the confrontation the neighbor had called police about. And nothing spilled outside in view of the camera.

A part of him wanted to rotate the video to see inside the house, but that was as impossible now as warning himself. He was a powerless witness at his own attack.

Growing impatient, he increased the playback speed. Suddenly the video jerked downward, showing dirty black boots and jeans, before the feed cut out.

What had happened? Who had removed the camera?

He replayed the video, dragging the playback bar over to the final few minutes of footage and slowing it down. There was nothing to see until the final ten seconds when the video dropped, turning fuzzy before focusing on the boots and jeans. Then it ended. There was nothing obvious to give away the identity of the person who had removed the camera.

He played it a third time, but his only takeaway was the boots and jeans looked like a man's. They were much too large for Mary for sure. They didn't belong to him either.

The limited footage still excited him. Investigator Wright might notice more than he had, and he had yet to watch the video from the back porch camera. Whoever had attacked him hadn't come in through the front, so maybe the back porch camera had more.

He found the latest footage from it and pressed play. The video showed the woods behind the property. The house was on the last block in the neighborhood, with several miles of forest behind it. As with the front porch camera, this footage started at midnight. He sped through the night hours. Occasionally some animal zipped past the screen. The video brightened as the sun rose, and nothing of interest appeared as the morning progressed to noon. His hope faded as the afternoon passed without event.

At the four-twenty mark, three men double-timed it out of the woods. He slowed the video down to normal speed. Two of the men were of average build. They looked older than him—late thirties or early forties if he had to guess. The pair sported beards and different shades of dark brown hair.

The third man was wiry and possessed a balding head with a little gray hair. As he drew closer, Brice spotted the dirty black work boots he'd seen on the front porch footage.

His pulse quickened. Who were these men? What had they been doing here?

He forgot the questions as he got his first glimpse of Mary. Not a front view, only her back. She was short, no more than five feet six or seven inches. Curly blonde hair stretched down to her shoulders. Her back arched from her efforts to balance her swollen belly. She crossed her arms, and the men stopped.

The one in the middle spoke. Brice wanted to scream at the lack of audio. He tried to read the man's lips, but failed.

It seemed to Brice that they all knew each other. There was a familiarity in the men's expressions and Mary showed no fear at their presence. They must've come for her, but why? What did they want with her?

Mary turned back to enter the house, her face lowered, preventing him from getting a good look at her. What he saw resembled the police sketch, but left him wishing for more.

To his unease, the three men followed her. The two bearded men marched straight inside, but the older man grabbed a porch chair and set it beneath the camera. He climbed onto the chair, giving Brice a good look at his face—yellowed teeth, plenty of wrinkles, and a grin that made him think of the creepy old drunks that every bar seemed to have. The old man reached up for the camera. The video shook for a few seconds, then cut off.

He had to get these to Investigator Wright.

He'd call him. It was almost two in the morning now, but he didn't care if the investigator was asleep. This was an emergency.

To his frustration, he realized he'd left his cell phone in the bedroom. Growling, he climbed to his feet using the desk and one chair arm. The chair slid backward as he stood, tipping him sideways away from the desk. He crashed to the floor, landing on his arm. The fall knocked his breath out. For several seconds he lay there, stunned. Once he caught his breath, he rolled onto his stomach and crawled toward the door.

Before he reached the doorframe, Mrs. Drew appeared. "Oh my, Mr. Dunn, what are you doing?"

"Phone," was all he managed as he lay there on the ground wearing only his boxers. She'd helped him change every day, but her finding him here like this still humiliated him.

She grabbed for his left arm, trying to lift him, but he was too heavy for her. It was one thing for her to support him while standing, but hauling him to his feet was a different matter.

He crawled closer to the doorframe and grabbed it with his right hand. With its support and her help, he climbed to his feet. He had to get to the phone.

"Why were you up?" Mrs. Drew asked, tone scolding as they hobbled to his room.

He pursed his lips, feeling his face begin to burn. He concentrated on putting one foot in front of the other. His phone remained on the floor by his nightstand, but when he pointed for it, she strong-armed him to the bed. He had no energy left to resist. A second later he lay on his side on the bed.

He pointed at the phone, waving for it. His words came out as a mumble.

"What?" she asked, but spotted the cell on the floor. She didn't retrieve it for him. "You've overexerted yourself. What were you thinking?"

He reached for the phone again, knowing if he pushed too far he'd fall out of bed. "I need… to call…"

"Call who? Do you realize what time it is?"

He wanted to scream that he didn't care about the time, or how tired he was. "Investigator…" he said as he pointed at the phone again.

"You want to call and wake him up?" she asked in disbelief.

All he managed was a nod.

Shaking her head and huffing disapproval, she grabbed the phone, hit the button to activate it, then turned the screen to show him.

"It's dead. You forgot to charge it."

He groaned. "Please. Call?"

She tossed the dead phone on the nightstand and crossed her arms. "It can wait until tomorrow."

He shook his head. "No. It's an em… it's urgent. About her."

"I don't have his number."

"His business… it's in my pocket. My wallet." He pointed toward his shorts on the chair in the corner.

For a few seconds she studied him, as if weighing whether to call Investigator Wright, or conclude he'd lost his mind.

"Fine," she said, clenching her jaw. "But you stay there. You are not to get out of bed again."

He almost laughed. He didn't think he could've summoned the strength to get up.

She retrieved his wallet, tossing it on the dresser after she removed the investigator's business card. Then she plugged in his cell phone and left the room without another word.

He lay back on the pillow, closing his eyes, listening for her to return with word from Investigator Wright.

Chapter 9

Brice's eyes stung and his skull throbbed when he awoke. He needed another hour or two of sleep, but his room was far too bright. The clock read noon. He groaned.

He'd slept too long. Why hadn't Mrs. Drew woken him?

He sat upright, clutching his head, his mouth dry with a rancid taste. Reaching for his water on his end table, he found only his cell phone sitting on his sudoku book.

Something tickled his brain. He looked around. His water remained on his dresser. The tickle became a flood. He'd gotten up for it last night, before heading to the computer room. Before discovering the security cameras. The men. Mary. Mrs. Drew had left to call Investigator Wright.

"Mrs. Drew!"

He grabbed his phone, disconnecting the power cord. When he searched the contacts list, he discovered he'd never entered Investigator Wright's number. And Mrs. Drew had taken the business card.

"Mrs. Drew!"

"Don't shout at me," she called from the hallway. A second later she pushed the door open. "Do you need to go to the bathroom?"

He did, but that could wait.

"Where's Wright's business card?"

"That again?" She frowned, turning and gesturing out the door. "Probably still in my room."

"Why did you let me sleep?"

Placing hands on her hips, she glared at him. "The man didn't answer his phone and when I came back you were asleep. I decided whatever it was could wait until morning. You need rest to recover. Much more than you realize."

He huffed and waved her over. "Help me out of bed."

She remained where she was. "You need to remember your manners."

"I need Investigator Wright," he said, slamming both fists into the bed. "Her life depends on it."

Concern and confusion flashed across Mrs. Drew's face. "Whose?"

"Mary. The baby."

She looked doubtful, but didn't argue. Instead, she retrieved clean clothes from his closet and helped him dress. Then, wrapping her arms around his torso, helped him stand. They swayed a little, like awkward teenagers at their first dance, before he steadied on his feet. She stepped back, letting go so that he had to reach out to hold on to her, forcing him to walk under his own power.

"We don't have time for this." He took a step forward, leaning toward her for help. "Take me to… computer."

She backed away, preventing him from leaning on her, but grabbed his hands to help him balance. "What's this about?"

"I found—" He focused on the floor, sliding his right foot forward. "Cameras. There were—" He tipped to his right and would've crashed into the nightstand if Mrs. Drew hadn't gripped his arm with a steadying hand. It surprised him how much strength she possessed.

"Concentrate on walking," she advised. "Your story can wait five minutes."

He nodded and followed her to the computer room. With a grunt, he dropped into the chair and maneuvered back to his desk, tapping on the mouse to wake it up.

"What's wrong with Mary?" she asked, hovering at his shoulder.

"I don't know. These men…" A log-in box popped up onscreen; he had to think to remember the password.

"What men?"

Rather than respond, he entered the password and waited on the computer to process so he could show her. His browser remained open from the previous session with the video frozen. He tried to start it up, but a message appeared. The session had timed out.

He swore and closed the browser, then reopened the site. Mrs. Drew said nothing at his side, but he sensed nervous tension in her posture. After several minutes he had the backyard camera footage running again.

"What is this?" she asked.

"Footage of the back yard."

"You have a security camera?"

"I did..."

He skipped to the arrival of the men. Speechless, she watched the entire encounter. The hairs on the back of his neck stood up when the men followed Mary inside. Something about their expressions, Brice couldn't quite come up with the word for them, but they bothered him. He sensed they troubled Mrs. Drew as well.

Her voice trembled as she said, "I'll get his number."

As she stepped toward the door he reached out and grabbed her arm.

"Can you drive me?" he asked.

"Drive you where?"

"To the police station."

He began downloading the videos from both the front and back cameras. There wasn't much to see on the front porch video, but the investigator might notice something. When he'd finished, he removed a USB from a drawer and copied both video files onto it. "I want to take it to them."

******

At a few minutes past one in the afternoon, Mrs. Drew pulled her maroon SUV into one of the four handicap parking spots out front of HPD's north precinct. Brice wrinkled his nose, bothered by her parking in the handicap spot, but he didn't mention it to her because she might move to a regular spot and make him walk.

Pushing the passenger door wide open, he regarded the blue-striped rectangle box on the pavement. The distance to the ground wasn't something he would've given a moment's thought to a couple weeks ago. Now he hesitated. The possibility of face planting in the parking lot made the scars on his head hurt.

Instead, he waited for Mrs. Drew to shimmy out on her side, squeezed between her SUV and a squad car. She unlocked the trunk and removed the walker, which she brought around and placed beside the door.

He stared at it, his frustration rising.

"I know you hate it," she said. "So far we've gotten by without it, but I can't catch you if you fall sliding out of the car. This will support your weight. And I can put it back when you're out."

She was right, but it didn't improve his mood. He also didn't want to be a show, lying on the ground, if any bystanders arrived, so he leaned forward and gripped the handlebars in both hands, clinging hard as he slid out.

Despite his effort to take it slow, he pitched forward onto the walker. It held under his weight and Mrs. Drew gripped his shoulders to help him steady. With her help, he stood and leaned back into the SUVs rear door to make room for her to put away the walker and close the passenger door.

The ordeal reminded him of chauffeuring his mother to doctor's appointments her last year. She'd weakened to the point he'd had to lift her into and out of the car. Even in her feeble state, it had required a good bit of effort for him to handle her.

This time Mrs. Drew returned with a metal cane with an arm brace. "I thought this might help. It's not the walker, and it will give you more independence to walk."

"Thank you," he said.

It took a few minutes of fumbling with the cane for the two of them to get his right arm into the brace and raised to a level that would help him keep his balance. Then he spent a few minutes walking around, getting used to it. He still had to go slow, but he could walk on his own. The small measure of independence exhilarated him. This was a lot better than Mrs. Drew standing in front of him as he baby-stepped through the precinct.

The North precinct was a red brick building, opened a few years earlier next door to Huntsville Fire Station 8. On the other side, a large field and parking lot led to the Alabama A&M football stadium.

The precinct's front entrance had beige brick with a large glass archway and door, providing plenty of light into the lobby. Near the top of the building, large dark letters spelled out North Public Safety Complex. Below them, in smaller letters, were the words North Police Precinct.

Inside, their footsteps and Brice's cane echoed off the tile floor as they approached the front desk. An older woman with olive skin, long black hair, and wrinkles around the eyes regarded them. The smell of coffee wafted out from a pot on a table behind her.

"May I help you?" she asked as Mrs. Drew helped him to the desk.

"Investigator Wright, please." Brice leaned one arm casually on the dark gray granite raised bar top, as if he didn't need the support to stand. "I've got evidence for him. About my case."

"Is he expecting you?"

"Yes, well… no. But he knows we're trying to reach him."

"And you are?"

"Brice. Brice Dunn."

"One moment, Mr. Dunn. I'll call him." She picked up the phone and dialed. After several seconds, she hung up. "He's not answering. He must be out at the moment. I can have another investigator come out and collect the evidence if you like?"

He grimaced. He hadn't considered the possibility that Wright wouldn't be in. "Do you have another number? It's important. A woman's life is in danger."

Her mouth tightened. "What's her name? Why's she in danger?"

"Mary Smith. Investigator Wright knows about her." His left elbow hurt, so he shifted his weight. "He's looking for her. I have evidence to help."

"Okay." She hesitated for a moment, weighing how to respond. Then she typed on her computer, looking for something. Should he volunteer more information or stay quiet and let her work?

Mrs. Drew remained silent at his elbow, so he followed suit.

After a few seconds, the woman grabbed the phone and punched in a number. After a brief pause, she said, "Hello, Investigator Wright? I've got a Mr. Dunn here who says he has some evidence about a Mary Smith."

Brice heard a man's voice from the receiver, but not well enough to understand anything said.

"Mhmm…okay, I'll tell him." She listened a moment longer, then hung up the phone. "He's ten minutes out. You're welcome to wait, or we can collect the evidence and give it to him."

"We'll wait," Brice responded, not about to give it to anyone else. Plus, he wanted to talk with Investigator Wright and let him know there was more footage if needed.

He and Mrs. Drew took a seat in the corner to wait. As they waited, he fingered the USB drive, wondering if this would be the break they needed. Would the videos help the investigator locate the men? He tried to banish the fear about how much time had passed since the men had shown up at his house.

Out the front entrance windows, Brice watched the traffic pass by on Memorial Parkway. Two other officers returned, and twenty minutes passed, before Investigator Wright arrived. He looked tired, his shoulders hunched. But he straightened as Brice used the cane to rise to his feet. Mrs. Drew placed her hands on Brice's shoulders for support as he stood.

Eyes assessing them, Investigator Wright stepped forward and offered a handshake. "Mr. Dunn, it's good to see how much progress you've made."

Brice accepted the handshake, but didn't reply to the comment. Instead, he held out the USB drive. "I've got some camera footage you need to see."

Investigator Wright accepted the drive. "Cameras from where?"

"My house."

"Your house?" Investigator Wright blinked, brow wrinkling. "I wasn't aware you had any cameras."

"They were removed. I only discovered them last night."

This seemed to perplex the investigator. "You just discovered cameras at your house?"

Brice's cheeks tightened in an uncomfortable smile. "I forgot. I've had trouble remembering things."

"Sure. Sure."

Brice couldn't tell from the investigator's tone if he accepted the explanation.

"They're gone now," Brice added.

"What happened to them?"

Brice gestured at the USB. "The videos show three men... walking to the house the day I was attacked. One took down the backyard camera. The front, too, I think."

Investigator Wright stiffened. "Did you recognize any of the men?"

"No. Never seen them before."

"Is it possible you've forgotten them?"

Brice bristled at the question. "They approached from the forest behind my house. Why would they do that if I knew them?"

"Well, let's look at this footage."

Investigator Wright led them through a door beyond the bathrooms, which led to a hall. The investigator directed them to a large room with rows of tables and chairs, and a few offices along the perimeter. A couple of officers stood in the doorway of one office, talking to someone inside. The officers regarded them as they entered, then went back to their conversation.

"This way." Investigator Wright ushered them into an office in the back corner of the room, gesturing for them to take a seat while he stepped behind a simple wooden desk with a laptop and monitor.

This time Mrs. Drew helped Brice sit in the confined space. Fortunately, Investigator Wright seemed more interested in finding out what was on the USB. He plugged it into his laptop and grabbed his mouse, clicking away at the screen.

"What's the time period for these videos?"

"The whole day I was attacked. Front and back cameras as I mentioned. The men arrived at four in the afternoon. I got home from work a little after six."

The investigator double-clicked his mouse, watching his screen. "Any volume?"

Brice grimaced. "No." Whenever he had installed the cameras, he should've chosen ones with audio. It was stupid not to get them. What if they never found Mary because of that?

For the next several minutes, they sat in silence while Investigator Wright watched the videos. Other officers filed into the main room, joking and sharing stories. One talked about a DUI arrest he'd made the previous night—a law student who had given his arresting officer an earful about how it had been an unlawful stop in front of his frat house, which wouldn't hold up in court.

"These men are definitely persons of interest," Investigator Wright said, drawing Brice's attention back. "Possible witnesses. We'll try to track them down for interviews."

Brice shook his head. "What do you mean, interviews?"

"We'll talk with them. See if they witnessed anything."

Brice leaned forward, wondering if the investigator had seen the part where they removed the cameras. "It must've been them who attacked me."

"We don't know that." Investigator Wright eyed him a moment, lips tight, before resuming his study of the video. "Witnesses only reported hearing you and Mary argue and only saw her leave."

"The man who took down the back camera removed the front after I got home. They were there during the attack on me."

Wright shook his head. "They may have left out the back again well before you returned. We don't know who took down the front camera."

"Who else would it be? It's not Mary."

"All we have to go on is the clothes from the front video. Anyone could've been wearing those."

"Are you saying I could've removed the front camera wearing the old guy's clothes?" His voice rose, but he didn't care.

Investigator Wright's eyes flashed. "I'm saying we need more information. We are going to look for these guys and get their story."

"Their story?" Brice rose to his feet, using the investigator's desk to stand. "These guys weren't innocent bystanders. They invaded my house."

The investigator stiffened. "From the look of the video, Mary allowed them inside."

"Let them? She was over nine months pregnant. How could she have stopped them?"

The officers in the main room quieted, a few peeking into the office.

"Mr. Dunn, I need you to calm down," Investigator Wright said, raising both hands in a placating gesture. "We are going to follow up on this lead."

Mrs. Drew laid one hand on Brice's arm. She had also risen to her feet at some point. "Please sit down, Brice."

Brice shook her off. "Mary's been missing for weeks. Who knows what these men did to her? You should be out there now, looking for them."

A couple of officers appeared at the doorway, but didn't enter.

"We are going to look into this. If you're so concerned, why have you been sitting on this evidence all this time?" Investigator Wright's face had reddened.

Brice slammed his fists down on the desk. The investigator jumped to his feet and the officers in the doorway shouted in alarm.

"Sitting on it? I told you I just found it. And I'm not the investigator. You are." Brice jabbed a finger at Investigator Wright. "You're not taking this seriously."

Again Mrs. Drew grabbed his arm, trying to pull him back. "Brice, calm down. You're overexerting yourself."

In pulling his arm free, he yanked too hard, almost toppling over backward. He caught himself with the corner of the desk. Investigator Wright moved forward, arms up to help catch Brice if he had fallen. More officers had appeared in the doorway, eyeing him. They all seemed more concerned with him than with finding the men.

"Why are you all staring at me?" Brice yelled at them. "I'm the victim. And this guy isn't doing his job." He swung an accusatory hand toward Investigator Wright, but they were close enough that he clipped the man.

"Brice, please."

Mrs. Drew's words seemed hushed as the closest officers decided they'd seen enough. They stepped forward. He tried to back away, but they grabbed both arms, holding him as if he were the perp they were after. Him. He shook, trying to wrench his arms free. This wasn't right.

His chest tightened, making it hard to breathe. The room was so small.

"Mr. Dunn, I must insist you calm down." This came from Investigator Wright, one hand dropped to cuffs at his waist.

The simple gesture ignited a blaze within Brice. "If Mary is harmed because you didn't act on this, I'm holding you responsible." The words didn't seem enough.

The laptop rested on the desk right in front of him. Raising a foot, Brice kicked it, sending it flying off the desk.

"Brice!" Mrs. Drew shouted.

The officers who held Brice's arms, slammed him forward on the desk where the laptop had been. Someone cuffed his hands behind his back. The cold metal dug into his wrists, only making him angrier.

"Do your jobs. Go find Mary. Let me go."

They hauled him from the office. Brice stumbled, but they kept him upright, maintaining his balance as long as he kept his feet moving. He cursed them, demanding they let him go and locate the men from the video.

The officers said nothing.

Chapter 10
(Twenty-two years past)

Beulah sat on the floor, huddled over the glass coffee table, drawing a picture of a princess in knight's armor storming a castle with a dragon perched atop it. She colored the princess's hair with a pair of braided ponytails. Her mama's soaps played on the TV, but she focused on her picture.

The large red dragon gripped the castle parapets in long golden talons, each as long as the princess's sword. Dark gray smoke shot from its nostrils, and a beard with a curly point descended from its lower jaw.

Returning a brown crayon to its box, she removed a purple one and added bows to the princess's braids, longing for a pair of her own.

"What're you doing?" her mama snapped, coming down the steps.

Beulah dropped the crayon, which thumped off the glass to the floor, as she swiveled toward her mama. Her eyes widened, recognizing the tone. She went rigid. What had she forgotten?

"I told you to straighten your room. Here it is almost lunchtime. Your room is filthy, and you're coloring and watching grown-up shows."

Beulah's mouth opened and closed like a fish on land. She wanted to tell her mama that she'd put all her clothes and toys away in her room. And she hadn't been watching her mama's show, not even listening.

The words wouldn't come. She longed to run and hide, but found herself rooted in place, unable to move.

Her mama crossed the room and snatched her arm, dragging her toward the den. "That's a timeout. You know better."

Tears filled Beulah's eyes. She wanted to pull away, but in her mama's vice-like grip, it was no use. She started to bawl.

"No… mama. Please. I—" Beulah hiccupped. She wanted to beg for forgiveness. "Don't."

Her mama stopped before a brown chest and lifted the lid. Claw marks covered the underside of the lid. At sight of the interior of the chest, Beulah struggled, desperate to slip free. She used her whole body to pull, but it was like trying to escape the dragon's clutches. Her mama grabbed her other arm and swung her around before the chest.

"Get in," her mama roared.

"No, please." Beulah held up her hands in supplication, her mama little more than a blur through her tears. "I wasn't watching. I'll go clean my room."

Her mama pushed her toward the chest. "This is your fault. You should've done it when I told you. Now get in!"

"I'm sorry mama, please. I don't want a timeout." Even as Beulah pleaded, she stepped into the chest. Despite her terror, she knew refusal would mean even worse.

"Lie down!"

"No, please. No." The chill flooding through her made her bladder hurt. Wetness flooded down her cheeks. She coughed so hard that she thought she'd get sick.

Her mama backhanded her, snapping her head sideways. "Lie down now! Don't make me tell you again."

The rage in her mama's voice forced Beulah's knees to buckle. She dropped, butt hitting the wooden bottom. She tucked her knees and rolled over on her side, lying down. Even as she begged her mama to forgive her, the chest lid closed.

"Stupid girl," her mama snarled. "Why won't you learn."

In the darkness, Beulah's heart thumped in her chest as if trying to escape on its own. Her cries cut off as her throat constricted. She gasped for air that seemed in short supply.

A lock snapped shut. A part of her wanted to lash out, to beat at the lid. She imagined somehow battering it to pieces. But she'd only broken nails trying that before. Instead, she hugged herself, shrinking inward, a lone buoy in a storm.

Chapter 11

Anger cooled as Brice sat on a bench in the intake room of the Madison County jail. A few others huddled on surrounding benches, while a young frat boy yelled obscenities at the guards from a cell along the perimeter.

Why had he gone off on Investigator Wright like that? The investigator's lack of urgency had frustrated him. No, the burning he'd felt was a lot more than frustration. More like pressure building inside a volcano until it erupted. But why?

He worried for Mary and the baby. And the video of the three men had crystallized the threat he'd sensed since awakening from his coma. Or perhaps it was the lack of progress that got to him. The failure of Investigator Wright and anyone else associated with the investigation to turn up any real leads on Mary's disappearance and discover what happened to him after more than a month.

Still, that hadn't warranted his explosion. Even as it had happened, during the heat of his fury, a part of him had been a surprised bystander, unable to do anything about the blowup.

Now he sat in a place his mother had sworn he and his brother would never see the inside of. She had ruled over their teenage years, planning out the hours of their days, weeks, and months to ensure they hadn't the time to get into trouble. And she'd punished any misbehavior or smart mouth with a wooden spoon, shoe, hairbrush, or whatever she could lay her hands on at the moment. Once, she even threatened Jaxon with his baseball bat when he came home drunk from partying with teammates after they took state in basketball. He'd only missed curfew by thirty minutes, but that had been enough to put her on the war path, preventing him from sneaking in to sleep it off.

If she were still alive, Brice knew he never would've called her to come bail him out. He would've stayed here until his court date rather than face her. It would've been safer in here where she couldn't reach him.

"Brice Dunn?" A guard stood in the doorway back near the phones, which resembled old fashioned pay phones.

Brice used the nearby wall to support himself as he climbed to his feet. He hobbled along the rows of benches, one hand against the wall to maintain his balance. The other inmates hooted and hurled insults at him, speculating crudely as to the reasons for his affliction.

The guard, large and muscular like a bouncer, watched him in silent bemusement, hands on his hips as if he had all day to wait on Brice to reach him. He had the smooth, babyish face of someone unable to grow facial hair, though he was likely only a few years younger than Brice himself.

As Brice neared, the guard shook his head. "Arrest for malicious mischief, assault, resisting arrest. All misdemeanor charges, but I'm curious how a man barely able to walk pulled those off. I bet it's some kind of story."

"Probably walked good until the officers who arrested him got their hands on 'im," an old, grizzle-bearded man said from a nearby bench.

"Nah." The guard shook his head. "Don't you know this man here's a celebrity? All over the news a month back. Beaten until he ended up in a coma for a week or so, isn't that right?" He gave Brice a questioning glance.

The others laughed and jeered even harder at this.

Brice said nothing, so the guard continued. "What I can see of your injuries are at least a month old, so what landed you in here?"

Brice ignored the question. "What did you need?"

The guard studied him a moment longer with that curious expression, waiting to see if Brice would spill. When Brice didn't, he nodded his head back down the hall behind him.

"Your bond's posted. You're being released." The guard retreated around the corner to out-processing.

To Brice's relief, he'd said nothing about Mary being the lone person of interest in his attack. If the guard knew his story well enough to recite it, he must know Mary was the only other person involved, according to public reports. He would've received more grief on his way out if the others had known, but the guard had spared him that humiliation.

Around the corner, Brice found the guard holding a door off to one side. He gestured for Brice to proceed to a large desk in the center of out-processing. Brice limped along the wall to the desk where a second guard gestured for him to take a seat. The guard handed him a sealed bag and a clipboard with some papers.

"The bag has the belongings on you at time of arrest," the guard said. He was older, with a mustache. Brice wondered if he ever teased the younger guard about his inability to grow facial hair.

"If everything is there, please sign and date the top sheet," the guard added.

"What about my cane?" Brice asked. The cane wouldn't fit in a bag.

"The contents of the bag are all that we have."

A small flame ignited inside him once more. Brice started to complain, but this time managed to halt himself. He wasn't sure the officer had the ability to revoke his bail, but didn't want to test it.

Instead, he took a deep breath to calm himself. Then he opened the bag to find his wallet, cell phone, and keys. He supposed it was ridiculous to carry around his keys when he could only use his house key at present. He couldn't drive, nor had any use for his work keys for now, but he refused to leave them behind. Something about carrying the full keychain gave him a small sense of normalcy. Same with his wallet, even though Mrs. Drew did all the grocery shopping at present.

After signing the sheet, the guard handed him a second form to sign.

"The next page lays out the amount of your bond and certifies that you will appear for your court date."

The page listed an overall bond of $1,500. Who had paid it? He supposed it had been Jaxon, arranged through a bail bondsman. It was something else he'd have to pay his brother back for later.

Brice signed then received two more pages with his court date and a place to sign that he'd been notified of it. He was scheduled for next month on the 21st at the Madison County courthouse. It was doubtful that he'd be driving by then. Mrs. Drew would have to bring him. He wondered if she'd ever had to drive a patient to their court hearing before.

While Brice finished signing the papers, the guard focused back on his computer.

"Give me a minute to finish your exit check," the guard said.

"Exit check?"

"We run your information through NCIC. Check for outstanding warrants."

While Brice knew he didn't have any, his stomach clenched anyway. He stared down at his hands.

After a few seconds, the guard turned back to him. "You're free to go." He pointed at the double doors behind him where the first guard waited.

Brice labored to his feet, the desk providing support. He wished he had his cane. Was it still back at the precinct?

He leaned on the desk as he made his way around it toward the doors, but there was a sizeable gap between the desk and the doors. Much more than the couple of feet he'd managed between his bed and dresser the previous night.

As he prepared himself for crossing to the doors, the original guard approached, holding out a raised arm.

"Would you like some help to the door?" His expression had no hint of condescension or amusement.

Brice didn't want the help, but he also didn't want to fall flat on his face. "Thank you," he forced himself to say as he grabbed the guard's forearm with his left hand and transferred his weight, though he maintained as much balance on his own as possible.

The guard shuffled, patient as Brice took each deliberate step toward the door.

"Look, I'm sorry about earlier," the guard said. "I have a brother who went through this kind of thing, too. Rolled his car and got hurt pretty bad. He had physical therapy for months in order to walk again.

"Anyway, after seeing you walk, it seemed bizarre that you got arrested, so I had to ask. Figured it must be a pretty good story."

Brice couldn't think of any way the story would sound amusing or anything but pathetic. "It was actually pretty sad."

"I guess they pretty much all are," the guard replied.

They continued in silence to the door where the guard opened it for him. Brice reached for the doorframe and let go of the guard.

"Good luck in your recovery," the guard said.

Brice nodded and exited, the door closing behind him.

The rest of the Public Safety Complex held courtrooms for city tickets and other minor offenses. There was also a place to pay traffic tickets or other fines.

Nate stood waiting near the main entrance, but approached once he saw Brice. To Brice's relief, Nate carried the cane from Mrs. Drew in one hand. Brice focused on the cane, unable to meet Nate's eyes. Had it been Nate instead of Jaxon who arranged his bail and paid the ten percent? That was even worse.

Nate held out the cane to him. "Mrs. Drew told me to give this to you."

Still using the wall for support, Brice accepted the cane with his free hand. He would have to thank Mrs. Drew on top of apologizing when he got back.

They exited to the parking lot and proceeded to Nate's beat up beige Ford Ranger in a handicapped parking spot. Between the cane and the door for support, Brice climbed into the passenger seat, thankful that Nate drove a small pickup. When Brice got his feet inside, Nate closed the door behind him.

Neither spoke as they set off. The awkwardness of the situation returned. Nate didn't turn on the radio to break it.

Brice didn't want to talk, so after a few minutes, he rolled down the window for the flow of air. He stared out at the businesses whipping past. Nate kept his eyes trained on the road, shifting gears as traffic slowed then sped up through stoplights. Twenty minutes later Nate pulled into Brice's driveway where Mrs. Drew's maroon SUV was parked.

Brice wasn't looking forward to speaking to her. After all, she'd been there for the whole arrest. She had tried to calm him to no avail. Perhaps he would go straight to bed, begging fatigue. He was exhausted at this point.

As he opened the door, Nate spoke. "I'll be by at eight thirty in the morning to pick you up for your doctor's appointment." He turned off the truck.

"Thanks," Brice mumbled as he opened the door. He eased out of the truck, using the cane to support his weight. He was getting more comfortable with it.

Nate climbed out as well, making his way around the truck.

As they headed up the walk to the porch, the front door opened and Mrs. Drew stepped outside. The moment her eyes landed on Brice, her mouth tightened. She crossed her arms.

Brice shifted his gaze to the broken swing in the yard, teeth bared in a grimace.

Mrs. Drew didn't make it easy on him. She remained rooted in place, staring at him so that he felt two pressure points on his head, as if her eyes drilled little holes. Nate also stood still, saying nothing. Both waited on him.

For a few uncomfortable moments, the silence hung between them, before Brice felt like a petulant teenager refusing to admit he was wrong.

"I'm sorry." He looked from the swing to Mrs. Drew. He repeated the apology loud enough for both to hear him, again not wanting to appear a sullen child.

Mrs. Drew waited, her expression unchanged. He half expected her to snap at him to standup straight like his mother used to do. Stop slouching.

"I don't know what happened. I mean, I know. Just not why." He stammered a little at this part, hoping Mrs. Drew would accept that, but she didn't budge. "It was like I had no control…"

Mrs. Drew's brow darkened. Once more he thought of his mother. She never accepted excuses. 'God didn't make you do it,' she would say if he or Jaxon ever tried to claim something they'd done wasn't their fault.

Brice shook his head. "Doesn't matter. I screwed up. I'm sorry I put you through that." He forced himself to return her gaze, to accept whatever she had to say on the matter.

She nodded once, then beckoned for him to enter. "I've got dinner reheating for you."

His stomach growled at that.

Nate coughed. "I better be getting home."

Brice paused and turned to his boss. "Thank you."

"Sure, kid." Nate returned to the Ranger. "See you in the morning."

Chapter 12

Nate pulled his pickup into the driveway at eight-thirty sharp the next morning. Using his new cane, Brice struggled to his feet and headed for the door. He'd gotten out of bed on his own and used the bathroom alone that morning for the first time, thanks to the cane. And when they'd done his morning workout routine, he'd completed each exercise with the cane instead of holding onto Mrs. Drew.

"You're doing good." She closed the book she was reading and set it on the end table. She didn't rise from her chair, which he took as another positive.

"Yes, ma'am." He limped toward the door, first grabbing his jacket from the coat rack beside the door. He had to set his cane aside and lean into the wall while he put on the jacket.

When he opened the door, Nate waited on the front porch, two McDonald's coffees in hand. He offered one to Brice.

"Thanks." Brice accepted the coffee. A chilly January wind wafted in, sending a chill through him.

Raising the second cup, Nate glanced past Brice. "Brought one for you as well."

Brice shifted to the side, not yet comfortable backing up with the cane, to make room for Nate to enter.

"You didn't have to do that." Mrs. Drew rose from the couch, a mug of coffee on the end table beside her seat. "We have plenty here."

Nate shrugged and offered her the coffee anyway. "Amy's out of town visiting her niece and I was running behind. Didn't have time to make coffee. Normally I'd wait till I got to the office—Lisa keeps a pot going all morning—but since I'm taking Brice to the doctor, I had to stop. My teachers always taught me to bring enough for the class."

"Well, I won't let it go to waste," Mrs. Drew said as she accepted the coffee. "I'll take this for the road."

After a smile, Nate turned back to Brice. "Ready?"

Brice nodded. As he made his way down the front walk, Mr. Langenberg was heading up the driveway, mail in hand. When his neighbor spotted him, Brice smiled and raised his mug in hello. The old man averted his gaze, frowning, and hurried back inside.

Mr. Langenberg had been the witness the night he was attacked. Brice had tried a couple times to thank him for likely saving his life, but the man acted as if he feared Brice would attack him. In fact, all his neighbors had shunned him since he'd returned home. Many of them had known him since he'd moved into the neighborhood as a kid. They'd known his mother and grandmother, too.

He wanted to yell that he'd been the victim and show them the footage of the men whom they should worry about, but Investigator Wright would never approve of him sharing evidence. Still, it was hard to accept all he'd lost. Not only the physical injuries, but becoming a pariah in the very neighborhood where he'd grown up.

Nate opened the pickup's passenger side door, and Brice climbed in. He leaned the cane against his seat, then gripped the coffee in both hands to warm them.

Mrs. Drew waved as she shuffled between the vehicles. "I should be back from my errands a little before noon."

"We'll grab lunch before we head back. Give you time," Nate said as he shut Brice's door and moved around to the driver's side.

Brice sipped his coffee as Nate drove out of the neighborhood. It tasted good. Black. Strong. Simple. He preferred it to the fancy gourmet brands Mrs. Drew made. Those came in too many exotic flavors that made him feel like a teenage diva queen spending her daddy's money every day on Starbucks, though he had to admit it smelled good with breakfast. Especially this morning when Mrs. Drew had prepared French toast with sausage links.

Traffic was good and they reached Dr. Korrapati's office fifteen minutes early. The neurologist's office was located in the medical mall, a small neighborhood of medical offices in southeast Huntsville. Like many offices in the medical mall, the building was bricked. Bright lights lit up the lobby as they entered, and Brice's cane clinked off the tile floor.

"Morning, Darlin'," the receptionist greeted as Brice approached. She eyed his cane with a broad smile. "Making progress, I see."

"Yes, ma'am." He'd managed a casual stroll instead of a hobble on his way in.

Her gaze diverted to Nate. "Mrs. Drew not with you this morning?" she asked.

"Not today," Brice answered. "This is my boss, Nate Day."

"I'm just the chauffeur," Nate countered.

The receptionist snorted as she retrieved Brice's folder from a file on the back wall and motioned for him to follow. She never made him wait in the lobby. He guessed she felt sorry for him.

Leaving Nate to take a seat in the waiting room, Brice followed the receptionist around a corner and into the first exam room. His vision blurred as he entered the room, a warning that he'd reached his walking limits. He remained standing while the receptionist told him Dr. Korrapati would be in with him shortly, left his file on the counter, and departed, closing the door behind her. Then he collapsed into a chair. He felt light-headed, but took deep breaths to relax.

For the first time, he was relieved it took Dr. Korrapati a full twenty minutes to enter, giving him plenty of time to regain control of his breathing.

"What a morning. I need to retire," Dr. Korrapati said as he went for Brice's chart.

Brice debated rising, but decided he needed a little more rest. He'd wait until the doctor directed him.

"How are you doing this week?" Dr. Korrapati looked up from the chart to study him.

Brice raised the cane. "Moving around a little on my own."

"Very good. And your balance with it?"

"Getting there."

"How about your head? Still getting headaches?"

"Some," Brice admitted. "Like when Mrs. Drew pushes me extra hard with exercises."

Dr. Korrapati chuckled. "How about your memory?"

Brice pursed his lips and shook his head. "Same."

The neurologist made a note in the folder, before pointing at the examination table. "Let's have a look at you."

Stacking both hands on his cane for support, Brice leaned forward and stood. His legs quivered as he rose, but he got to his feet and managed to walk to the table. Then he laid the cane on the edge and placed both hands on the end of the table as he stepped up and rotated to sit, exhaling in relief that he hadn't fallen.

Wielding an ophthalmoscope, Dr. Korrapati shined a light in Brice's eyes, checking one and then the other. Brice looked past the light to ease the strain.

"Anything I should know about?" the doctor asked.

Brice shook his head. "Not really. I'm impro… getting better, but the last year's still a blank."

"And your mood? Mrs. Drew said last time that you're a tad volatile, especially when tired. Do you still have issues with that?"

Brice hesitated.

Dr. Korrapati looked up at him questioningly. Brice didn't want to tell him. He didn't want to speak of it ever again. But the fury had been overwhelming, like an independent force controlling him. He'd lashed out, like a bullet fired from a gun, headed straight for impact with nothing he could do to stop it.

"Whatever it is, tell me," Dr. Korrapati said, taking a step back. "The more I know, the better I can help you."

"I got arrested yesterday," Brice said, feeling his face begin to burn. "Lost my temper with the investigator working my case. Bad."

Dr. Korrapati nodded and crossed his arms. "Talk me through it." He sounded like a researcher wanting the details. No hint of judgment.

"I don't know." Brice shrugged, unsure how to elaborate. "I just lost my temper."

"How angry were you?"

"Bad. But it was like... I couldn't…."

"It was like you'd lost your ability to control yourself?" Dr. Korrapati asked.

"Yes."

The doctor retrieved his file and read through it again for about thirty seconds. "With your injuries, damage to the limbic system, that's not unusual, I'm afraid. That's an area that not only controls memory but also emotion. Your injuries may have inhibited your ability to control your feelings."

Brice grimaced. Instead of relief at the explanation, he felt horrified at what this meant. It was a bit of himself he'd lost. "I'll heal. Get better. Right?"

Dr. Korrapati pursed his lips and rubbed at his chin for a moment. "It's impossible to say. We can't predict how the brain will heal."

Heat ignited within Brice. Not to the same intensity as with Investigator Wright, but definitely there. He wanted to lash out and demand Dr. Korrapati fix him. It was his job.

"Did you have trouble breathing?" Dr. Korrapati asked.

Brice frowned. "Yes. Some."

"Maybe it was the situation that caused your problem."

"What do you mean?"

"Were you alone with the investigator when you were arrested?"

"No. Mrs. Drew was there. And other officers. We were at the investigator's precinct."

Dr. Korrapati nodded, this time as if things were falling into place. "With your injuries, your brain may not process a lot of people well. Or chaos. You were likely dealing with claustrophobia, and the stress of being arrested isn't easy on anyone."

"But I've never been claustrophobic," Brice protested. Thinking about it, though, he had felt overwhelmed.

Dr. Korrapati set the chart aside. "You're not the same as you've always been. Your brain isn't processing stimuli in the same way."

"What do I do?" Brice asked, afraid to hear the response.

"You need to stay out of high stress environments. Too many people, too much going on, is likely too much for you to handle. At least for a while."

"So, I should hide at home? I can't go anywhere?"

Dr. Korrapati shook his head. "Not at all. Getting out is important to recovery. Just not places with sizeable crowds, and make sure someone is always with you to help out."

"Mrs. Drew went to the police station with me. She tried to stop me, but nothing she did helped," he snapped, the fire inside still simmering.

The doctor raised his hands in supplication. "Because you need calmer environments. Ones that don't introduce stress."

Brice exhaled through his nose. Was this his life now? Was he doomed to be a lonely, crippled hermit? Shunned by his neighbors and unable to venture out in public for fear he'd snap and hurt someone…

"How're your mental exercises going?" the doctor asked.

Brice wanted to shout at the doctor to forget the damn exercises. What did they matter if his injuries were beyond his control? How would the exercises help? As if a sudoku puzzle could stop his outbursts. They were more likely to cause them than help. If Mrs. Drew told him one more time that he had to finish his sudoku puzzle before she'd serve him dinner....

Thinking of Mrs. Drew insisting he finish his exercise before eating calmed him. Perhaps the familiarity of it or the routine.

"I do them some," Brice admitted.

"You may not feel it, but these exercises help the brain heal, or develop new pathways," Dr. Korrapati said. "The same way physical therapy helps the body heal."

Brice accepted that without comment.

Dr. Korrapati approached and laid a hand on Brice's shoulder, squeezing. "It's going to be difficult, most likely for a long time, but some things will improve. Take it slow."

The doctor had said the same things in his previous appointments. Mrs. Drew had as well. Believing that was difficult, when he dealt with more hitches and failures than successes. How many more losses were ahead? And would any gains he made ever match up?

"There's one other thing I'd like you to do," the doctor added.

"What's that?" Brice asked, unenthused about something new on his checklist.

"I'd like you to keep a journal."

"A journal?" Brice wrinkled his nose. "Of what? My exercises? My days?" He said this last bit as though it were ridiculous.

"If you want," Dr. Korrapati replied. "Or things you remember. Whatever you want. It's the activity that matters, forcing your brain to process your day. And it's less taxing than your exercises."

"I'll try," Brice replied, unsure if he meant it or not.

Dr. Korrapati retrieved Brice's folder and made a few additional notes. "I'd like to see you again in two weeks. In the meantime, if you have any more issues, tell Mrs. Drew so she can keep me informed." With that, he left.

Brice grabbed his cane from behind him, but didn't stand. He needed a minute alone.

Perhaps Mary leaving had been for the best. What good was he to her or the baby like this?

He wanted to know where they were. And that they were safe. After that, he wasn't any good to them in his present condition.

Chapter 13

Brice woke in a cold sweat, the baby's cries ringing in his ears. It was only a dream, but that did nothing to calm his runaway heart. Instead of a white fog, this time he'd wandered through a forest of aspens devoid of leaves. Every time he'd pin-pointed the baby's cries, behind a tree trunk or boulder or beneath a log, he'd hurry to look, only to find nothing. The cries would then echo from another direction. He'd try to run, only to feel as though he slogged through water.

He was chasing the baby. Mary's baby. His baby? He never chased Mary, just the baby. Did that mean he prioritized the baby over Mary? Or was he receiving some sort of cosmic message that it was too late for Mary, but not for the baby?

The image of the three men sauntering up to the house flashed into his mind. Those men hadn't been here out of kindness. They posed a threat to Mary and the baby, but he had to believe it wasn't too late. Had to believe there was time for him to locate Mary, the baby, and those men, so he could make things right.

The clock on the end table read four-thirty. The sun wouldn't rise for a couple more hours, but Brice knew he wouldn't relax enough to sleep. He pulled back the blanket and swung his legs out of bed. He checked his phone. Investigator Wright had never returned his call. Brice told himself it was because Investigator Wright was too busy tracking down the men.

After returning home post lunch yesterday—a small café with cheap food and only a handful of customers—Brice had called Investigator Wright to apologize. The call had gone straight to voicemail, which made the apology a little easier for Brice. When he'd hung up, his mother's voice had scolded him that he wasn't getting off that easy. He would apologize again the next time he spoke to the investigator.

The apology wouldn't happen now, in the middle of the night. Not wanting to wake Mrs. Drew, Brice reached for his cane and struggled to his feet. He went through the slow process of retrieving jeans and a shirt, then sat on the end of the bed to dress, enjoying the ability to do it himself. As he pulled his jeans up his thighs, he started to slide off the bed. He fell backward on the mattress and adjusted himself before resuming dressing. Once he'd pulled on his shirt, he debated what to do now.

After the nightmare, he wanted to find something to help locate Mary and the baby, yet he was at a loss on what to do. He'd finished searching through the remaining stored footage from the security cameras, using whatever free moments he got from Mrs. Drew; she'd been increasing his exercise load of late. The stored footage went back a month before his accident, but had shown nothing but himself and Mary, and occasional animals meandering past in the back yard. And it appeared that no one special had passed by the front yard.

He'd spent some time observing Mary in those videos, willing himself to remember her. She'd lived in his house for a year, but the videos offered the only proof. She'd left nothing behind, at least as far as he and Jaxon knew. It was as if she'd been no more than a guest here. Or as if she'd always expected those men to find her.

Had she? She hadn't acted surprised when the men arrived. Had she known what they'd do to him? Had she stood by and watched them beat him to near death, then walked out, taken the car, and driven away?

Easing down the hallway past Mrs. Drew's room, he used the wall for support, placing the cane carefully to minimize noise and avoid waking her.

It was too early for breakfast, so he proceeded to the living room and turned on a lamp. Taking a seat on the couch, he pondered doing a sudoku or crossword, but he wasn't in the mood to concentrate. He grabbed the remote but didn't turn on the television. He didn't feel like watching anything, especially not the news.

Growing restless, he stood and walked over to the pictures hanging on the wall. Mrs. Drew insisted that studying things from his past should help with his lost memories, but these were all from his childhood. He'd found none of Mary.

There were the pictures for Jaxon's baptism, as well as his, both up in Michigan. Next came Jaxon's freshman football pic, kneeling on the ground in his blue and gold Johnson High uniform. Jaxon had played wide receiver for four years and gotten a few scholarship offers to small colleges, but he'd had enough at that point, even then knowing he wanted to work for the FBI. Jaxon had pretty much always known what he wanted growing up, unlike Brice.

That had changed the day he began working for Nate. His mother had hung a picture on the wall of him standing next to a Subaru in the shop, the first vehicle Brice had ever worked on. It had been a simple oil change, rather than a repair job. It surprised him that he still remembered that more than a decade after he'd started working there.

The clang of his cane hitting the ash bin by the wood stove, followed by the lid hitting the brick hearth, made him freeze. He listened, hoping he hadn't woken Mrs. Drew, but doubting she had slept through that. Yet after several breaths, her door didn't open. The only noise in the place was the sound of his breathing and the hum from the heater.

He bent to pick up the lid, using the wall and cane to keep himself from toppling over. The bin had ash in it. He'd have to tell Mrs. Drew that anytime there was a fire, they needed to dump out the ashes as soon as they'd cooled.

Except they hadn't made a fire since he'd been home from the hospital. How did it get in here?

He never left ash in the bin like this. His mother would've been furious. She'd always insisted he clean the ashes out of the bin first thing the next morning any time they'd had a fire. He had continued the practice after her death. It was the way things were done in the Dunn household. A couple years back he'd discussed the habit with Jaxon and learned his older brother did the same in his own place up in Chicago. Funny, the things children learned from their parents and never once thought to question.

As he reached for the bin to go dump it out, he noticed a corner of newspaper poking up out of the ashes. He pursed his lips. He never started a fire with newspaper.

Curious, he picked up the bit of paper. The top half was blank, but when he flipped it over, he found a date—November 14, 2014. Almost eight years ago.

The Huntsville Times hadn't been delivered to their house since his mother's death. Even then, they had never kept the paper. They'd read each day's edition, collected them in plastic bags for a couple weeks, then dropped the lot off for recycling.

He dropped the paper back in the bin and grunted as he struggled to his feet, putting all his weight on his cane. He carried the bin to the kitchen and dumped the ashes in the trash can, where they spread over a couple of empty tomato sauce cans, some carrot peels, and a ground beef wrapper. A couple of other pieces of newspaper landed on top.

He picked up a second piece, checking both sides. This one was blank. On a third, he found the letters A, t, and l printed on it. The rest had burned away.

Atlanta, he guessed. Why had there been an Atlanta paper here? And which one?

Fishing out the last couple bits of paper, he found the one with the date again but nothing on the last. He set them on the counter. Had Mrs. Drew brought an old copy of a newspaper over with her? If she'd kept an old newspaper for close to a decade, it seemed unlikely she'd bring it here only to burn it.

Yet someone had brought it here and burned it. And while the date and three letters weren't much to go on, he'd bet he could figure out which newspaper it had come from and find a copy of that issue online.

Before he looked it up, he needed some coffee. He shuffled to the corner cabinet above the coffee pot. Mrs. Drew's coffee—coconut macaroon—sat in front. He pushed it off to the side and retrieved a can from the back, along with the sugar shaker.

After setting up the pot to brew six cups, he stood back to wait. How long had those ashes been in the bin? If Mary had moved in last winter, they would've had some occasion to build a fire, and he would've mentioned the whole cleaning out the ashes bit. Right? Or would he have done it himself without telling her? But if he hadn't told her, she would've left the ashes in the wood stove to cool until he cleaned them up.

Unless she'd done the fire the day of the attack. Maybe while the men had been here? That explained why he'd never emptied the bin later.

He kept coming back to the question of why she or anyone else would have an eight-year-old newspaper on hand unless it possessed something of value. And if it did, why burn it?

He grabbed a maroon Alabama A&M coffee mug and poured himself a cup, adding a little sugar. Taking a sip, he spit it out in the sink and wiped his mouth clean. He glanced over at the jar on the counter. It was hot chocolate.

He dumped the mug's contents down the sink. What was wrong with him? Couldn't he even make coffee right? Coffee grounds and hot chocolate powder looked nothing alike. Nor did coffee and hot chocolate.

Shaking his head, he grabbed the coffee pot, dumped the whole batch in the sink, and rinsed the pot. He washed out the reusable filter and set it aside, wondering if he'd need to do a more thorough cleaning of the coffee pot later to get the hot chocolate residue out.

Disgusted, he resigned himself to a coke from the fridge. Then he retrieved the newspaper pieces from the counter, slipped them into his pocket, and made his way back to his office.

*****

It took Brice only a few minutes searching the web to discover that there was only one major daily newspaper in Atlanta—The Atlanta Journal-Constitution. According to Wikipedia, the AJC had been around since 2001 when the Atlanta Journal and the Atlanta Constitution had combined.

He pulled up the AJC site, and the font type on his pieces of paper matched that of an edition shown onscreen. He surfed the site, checking the latest news stories, before locating the archives. From there he had access to any edition of the paper dating back to June 17th, 1868. The archive also held four years of backlog of the Mundo Hispanico, Atlanta's largest Spanish-language newspaper.

Brice looked up the November 14 edition from 2014. A window popped up, giving him the option to buy a monthly subscription to the full archive or sign up for a free trial. He signed up for a trial. The cover page of the AJC for that date appeared onscreen. The feature story covered some dispute related to the Atlantic Symphony Orchestra, followed by articles with titles that didn't appear relevant.

He sipped his coke as he flipped through page after page until he reached the legal notices. A name jumped out at him. An obituary for a Mary Smith, with a funeral planned for November 16.

His stomach churned.

The notice mentioned that her father, Rick Smith, had survived her. The notice didn't have a picture.

Both Mary and Smith were common names, but if his assumptions were correct about the newspaper, why would his Mary have one with an obituary for another Mary Smith? And based upon the date of birth, one who would've been roughly the same age.

It was too far-fetched that Mary would have the paper coincidentally. So why had it been in her possession? And why had she burned it?

Since the AJC was Atlanta's only major newspaper, he had no other sources to check for a picture. Even if he found one, what would that tell him? The notice didn't note how she died, so he flipped through the previous week's papers, searching for an article that might report her death. He found nothing.

Had his Mary known this other one? Had she been this other Mary and somehow faked her death? But if she was the Mary from the obituary, why carry around the clip?

The one other option that came to mind was that his Mary had assumed this dead girl's identity, which led to more questions. Who was she? Why had she taken this identity? Had she used it to hide from the men? How had they found her?

Or was he concocting some crazy story because he had no answers?

The obit write-up didn't mention foul play in this Mary Smith's death. The only useful thing he found was the name of Mary Smith's father, Rick. But after googling the name and Atlanta, Georgia, he discovered two hundred sixty-nine Rick Smiths in Atlanta alone, and five hundred seventy-two in the state, assuming Mary's father still lived in Georgia.

Brice searched the white pages listing of the Rick Smiths in Atlanta, hoping to find something that would help. For some listings the site noted family members, but he didn't find a Mary Smith under any of them.

What about Mary? He googled her name, but came up with over one thousand Mary Smiths in Atlanta alone.

He slumped back in his chair. It would take forever to search every Mary on the site, hoping to find one with a family member named Rick Smith. That also assumed the correct Mary Smith still existed in the white pages. She might've long since been deleted. And even if he tracked down the correct Rick Smith, what would that tell him? It would confirm if she was the same Mary Smith, but that wouldn't get him any nearer to finding her or the baby.

Would Investigator Wright have some ideas of what to do with this information?

Mrs. Drew stirred in her room. Brice hoped he hadn't woken her.

If she was up, he didn't want her to find him in here digging into this again. He didn't need another lecture.

Instead, he struggled to his feet and hobbled down the hall. He wanted coffee now, so he resolved to clean out the coffee maker and make a fresh pot.

Chapter 14

Brice sat at the dining room table with a black journal while Mrs. Drew loaded dishes into the dishwasher. She had picked up the journal for him while out grocery shopping, agreeing with Dr. Korrapati that it would aid his recovery.

The journal was nice, with a black leather cover and a mini calendar on the inside. At first, he'd argued that he worked easiest on a computer, it being the twenty-first century and all, but Mrs. Drew had insisted the physical aspect of handwriting his thoughts was better for him. It would make him think about what he wanted to write. A journal also offered fewer distractions than a computer.

Now, as he sat at the table staring at the first blank page in the journal, he wondered where to begin. Should he write about the day's exercises? He wrinkled his nose. How would this help if it bored him? Nor could he imagine ever wanting to remember this time or share it with anyone else.

He debated recording his discovery about Mary from the newspaper, except he'd learned nothing that would help him find her. During their brief conversation, Investigator Wright hadn't sounded all that enthusiastic about the information, though he had said he would do a little research to see if it turned up anything.

Of course, his handling of the newspapers had left his prints on them. That had been one of Investigator Wright's first questions, and Brice had groaned to himself that he hadn't thought of that before touching them. Wright had dismissed the issue, noting that they didn't know how the papers had gotten there in the first place, and that the chances anyone had touched the paper in those spots that didn't get burned were slim.

Brice knew those were excuses. He had screwed up.

He picked at the worn blue linen placemat beneath his journal. It had the "For God so loved the world" Bible verse stitched into it. Matching placemats, each with a different bible verse, adorned each place at the table, a wedding gift from Grandma Dunn to his mother. They represented home as much as anything else in the house.

Brice shook his head to clear his thoughts. The placemats weren't helping him come up with anything for his journal. Why was this so hard? His mother had always made writing in a journal look easy. Every night she'd written in her journal after dinner while he or Jaxon had done the dishes. Some entries had been short and completed by the time they'd finished cleaning up. Other days she'd written several pages before joining them for a show or to read before bed.

She'd never showed her journal to him. He remembered asking once what she wrote. Her response had been that they were her private thoughts, and he needed to respect her privacy.

When she'd finished each night, she'd slipped the little journal back into a drawer in the antique desk against the back wall. That was where she'd also stored the mail, stamps, and bills. She'd always written out checks at the dining room table as well, and balanced her checkbook at the end of every month. Even when she'd upgraded from paper to an Excel spreadsheet and paying bills online, she'd still sat at the table to do them.

Was the journal still in the desk? He'd never removed it after her death. Had never thought about it, or even gone through the desk, and he doubted Jaxon had either.

Using his cane and the table for support, Brice rose and started for the desk.

"Didn't spend much time writing," Mrs. Drew said in a chiding tone.

"I'm looking for something," he replied over his shoulder.

The desk, originally white, had yellowed with age. It had one of the breadbox-style lids that closed down over the desk. It was where his mother had kept her laptop and the stacks of mail and bills.

But her journal, she'd always kept that in the small top drawer on the left. He reached for the drawer, feeling both anticipation and guilt at doing so. They were her private thoughts. But she was gone. Would it bother her for him to read them now?

He opened the drawer and found a stack of journals, each with a different color flower on the front. They'd been waiting here for fifteen years. Had his mother been gone so long? Half his life now, though it didn't feel like it.

He chose a journal at random—white with purple delphinium flowers on the front. The journal wasn't much larger than one of his hands. He slid free the purple strap holding it shut and opened the journal, ignoring the tightening in his gut at the trespass.

The familiar scrawl stung his eyes. Her handwriting was like his, but smaller. He supposed his was like hers instead.

Observing her handwriting was like seeing her again. He stared at the page, taking in the cursive text the way one might a loved one they hadn't seen in years. She'd been the one to teach him to write, first in print on construction paper with crayons, then in cursive on the backs of the envelopes from their opened mail. He'd asked her for a notebook to practice his cursive on, like the ones he and Jaxon took to school, but she said she wasn't buying extra paper when the stuff that came in the mail worked just fine.

His eyes focused on the date at the top of the first page and his smile dissipated. The date was January 27th. He skimmed the text and confirmed that this first entry detailed him arriving home from the hospital after falling through the ice up in Michigan.

He turned the page. Now wasn't the time for that memory. Nor could he bear to peek through that window into his mother's heart.

Had that been when she had started journaling? Because of him? Or had she just started a new journal then? He tried to recall if he'd seen her journal up in Michigan, but his clearest memories of her doing it were all in this house. He couldn't remember for sure. In those days up north, as soon as dinner ended, he would've been outside in the summer or off to his room to play in the winter. It wasn't until his teenage years that he'd started doing dishes some nights, and that was when he recalled her hunched over this journal. But she'd obviously at least started up in Michigan.

He skipped past several pages—the dates revealing that she hadn't yet started daily entries—until he hit one from early March that made his breath curl up in his mouth and slide back down his throat to create a lump around his Adam's apple.

March 4
The bastard left. Packed a suitcase and walked out the door while the boys were at school. Coward.

Couldn't even face his own sons.

How am I supposed to tell Brice that his father left because he couldn't cope with the difficulties of raising a child with impairments? Or with trying to keep up with the medical bills.

Oh God. How am I going to provide for these boys and cover Brice's medical expenses on my wages from the law firm?

If that bastard were standing in front of me right now, I'd claw his eyes out. Only reason I didn't earlier was I was too shocked to do more than numbly watch. I'd never imagined him capable of walking out on his sons.

Me maybe, but never his sons.

Bryce's eyes burned. He scrunched up his nose, forcing back any threat of tears. That day he'd come home to find his mother sitting on the couch, eyes red-rimmed, a beer in one hand and two crushed cans on the coffee table. He'd known something was wrong more by the beer than her eyes. She rarely drank. Only at special events, and then only one. To find her on a third beer in the middle of the afternoon, he'd thought someone had died. His first thought had been Grandma Dunn. She'd had her own health problems the last couple of years. Instead, a few weeks later they were down here, living under this roof with Grandma Dunn.

In a sense, his first instinct had been right. He had never seen his father again. Before the move, Jaxon had gone to beg their father to return so they wouldn't have to leave. Jaxon also had been the one to rage at their mother while she packed up their things.

Not Brice. Though he'd never received direct confirmation until now, he'd always known his father had left because of him. His mother had given him plenty of excuses, but he'd seen the guilt in her eyes, as if she had been the one to leave. He had curled his young hands into fists, refusing to show any concern over the news. Later that night he'd cried into his pillow so she and Jaxon wouldn't hear him. The next day, he had gone to school even though she'd given him permission to stay home. He'd refused to go with Jaxon to plead with their dad to return.

And when Mom had announced they were moving down to live with Grandma Dunn, which she'd claimed was because Grandma was too old to live alone, he'd packed up the house right alongside her, skipping school because what was the point in finishing those final few days?

He'd shed no further tears after that first night. If his father was through with him, he was through with his father. And with Michigan by extension.

"Dinner will be ready in a few minutes," Mrs. Drew announced, jolting Brice.

He'd forgotten where he was.

"Will you set the table?"

"Yes, ma'am." Closing the journal and slipping the strap back over the cover, he returned it to the top drawer.

It had been years since he'd thought about his father. As he had on every previous occasion since that winter, he forced those thoughts away, choosing instead to focus on his mom. On how hard she'd worked and how much she had given up to raise them; he'd been aware of it even back then. Jaxon hadn't. Brice supposed that was why Jaxon had chosen a career that forced him to move away, while he had stayed home, taking care of their mother in her last days and remaining here after her passing.

When their father had left, Brice had realized she could've done so, too. But she had done the exact opposite for him.

And he had done the same.

Chapter 15

Mary lay naked in bed, eyelids sore. She needed sleep. A shiver rippled through her, but the sheet and a corner of the comforter were all she had to cover herself. The rest, Spencer clutched to his chest.

She hated sleeping next to him because of it. He also snored like a lawnmower with engine troubles. But he'd wanted *his* tonight, so she'd had no choice but to come to his bed. It had hurt like hell. She'd spent the whole time hoping her stitches didn't rip. The saving grace was that at Spencer's age he wasn't as vigorous.

After he'd finished, she hadn't bothered going out to the couch to sleep. She'd grabbed what she could of the covers and hoped her exhaustion would overcome the cold.

Patty's cries filled the living room and trumpeted their way into the bedroom. Mary groaned as tears welled up in her eyes. She forced herself out of bed despite wanting nothing more than to lie there and cover her head with the pillow.

Or smother Spencer with it. Not that she could've, but it was fun to imagine.

She snatched her medical underpants from the floor and slipped them on, before grabbing her pants and sweater and heading for the door. She didn't bother with her bra. It was time for the baby to eat.

She limped, groin aching with every step, to the fridge. They were out of beer.

"Fuck."

There'd been a six pack in there at dinner. She should've known Spencer wouldn't let that last the night.

"Shut that baby up," Garrett yelled from his room, where her medications were. She didn't dare go for them until she'd tended to Patty.

Since the men had taken up both bedrooms, Patty lay swaddled on the floor in the living room, pinned between two couch pillows to keep her from rolling over on her face, since she was too young to lift her head. Patty had freed one arm from the swaddle and it shook above her head, punctuating her cries. Mary tossed her clothes on the couch, then scooped up Patty and offered the left breast. Patty didn't latch on. Instead, she cried around the nipple.

Mary carried her to the changing station—a wide square footrest that belonged to a blue chair. Diapers and wipes lay between the chair and end table.

"I said shut the damn baby up!"

"Shhh. Shhh," Mary soothed as she unswaddled Patty, changed the wet diaper, and wrapped her back up.

Patty continued crying, struggling against her confinement. Mary returned the baby to her breast and this time Patty latched on, her little tongue licking at the nipple to encourage milk to come.

As the baby drank, Mary sat on the couch. She shivered.

Why hadn't Arden come? She'd expected to be back in the Community by now. Back in her mother's home, but at least away from Garrett and Spencer. Instead, they remained in this waiting house where everyone, returning or new, abided until Arden came for them.

No one came into the Community without Arden leading them. He claimed it was to ensure the Community's safety. Mary guessed it had more to do with him enjoying the fact that everyone needed his permission to come or go.

Patty unlatched from the left breast and Mary switched her over to the other before she had time to cry again.

Arden would want to make a spectacle of Patty's first time into the Community, but it had been five days already. What was he waiting on? Was he just reminding her he could make her wait?

The right breast drained, Patty disengaged and resumed crying. Mary burped her, but it did nothing to satisfy her. Not wanting to risk Garrett getting angry enough to come out here, she set the baby on the couch and pulled on her clothes. She lifted her left leg where a thorny vine tattoo circled the right ankle—the Community symbol. Every member of the Community possessed the tattoo. According to Arden, the symbol meant they were all connected, and that made them whole. Also, they had thorns because they were tough. They defended themselves.

To Mary, the tattoo was a brand. And also a whip. Every woman in the Community had felt those thorns. Some, every single day.

Once more she debated going to Garrett's room for her meds. She needed a couple pills to dull her senses. She even rose from the couch and took a step toward the room, but she halted. Garrett would notice her searching for them, and with Patty still upset, he'd punish her for not following his orders.

She almost went anyway.

But Patty grew louder, so Mary scooped her up and exited out the sliding glass door to the rear driveway to reduce the noise for the men.

She walked around the brown 80s Volvo, wishing as she did so that she dared to steal the keys and run. Instead, she opened the passenger side door and climbed in. Her breath fogged; the overnight low would be below thirty. She couldn't stay out here long. Already she wished she'd brought out a jacket.

Patty didn't like the cold either, and her cries were louder in the confined space of the car.

"Shhh. Shhh." Mary bounced Patty and tapped her back, hoping to quiet her. She fought the urge to shake Patty and scream at her to shut up for five minutes. Patty had eaten and had a clean diaper. She'd burped. There was no reason for these continued histrionics.

And if Patty didn't quiet, she couldn't go back inside.

They needed warmth.

Mary opened the glove box and pawed around with one hand, getting lucky and finding a car key. She reached over, shoved the key in the ignition, and turned the car on. Her hands going numb, she flipped the temperature control to the far right, but didn't turn on the heater yet, not wanting to blow cold air on them.

Again, she fantasized stealing the car. But she knew she wouldn't get far. They'd find her. They always did. And those times when she tried to run were when the thorns cut the most.

While she waited, she hummed, hoping the melody might soothe Patty, but the baby took no notice of it. She clutched Patty close, attempting to warm her until she dared turn on the heater.

Somewhat warm air filtered into the car. Patty's cries finally subsided and Mary slumped back into the seat in relief. She continued to hum. Patty mewled and snuggled against her chest before settling.

Exhaustion took hold of Mary again, pounding her head. She craved at least an hour of sleep, but not out here. The chilly nights this time of year weren't good for her or the baby, even with the heater from the car. She needed a few minutes to gather herself, before she attempted the trek back inside. Plus, she wanted to make sure Patty was fast asleep. Far be it from her to risk making the men lose a single hour of sleep.

If Arden didn't come for them tomorrow, she was heading to the Community herself, regardless of the rules. Arden could escort her in from the front gate.

Chapter 16

Brice answered his cell on the third ring. "Hello?"

"Buenos días, Brice. How are you?" A woman asked with a strong Spanish accent.

"Uh… good… you?" he replied, struggling to place the familiar voice. Had he forgotten someone else?

"Muy bien. I heard what happened to you. You are getting better?" She must know him from somewhere.

It was frustrating. A face appeared with long, dark, frizzy hair, but the facial features wouldn't come into focus. He rubbed his eyebrows.

"I'm making progress."

In some ways anyway. Not so much in others, but he wasn't comfortable telling her that.

"That's great! Do you need anything?"

"No, I'm okay, but thanks."

For a moment there was a pause, neither of them saying anything. He sensed there was more she wanted to say. He hoped it wasn't for a firsthand account of what happened to him, since he couldn't give one, even though he was the victim, which would lead to more awkward questions.

To be polite, he asked, "Did you need anything?"

"Yes, um." Another pause. "I'm having a little trouble with the truck. You are back to work now? Maybe I should've called Nate?" The words spilled out of her.

He sighed, relieved. More than relieved. Thrilled.

"No, you're fine," he said. "What's wrong with it?"

"The engine's sputtering. It sounds weak when I'm driving. Papa told me to get it checked out over the weekend, but I was hesitant to call you. I guess I should've called Nate, but you've been handling my trucks for so long…"

Dora! Her face came into focus. A couple of years younger than him, she always wore large hoop earrings poking out from brown curly hair, which had highlights. Her lips were thick and every time she came in needing repairs, it appeared as though she'd just put on lipstick.

And she always drove a truck. She used to drive a Tacoma. He couldn't quite picture what she drove now, but he didn't think it was still the beige Tacoma.

She'd been coming to the shop for her repair work almost as long as he'd been working there. Her father had insisted she learn to deal with mechanics as soon as she learned to drive, so she gave him better descriptions of what was wrong than most people.

"Should I call Nate?" she asked, drawing him out of thought.

"No. I'd be… I can look at it." He started to say bring it into the shop and he'd check it out, but caught himself. If he went to the shop, Nate would send him home and put Warren on it instead, or do the repairs himself.

Brice had been to her place a few times when she couldn't get the truck to the shop, rather than making her call in a tow. It would get him out of the house and let him accomplish something other than exercises or puzzles.

"I'm not back at work yet, but you're special. How about I come to you?" he suggested.

"Are you sure? I don't want to ask if you're not ready."

"It's fine. It may take a couple hours, but I'll be there."

First, he had to figure out how. He couldn't drive yet, nor could he ask Mrs. Drew to take him. She'd try to stop him from working.

"Any time," Dora replied. "I'm off today, which is why I waited. I'll be home all day."

"Great, I'll see you soon."

"Gracias, Brice!"

"You're welcome, Dora."

As he hung up the phone, he debated the best way to get to her place. She lived in the Mt. Carmel area, a twenty-minute drive. He marveled that her location came back to him so quickly when he hadn't been sure who she was when they started talking.

Now to figure out how to get to her. Mrs. Drew had told him she needed to buy groceries before lunch. She'd invited him to come, but he'd declined, telling her he'd work crosswords or Sudoku. In truth, he didn't wish to go to the grocery store. Ever since the incident at the police station, he found it difficult to go anywhere that was likely to have more than a couple of people.

Now he had something better to do, if he figured out how to get there.

Uber.

He could call an Uber to drive him out to Dora's. He'd never used one before, but figured it couldn't be all that hard.

Chapter 17

After downloading the Uber app to his phone, registering an account and ordering a ride took longer than Brice cared to admit. He was sure he would've done it in less time—with fewer inquiries from Mrs. Drew about what he was up to that he had to dodge—before his accident. Of course, before his accident Mrs. Drew wouldn't have been around to question him. And he would've driven.

A twenty-something named Luke, dressed in a gray jacket, khakis, a visor, and sunglasses, arrived in a ricer. The black Camry had a spoiler on the back, tinted windows, and undercarriage lighting. If he hadn't been in a hurry to get out to Dora's to fix her truck, he might've cancelled the ride and waited for another without the useless modifications.

Around lunch time, Luke turned into the neighborhood right before the Winchester Road bridge crossed the Flint River. A shiver rippled through Brice at the closeness of the bridge and river. In fact, the houses on the left side of the block were less than a hundred yards from the river. Fortunately, Dora lived on the right side of the street, elevated on a hill.

Exiting the ricer, Brice pulled out his toolbox. An icy wind picked up, stinging every inch of exposed skin. Each foggy breath billowed in front of his face. It wasn't the warmest weather for turning a wrench, but he didn't want to let Dora down, especially after he'd come all this way. Besides, he looked forward to working on a vehicle again.

With the toolbox in one hand and his cane in the other, he labored up the hill of Dora's driveway, hoping he didn't fall and roll back down.

Sky blue vinyl siding covered her two-story house, a nice change from the dirty yellow it had been when she'd bought it. He'd helped her repaint it about a month after she'd moved in, along with her father and brother.

As he neared the top of the driveway, the garage door droned up. Dora emerged, wearing a thick flannel button-down shirt, jacket, and gloves. A single blonde lock of hair lay on her right shoulder. She'd pulled the rest of her dark brown hair back in a ponytail. As usual, she wore steel-toed boots.

"Gracias for coming," Dora said, her full lips bright red. She eyed his cane and her brow darkened. "Are you sure you're okay to look at the truck?"

"Sure, the cane is for balance." He raised his toolbox a little. "But do you have something I can set this down on?"

"Of course." She shivered, rubbing her gloved hands together before grabbing a folding chair from the wall and placing it in front of the cab of her truck, a jungle-green Nissan Frontier. "Sorry for asking you to work on my truck in such frigid weather." She rubbed her hands again.

"It's no problem," he assured her.

He wanted to ask for a second chair so he could rest a moment after the hike up the driveway, which had left him more winded than he cared to admit. He would just take it slow for a few minutes.

Dora opened the driver's door. "The engine's sputtering, but I don't know why." She popped the hood.

He dropped the toolbox on the chair and stepped closer to the engine to look, tracing the labyrinthine block of dusty hoses, wires, belts, and metal. There was nothing obvious to the eye.

"Start her up for me?"

She hopped into the driver's seat. A couple clicks from the ignition and the engine sputtered to life.

"Give it a little gas."

She did and the engine sounded strained, coughing on too little air.

"Kill it."

The engine stopped. Dora hopped out of the truck and came up, arms crossed in front of her.

"What do you think?"

He shrugged. "Cap and rotor, maybe. Let me check."

He grabbed a screwdriver from his toolbox. Pushing aside the cables plugged into the distributor cap, he unscrewed it.

While he worked, she leaned over the side, watching him. The sweet scent of perfume reminded him of something. It made him wonder what kind Mary wore. Did he know before the attack? He must have. Another thing he'd lost of her.

The screws fell into his hand, and he popped off the distributor cap. It was scorched and worn.

"This is the problem?" she asked, leaning in to see them.

He felt her closeness even without touching. He nodded. "Probably. Even if it's something else, this isn't helping."

"You can fix this?" she asked.

He set the cap and rotor on the lid of his open toolbox. "They should have aftermarket parts at O'Reilly's. I'll go pick one and should have you fixed up in no time."

Her beaming smile was pure delight, eliciting a smile from him. She turned and stared down the empty driveway and street, likely noticing for the first time that his car wasn't there. "You didn't drive?"

"No, can't drive yet," he answered.

"If you hook the truck back up, I can drive that far."

He shook his head. Now that he had the cap and rotor removed, he didn't want to put them back on, even if it hadn't taken that long. And something about her having to drive him bothered him. He wasn't sure why. After all, Mrs. Drew drove him all the time, but with Dora it felt different.

"It's okay. I can walk," he said. It was a half mile at most to O'Reilly's.

Her brow wrinkled with concern. "That's too far. And it's cold out. I'll feel bad."

He wasn't thrilled about the possibility of walking that far either, not at his current pace. Then he spotted a Segway at the back of the garage.

"That thing still work?" he asked, pointing at the electric scooter.

"The Segway?" she asked, moving around her side of the truck toward it. "As far as I know. Alfredo left it when he re-upped last time."

Alfredo was her younger brother. A big, muscular man, he'd signed up with the Army after high school. Brice had only seen him on a couple of occasions.

She grabbed the handlebars and steered it toward him.

"Where is he now?" Brice asked.

She shrugged. "He's a Ranger. I only hear where he's been after he's back. If it's something he can talk about." She offered the handles to him. He set his cane against the chair.

"I'll get the keys," she said.

While she was inside, he gripped the handlebars and stared down at the thin footboard, wondering how fast the thing went and if he could maintain balance on it. He might be better off walking. But now that he'd asked to use the Segway, he didn't want to back out.

She emerged from the house with a single key on a thin wire hoop in one hand and a bottled water in the other. She offered the water to him first. "Would you like a drink?"

"Thanks." He leaned the Segway against the truck and accepted the water.

"Are you sure you don't want me to drive?" she asked as he drank.

After a couple swigs, he waved dismissively with the hand holding the bottle. "I'll be fine. Don't worry. I'll be back before you know it."

Chapter 18

Brice narrowly avoided crashing into a parked car leaving Dora's block. Only by focusing hard on keeping himself centered on the Segway did he smooth out the ride.

Once he turned onto the busier Winchester Road, only a narrow strip of pavement between the hayfield on his left and the street on his right provided room to steer the Segway.

The cold air seeped into his face and hands, freezing his skin so that it throbbed. He wished he'd thought to bring gloves.

Every time a car sped past, wind pressure from it rocked him, sending the Segway wobbling. Three times he came close to crashing into the hayfield.

He debated ditching the Segway until his return, but someone might steal it. Instead, he motored along to a side road that led into the O'Reilly's parking lot and the shopping center behind it. His stomach rumbled. He debated going to Publix for a sandwich after getting the parts he needed to fix Dora's truck.

Unstrapping his cane from the Segway, he left the ride propped up against the glass front. He entered, relieved for the warm shield of heat he got the moment he stepped inside. Movement out of the corner of his eye drew his attention, but the person moved down an aisle.

No employee stood behind the counter as Brice approached, so he waited a few minutes until a young girl in an O'Reilly's cap returned from a restricted aisle of parts in the back.

"Can I help you?" she asked.

May I help you, his mother's voice corrected, causing his lips to curl in a small smile. He squashed it, hoping the girl took it as a greeting.

"Need to pick up a new distributor cap and rotor," he said. "For a 2015 Nissan Frontier SV. A six banger."

"A what?" the girl asked, brow wrinkling.

"Sorry, mechanic slang. It has a V6 engine."

She typed away on the nearest computer. After a minute, she bit her lower lip. "Hmm. Yeah, we'll have to order it."

He groaned. He'd assumed it would be in stock. "How long does that take? I sort of need it today."

The girl hit a couple keys and bit her lip again. "Tomorrow. Maybe the day after."

He grimaced. Should he order it or try somewhere else? There was an Advance Auto Parts a few miles away, but he didn't relish traveling further along Winchester on the Segway.

As he waffled over what to do, a man emerged from another aisle, approaching a different register where another employee had come up from the back.

Brice's stomach knotted. He'd seen this man before, on the footage from his security camera. The man had a thick brown beard with flecks of red and a gray hat on his head. A tattoo adorned his left hand, though from this distance Brice couldn't make it out.

"Sir? Would you like me to order this?" the girl asked.

Brice turned his back to the man, heart pounding. Would the man recognize him?

"Um, sure," he replied without thinking.

He immediately regretted the response, because now he'd have to stay longer to pay. He wanted to run, but that would draw the man's attention. What should he do?

"Do you want to pick it up here in store or have it shipped to your address?" she asked.

While he knew how to get to Dora's house, he didn't remember the exact address. "Here is fine." His back burned as he imagined the man studying him.

He fished out his phone, looking up Investigator Wright's number.

"How would you like to pay?" the girl asked, oblivious to his unease.

Setting his phone on the counter, he grabbed his credit card from his wallet and tapped the card reader. His breath caught in his throat as the man strolled past him, a bag in one hand. The man exited the store and headed for a beat-up blue pickup at the back of the parking lot.

"If you'll sign this." The cashier handed him a receipt.

He grabbed a pen and scribbled on it, pushing it to her. When she offered him a receipt, he stuffed it in his back pocket, grabbed his phone and cane, and started for the door. He hoped the man didn't drive away before he got out and saw the license plate.

"Have a nice day," the girl called after him.

He ignored her as he hobbled toward the door, searching for Investigator Wright's number. The pickup backed out of its spot. Brice half-caught the license plate. An Alabama plate, but the letters and numbers ran together on him. He thought he saw an eight and a three. Or an S.

As he pushed out the door, he took a quick picture with his phone before calling Investigator Wright. The call went to voicemail. He cursed. Dumping the phone in his pocket, he hurried to the Segway. The truck headed out the small side road he'd come in on.

He stepped onto the Segway, knowing he'd never keep up, but he had to do something. Setting off after the truck, he watched as it turned right to head back the way he'd come.

For an irrational second, he feared the man was headed for Dora's house. How would he know about her?

Brice floored the Segway, which wasn't fast. Still, the speed forced him to focus. By the time he reached Winchester, the truck was well down the road. It had shifted into the far-left lane, before pulling into a turn lane; the opposite direction from Dora's block.

The Segway pitched, causing him to weave. He slowed and struggled to steady himself, terrified he'd fall into the road and someone would run him over. When he'd righted the Segway, the truck had turned down a side road, passing an abandoned storefront.

Brice checked behind him, but several vehicles were too close for him to cross. Once he reached the light, there was a break in the oncoming traffic for both directions. Rather than wait for the light, he risked speeding across the intersection. The truck was long gone.

As he reached the far side of the intersection, he discovered the road crossed a two-lane bridge above the Flint River. The river was shallow here. He wouldn't drown. Unless... what if a car crossed while he was on the bridge and ran him off the side? The fall would cripple, if not paralyze him. He might drown in the river, unable to crawl out. He told himself that was ridiculous, but his limbs went slack. Dread poured through him at the prospect of crossing the bridge.

The Segway slowed despite his intention to push on through. He could cross the bridge. He'd be fine.

But his eyes locked onto the icy waters, which filled his vision—

He chased after Jaxon and his friends. They ran for the Dunes—a collection of dirt hills the local kids raced bikes over in the summer. Today, with all the fresh snow, they planned snowball fights. The first hour the kids would build up snow walls, then divide into teams and spend the rest of the day at war.

Brice hollered for his brother, but the moment Jaxon had his jacket, boots, and gloves on, he sprinted out the door. The first kids at the Dunes always teamed up on the best spots. And he didn't want to get stuck on one of the crummy teams. Or worse, on his own.

As he raced out of the house, Jaxon had already reached the end of the block. His brother didn't have a long head start, but other kids might be there now. His best chance to make up time was to cross the pond. It had frozen over a week ago. Hopefully the Benjamin brothers didn't take pot shots at him with their hockey pucks as he crossed. But when he reached the pond, the brothers and their crew weren't out playing hockey as normal. What a break!

As he ran out onto the pond, he discovered the ice was extra slick. He held his arms out wide, adjusting to his sliding feet. Jaxon rounded the far side. Brice debated calling for his brother once more to wait, but that would only ensure Jaxon wouldn't team up with him.

The first crack in the ice sounded like ice cubes popping when dropped into a glass of warm tea. He thought it was an echo from somewhere. After the second, the ice shifted beneath his feet. His whole body tightened, mind scrambling between press on or retreat.

On the third step he plunged through the ice. Every inch of him burned. He wanted to scream. He thrashed, kicking upward, desperate to get out.

Three kicks didn't propel him to the surface. He hadn't sunk that deep, had he?

His chest throbbed. It felt like any second it might explode. His insides were turning to ice, he was sure of it. He had to get out now.

He punched the ice with his hands again and again, but it didn't crack. Where was the hole? How could he get out?

Jaxon, help! Please God! Someone save him!

"Sir, are you okay?"

Brice was free of the water. He was cold, but not like he'd been moments before. An older man with a white beard stared down at him, concern etched into his features.

Brice realized he lay in the middle of the road short of the bridge. He scrambled backward.

"It's okay." The man held up both hands to show he posed no threat. "Are you hurt? Did you crash?"

Brice's heart pounded. His breath came in ragged gasps. He hadn't been underwater. He'd been following a man involved in Mary's disappearance.

Where was his cane? Brice looked for it. The cane had ended up in the middle of the bridge, along with the Segway.

No, no, no.

He had to catch up to the man. It was his only lead to Mary and the baby, but the water.

It's shallow.

You can't swim. The current will pull you under.

The bridge is safe.

You thought the ice was safe.

I have to go.

You'll drown.

Please.

No.

Get up.

No!

Damn you, get up!

A sob broke from his mouth, which turned to a moan. He rocked, staring at the bridge.

"I'm calling 911," the old man said, his phone out, expression worried.

Brice's own cell rang. Dazed, he pulled it out. Investigator Wright's name popped up on his screen, with green and red buttons below it. Instinct made him press the green button.

"Hello?"

Chapter 19

After telling Investigator Wright his location and what had happened, Brice called Mrs. Drew. While he gave her directions to come pick him up, a police officer arrived. The officer retrieved Dora's Segway from the middle of the bridge, and they moved to the parking lot of an abandoned building beside the bridge. The simple act of retreating from the bridge alleviated some of Brice's tension.

Mrs. Drew and Investigator Wright arrived while Brice recounted the events from O'Reilly's up to the crash. Then Mrs. Drew checked him for injuries, while Investigator Wright and the other officer questioned the old man.

Brice endured Mrs. Drew's examination while sitting on the edge of the floorboard at the back of her SUV. He wished she would check him out from inside the SUV with the heat on.

Beside him lay his cane, which the old man had retrieved for him. The Segway leaned against the side of the SUV. The crash had scuffed the paint in several places. He'd tell Dora when he returned it that he'd pay for the repairs.

"You don't seem to have any serious bruises," Mrs. Drew said, stepping back. "You're lucky."

He grimaced. A dull ache had developed in his left knee, but it wasn't too bad. It was his own fault anyway, panicking about crossing a bridge. What kind of coward let down the woman he loved and his child because of a foolish childhood fear?

"The man was driving a blue truck?" Investigator Wright asked, as he approached.

The other officer and the old man headed for their cars.

"Thank you!" Brice called to the old man.

The old man looked back and nodded. "Glad you're okay." He climbed in his car and drove away.

Investigator Wright moved into Brice's line of sight, repeating the question, which reminded him of the picture he'd taken. Brice pulled out his phone and showed Wright the picture. The license plate numbers weren't clear in the picture either. Yet another failure. Maybe that was why Mary had left. She'd known he would only let them down.

"Send that to me." Investigator Wright held up his phone.

Brice nodded. As he did so, the investigator turned to study the street beyond the bridge.

"I'm going to drive on back there a bit," he said. "See if we get lucky. I'll send the pic back to the station to get someone working on the license plate."

"I'll come with you." Brice didn't want to cross the bridge, but if he wasn't driving, he could close his eyes. "I can help look for the vehicle."

"No, sir." The investigator shook his head. "I'll handle this. Go home and rest."

"I second that," Mrs. Drew chimed in.

"No." Brice grabbed his cane and stood, his body protesting. "If it wasn't for me *falling*, you'd have this guy or… location by now."

"More likely, the guy noticed you following him, ditched you, and is on the alert now," Investigator Wright corrected. "Or worse, he finishes what they started by taking you out."

Brice studied the road, biting his lip.

"Look, I get it." The investigator's tone had softened. "You want answers. I even understand following the guy when you ran into him. But you're in no condition to do more. Even if you were, this isn't a movie. I can't let a civilian assist in an investigation."

Brice managed a nod as Mrs. Drew grabbed his arm.

"Oh, Brice." Investigator Wright picked up the Segway and put it in the SUV's trunk. "I tracked down the Rick Smith from the paper you found. There was no foul play involved in the Mary Smith's death from the obituary. Nor did he recognize your Mary's photo. Based on the circumstances, I'm guessing your Mary stole the other girl's identity. Or maybe just the name.

"We also checked the bits of paper for fingerprints, but didn't find any beyond yours. But that was always a long shot."

"Okay, thanks." Brice let Mrs. Drew lead him to the passenger seat and got inside. Another lead shot down.

His phone started ringing again. Dora. She'd called three times already. There were another half dozen texts from her. At first checking in, then growing increasingly worried. It had been two hours since he'd left her house to go to the parts store.

He texted her an apology, telling her something critical had come up, and promising to call later. He didn't tell her he'd have to pass off her repairs to Nate now. Mrs. Drew wouldn't allow him out of the house again anytime soon on his own.

As she drove them home, he thought about Mary. He didn't even know her real name. Who was she? Did he have any actual connection with her or the baby at all?

All his energy, his efforts at recovery, had revolved around finding Mary and the baby. First to make sure they were okay, then to get answers for what had happened to him. If they were beyond finding, what was he doing all this for? He couldn't just go back to working and living alone again like they had never existed. It wasn't enough.

Despite his lack of memories, he felt their loss acutely. He had a void inside him like a missing limb, and with each passing day, the loss grew.

Chapter 20

During the ride home, the dull ache in Brice's left knee grew. When they arrived at the house, he kept his weight on his right leg as he exited the SUV. Even so, a jolt of pain flared through his left knee when he slid to the ground. He groaned and took a few deep breaths before walking.

With each step, he felt as if an amateur carver chiseled at his knee. "What's wrong?" Mrs. Drew asked, noticing his growing limp.

"Think I hurt my knee," he said through clenched teeth.

Her eyes dropped to his knees. "Do you need help?"

He shook his head, and when her eyes rose to him, he said, "No. I can manage."

She didn't argue, but her whole body tensed as if she expected him to topple over at any moment. He made it inside on his own but collapsed on the couch. She then examined his knee despite his protests, before ordering him to rest while she prepared a proper meal.

His stomach grumbled as the smell of cooking food filtered out from the kitchen. He hadn't eaten since breakfast. More than food, he wanted to sleep a couple hours. Only his aching left knee had kept him from crashing on the ride home. Now he wasn't sure even that would keep him awake much longer.

His cell rang again. His first thought was Dora was checking on him again, and he didn't have the energy to talk with her.

Instead, it was Jaxon on his caller ID. He grimaced, hoping Mrs. Drew hadn't called his brother after he'd called her earlier. He didn't want to recount today's events again. Nor did he want Jaxon berating him to let others handle things, while he sat here like an invalid incapable of accomplishing anything useful.

He almost hit the ignore call button, but if Jaxon had heard from Mrs. Drew, he'd keep trying. Or call Mrs. Drew.

"Hello," Brice answered, cringing at the weariness in his voice.

"Brice, I've got news." There was excitement in Jaxon's voice that gave him a lift.

"What is it?"

"We've identified two of the men from your camera footage."

Brice's heart leaped. "Who are they?"

"I can't answer that. They're in our databases, but linked to an active investigation. I can't elaborate other than to say they're suspected human traffickers."

"Human traffickers?" Brice felt as though every muscle in his body was suddenly immobile. What does that…?" He didn't know how to finish the question. Or how to process this revelation. His body processed it, however, a chill sweeping through him.

"Yes, and we have a lead on where to find them."

Questions began firing in Brice's head, though he knew Jaxon wouldn't answer any of them. Jaxon had communicated with Investigator Wright, offering FBI resources to the extent possible, which was how he'd ended up with the video evidence. That irked Brice a little. They were brothers. Wasn't blood supposed to be thicker than water?

"What about Mary?" Brice asked.

"Nothing so far. We don't know how she's tied in with them."

He nodded to himself, before halting the nod. He didn't want to get used to the lack of progress on finding Mary and the baby. Getting used to it wasn't much different from accepting it.

"This lead is solid," Jaxon said, guessing his thoughts from the silence. "We're going to track these men down and get answers."

"I saw one of them," he began.

"What? Where?" Jaxon asked.

Mrs. Drew returned with water, raising a questioning eyebrow at him. He mouthed Jaxon and accepted the water from her before setting it on the end table.

As she departed, he reluctantly recounted the day's events again. His pulse quickened with shame when he talked about crashing at the bridge. Jaxon interrupted a few times with questions, probing for details about the truck and the man.

"I wish I had more to offer," Brice said.

"It's likely for the best that you don't," Jaxon responded. "Had you scrutinized him too much, he likely would've recognized you. That could've led to a dangerous confrontation."

Brice tried not to let the implication that he wasn't strong enough bother him, but it was all too similar to what Investigator Wright had said earlier.

"I'm going to share this with the agent in charge of the FBI investigation," Jaxon said.

"There's an investigation on it?" He'd known Jaxon provided resources, but he hadn't expected a separate investigation.

"I told you that. An investigation on the human traffickers," Jaxon said. "Something that's been ongoing for a while, and there's a connection with these men."

"You're not on this?" Brice wanted Jaxon to assure him of his involvement and that he was doing everything possible to find Mary and the baby and protect them.

"I'm coordinating between Investigator Wright and the agents involved in this other investigation," Jaxon answered.

Brice didn't like the word coordinate, as if his brother was an administrator while others did the real work. Brice knew that wasn't true—his brother was a field agent—just not on this case. Not when Brice needed him.

"There'll be a pair of special agents coming to see you tomorrow," Jaxon added. "The evidence in your case is a bit of a breakthrough for them. They'll want to speak with Investigator Wright and see if they can't find the man you saw. And they'll have questions of their own for you."

"When?" Brice asked.

"Not sure yet, but they've got your contact info. I'd expect them to reach out a little later today. They'll meet with the investigator first. Then you."

"Okay."

"Look, Brice." Jaxon hesitated. "I know this has been hard. I can't pretend to know what you're going through, but I can recognize it's not easy. Any of it."

Brice waited. Whenever people admitted they didn't understand your troubles, the acknowledgement always felt disingenuous, because it never stopped them from telling you how to handle your situation.

"Right now, your primary concern should be to rest and recover. You don't need to work. There's no shame in taking time off to get better. Nate can handle the business for now."

Brice almost quipped that he might never get better. That this might be the best he could hope for now, but he kept silent. He didn't want to get into that discussion right now.

"And if you see that man again, please don't follow him. Let Investigator Wright do his job. Let the agents visiting you tomorrow do theirs. The men after Mary are dangerous."

Brice tightened his grip on the phone until his hand hurt.

"Please, Brice. This is your big brother talking right now. I'm worried about you, and I want you to be safe. Okay?"

"Yeah," Brice mumbled.

"Look, I'm hoping to get back down there in the next few weekends to check on you. I'd come now if I could, but let's talk after the agents visit you tomorrow."

"Sure."

"Good." Jaxon sounded relieved. "I've got to go for now."

"Bye." Brice ended the call and tossed the phone on the couch beside him.

His whole body hummed with nervous energy. On the one hand, he felt relief that the FBI had gotten involved in the case, helping to search for Mary and the baby—his little girl.

Were they okay? No, that was a stupid question. Not okay in the hands of those men, or with those men after them. He just hoped they weren't hurt or suffering, and that there was still time for him to find and help them.

Mrs. Drew entered with a tray holding a plate of chicken pasta, asparagus, and apple slices. She offered it to him.

"What did your brother want?"

Brice didn't want the food anymore, but he accepted it anyway, knowing she'd monitor him until he'd eaten something.

"FBI is getting involved," he said, picking up an apple slice. "They're sending a couple agents to question me tomorrow."

"Any idea when?"

"No."

She squeezed his left shoulder, then returned to the kitchen. He bit into the apple, but he didn't taste it.

Chapter 21
(Fifteen Years Past)

Beulah stared into the mirror as her mother finished braiding her hair. Her golden dress glowed in the sunlight blazing through the bathroom window.

"You look beautiful, baby." Her mother smoothed the back of the dress to hide the safety pin that hemmed it in behind the shoulders. "I can't believe you're already thirteen and fitting into my old dresses."

Beulah's bare arms shivered with delight as she stared down at the dress, unable to believe her mother had given it to her, a present for her birthday.

"Don't forget your new shoes." Her mother grabbed the box from the toilet seat, opening the lid to reveal a pair of simple white slippers. "Chloe got these special for you."

Beulah gasped. Her first brand new pair of shoes, instead of the usual hand-me-downs from older girls in the Community. Or donations brought in from elsewhere.

"Hop up." Her mother pointed at the counter between the sinks.

Beulah lifted herself up and raised her feet, so that her mom could put on the shoes. The yellow alpine buttercup flower slipped from the top of her braid. She pressed it back in, taking care not to mush it.

"Perfect," her mother said as she fit the second slipper on, then stood back in admiration. "You look like a princess."

Beulah smiled. She felt bigger. Taller. Older. The ticking clock during the night had been a switch. Climbing out of bed this morning, pulling back the sheets, had marked the end of her childhood. She was grownup.

"Come now, we don't want to be late for your ceremony." Her mother guided her out of the bathroom.

"What will happen?" Beulah asked. All she knew for sure was that it took place in the Sanctuary. She imagined everyone sitting in the pews, admiring her in her dress with her new slippers.

"I won't ruin the surprise." Her mother beamed as she headed for her room. "But it's a blessing. You confirm your place in the Community."

Beulah didn't understand what that meant, beyond that it was a tradition when any child turned thirteen.

Her mother wore a dark red dress with matching shoes. She grabbed golden bangles from her jewelry box, slipping them onto her wrists and part of her forearms. The bangles reminded Beulah of a Chinese dragon.

Coming back from her bedroom, her mother hugged her, squeezing tight. "My little girl on her special day. You're growing up so fast."

Beulah reveled in the attention, unable to remember another time when her mother had fawned over her so much.

As they left the house for the sanctuary, little Tommy next door dug in the flower bed by his family's mailbox. His older sister Helen usually watched him, but she was nowhere in sight. On a normal day, Beulah would've been with her, rocking on the front porch swing or drawing on easels in the yard.

Helen was probably inside getting ready, or had gone ahead to the sanctuary to get a good seat. Beulah had needled the older girl for weeks to give her a hint. Helen had gone through the ceremony only last year. But each time she'd asked, Helen had clammed up.

That didn't matter now. Beulah would soon share the secret.

When they reached the sanctuary, Beulah pranced up the front steps, following her mother inside. Beulah swept toward the main hall. To her surprise, it was empty. Not even Arden in there. Would they arrive later? Did she have something to do first? She knew others would attend. They'd told her so.

"This way." Her mother marched toward a thick wooden door off to the side, one that stood ajar.

Beulah stopped in her tracks. She'd never seen that door open before. It led down to the crypt, where the Community buried their dead. Why would they go down there?

"We're going to the crypt?" Beulah hoped this was a misunderstanding. She didn't want her ceremony down there.

Her mother laughed. "There's no crypt down there. You've heard too many childish rumors." She waved for Beulah to join her. "Come now. It's time."

Reluctant to go down, but not wanting to argue and risk angering her mother, Beulah followed. The door opened on a staircase descending toward torchlight. She placed a hand on one stone wall to maintain balance. Shadows covered the frigid walls. Lifting her dress, she eased down the narrow stone steps, not wanting to stumble and fall. The last thing she needed was to get hurt before her ceremony, or worse, ruin her dress.

She listened for others, but found only her shoes clapping the stone in counterpoint to her mother's steps. Torches hung from the walls along a corridor at the base of the steps, casting out some shadows, but offering little warmth. Beulah's arms pimpled in the cold. How long would they be down here?

Her mother led her into another torch-lit room to one side. Beulah gasped. Figures in red robes, or dresses like her mother's, stood along the walls, faces covered with gold masks. In the center of the room, a man wearing a golden, dragon-like mask stood beside a stone altar. Like her mother, he wore golden bangles on his arms, though his resembled talons. He held two chalices.

"Go ahead." Her mother pushed her toward the altar, before retreating. She joined the figures lining the wall, and someone handed her a mask.

Beulah stood there, confused. She hesitated to go to the altar, but she knew she had no choice. This was *her* ceremony. Everyone would know if she didn't go through with it.

She took a couple of tentative steps forward.

"Welcome, daughter." The man beside the altar held up two chalices.

She recognized his voice. Arden, leader of the Community. He'd conduct the ceremony. She'd expected him, and observers, just not underground with faint lighting.

As she smoothed her dress with both hands, she realized it was the only thing shining in the room. The light from the torches reflected off it. And her.

"Do not be afraid, daughter." Arden offered one of the chalices to her. A dark liquid filled the chalice to the brim. "This is a celebration."

Beulah took another step forward and accepted the chalice in both hands. She didn't drink. It smelled of wine.

Arden raised his own chalice. "Brothers. Sisters. We're gathered to commemorate Beulah Clarke, as she sheds her childhood. What came before was sacred, innocent, and good. A time of purity and joy.

"But there comes a day when each of us must leave that simplicity behind. We must choose to commit our self to this Community. To Home. To Family. Or walk away forever."

Arden lowered his chalice and aligned it with hers, which she clasped in both hands because she didn't trust herself not to drop it.

"Beulah Clarke, thus far you have enjoyed the blessings of this Community as a right. A right to life, love, and care that every child deserves." Arden let the words hang in the air.

Was she expected to say something? Her mother had given her no instructions. She didn't know how to respond.

His gaze had taken in the room to this point, but now he focused his attention on her. "Today, and henceforth, you must earn that right. Earn your place within the Community, the same as every adult. Do you promise yourself to the Community, to contribute as an equal among us?"

"I do," she answered, eager to agree with whatever he asked of her.

"Do you promise to honor the Community in all things?"

"I do."

"Do you promise to put the needs of your Community first always, ensuring its well-being?"

"I do." Her eyes clouded with relieved tears, but she hesitated to wipe them away, or do anything besides wait for direction from him.

"Drink, daughter. Drink as a symbol of your commitment, of your pledge to us all and our mutual future."

She raised the chalice to her lips and sipped. The bitter taste made her wince, then cough. Arden lifted the bottom of her chalice, forcing her to drink. The wine burned rushing down her throat, but she dared not shrink away. She gulped until it all churned in her belly.

With hers finished, Arden drank. Those along the walls drank as well, chalices seeming to have appeared from nowhere.

Her stomach burned, threatening to toss the wine back up. She took deep breaths, determined not to humiliate herself. At the same time a warmth spread through her, numbing the chill somewhat, which was a relief.

Arden finished and took her chalice, setting the pair on a stand that she hadn't noticed before. He placed his hands on her shoulders and moved her over to the altar. It made her uneasy, but she didn't resist. He was the leader. She must do as he instructed.

From beneath the mask, he smiled. She had responded correctly. Things were fine, even if strange and unexpected.

His hands clasped the straps of her dress and slid them off her shoulders, then down her arms. The dress fell, revealing her breasts. She gasped, whole body tensing. She raised her arms to stop the dress and pull it back up.

"It's okay, daughter." He stopped her arms. She froze, conscious of his eyes on her. Everyone else's as well. She wished to disappear. Wished she'd never come.

"It's alright to be nervous," Arden whispered, "but you mustn't shirk your duty to your Community."

She didn't understand. What did that have to do with removing her dress?

He slid the dress to the ground, baring her belly, hips, her white underwear, and her legs. Then he knelt, holding the dress wide for her to step out of it.

She looked toward her mother, wanting rescue. Wanting her mother to halt this, help her re-clothe, and take her home. But her mother only nodded, her smile as broad as it had been in the bathroom.

A tear slid down Beulah's right cheek as she stepped out of the dress. She crossed her arms to cover her breasts, wanting to run out the open door and up the steps, dress or no dress.

But her legs didn't move.

Arden stood, her dress still in his hand. He spread it out on the altar. Then he grabbed her shoulders again. Her skin crawled this time. She longed to pull away, but he drew her to the altar, forcing her to sit. He swept a hand under her legs and made her lie down on the cold stone. Even through the dress it chilled her skin. It seeped into her entire body. Control of her limbs, her head, herself slipped away.

Arden removed her underwear. She barely felt it. She felt she was rising above herself. Arden stood over her, yet somehow below as well. Just the two of them. Everything else dimmed.

His body was bare, the robes gone. Only his mask remained, the golden dragon covering all but the upward curve of his lips.

She felt a sharp pain, and then he was gone. She was gone. Her thoughts felt muddled. Flickering blackness. Swirling confusion, her entire world spinning. The only thing she could cling to was why.

Why was this happening to her?

Chapter 22
(Fifteen Years Past)

Beulah awoke alone in the torch-lit room, lying naked on the altar. Her head throbbed, unconsciousness threatening to overwhelm her again. As she rose onto her elbows, her vision spun, becoming splotchy, like a Rorschach test.

Her stomach bubbled.

She closed her eyes and took deep breaths, trying not to vomit. The room smelled of sweat and something else. A scent that reminded her of deer, though she wasn't sure she was thinking right. Whatever it was, it heightened her urgency to leave.

As did the memories surging back like a mountain slide.

Tears filled her eyes. She wanted to sob, but not here.

Her right knee brushed her underwear. She pulled it on, then eased off the altar. When her feet hit the ground, her legs almost gave out on her. Her groin throbbed, causing her to cry out as she fell against the altar for support, and her skin itched where it touched the cold stone.

Her dress lay rumpled on the altar from where she'd been lying on it. A quarter-sized blob of blood marred it around the waistline. Her mother would be furious with her for ruining the dress. Still, she pulled it back on to cover her nakedness. It was the only way she could leave.

She no longer felt beautiful in it. No longer special.

Her mother had called this ceremony a blessing. It felt like a punishment, like she'd committed a grave sin against the Community and they'd shamed her as a warning to others. Except what had she done wrong?

The white slippers waited beside her feet for her to step into them, but she didn't. Gift or no, she'd never touch them again. Those she could leave without.

She stumbled toward the door, a moan escaping her lips. After a couple of steps, she toppled to the ground. A part of her wanted to stay there and give in to her tears. Her terror and guilt threatened to overwhelm her.

But the rest of her was desperate to get out of here. To not spend another moment in this room. Ever.

She rose, struggling to breathe. Her chest felt constricted, as if an invisible snake encircled her and was squeezing the life out of her. She shuffled toward the open door. The frigid stone floor stung the bottoms of her feet.

Outside the room, the stairwell was dark except for the faint torchlight. At the top of the staircase, the massive wooden door stood closed once more.

What if it wouldn't open? What if she was stuck down here?

She rushed up the staircase, bent over with hands on the steps to maintain her balance. She expected some unspeakable horror to jump out of the shadows at any moment.

There was the door. A few more steps.

When her hands reached it, she clawed the wood, searching for the handle. She didn't find it and almost resorted to pounding on the door, screaming for someone to let her out. Then her knuckles scraped the handle. She grasped it in both hands and jerked hard. It turned, and she pushed with all her might. The heavy door creaked open partway, enough for the fading daylight to blind her. Still, it was a lifeline. A single buoy in the sea of loss that assaulted her from all sides.

There was no one else in the sanctuary, and she wouldn't have paid them any mind if there had been. She barreled through the front door and down the steps, half tumbling in her haste.

As she crossed the field from the sanctuary, Community members stopped to watch her run past. The blood on her dress showed for all to see. A mark of her shame.

There were calls or shouts, but she understood none of it, as if they all spoke in a foreign language. Nor did she care. All her focus was on the path to her house until it was in sight. Then her driving need became getting through those doors and away from everyone. She was desperate to reclaim some measure of safety.

A couple of people moved into her path. She darted around them, skin crawling in fear at the possibility of someone touching her. She balled her hands into fists, ready to attack anything that tried.

Home was so close. Her place to hide. Her refuge. And then she was inside, the door slamming shut behind her. Lock thrown. Back against the wall. Breath coming in ragged gasps.

Her mother's face appeared in the kitchen doorway and lit up, mouth open in a clown's smile, which gave way to disappointment as her eyes focused on the bloodstain. "You ruined your dress."

As if Beulah had gotten it dirty playing outside in the mud.

Her mother's eyes dropped to her bare feet. "You forgot your new shoes."

Beulah gaped.

Then her mother shook her head and sighed. "I guess that was to be expected." She waved Beulah to follow. "I've a surprise for you." She disappeared back into the kitchen.

Beulah stared at the doorway, unable to move. A surprise? She'd had enough of surprises. She needed comfort. Some sort of explanation.

She stumbled toward the kitchen where her mother bent over the island, putting the finishing touches on a cake. The smell of meat filled Beulah's nostrils, turning her stomach. She swallowed back bile.

"It's your favorite." Her mother raised the top of the cake. *Happy Birthday Beulah* written in pink icing.

Everything was off-kilter, as if the entire house had rotated five degrees. Beulah sensed the change was permanent.

"Did I ever tell you what your name means?" Her mother asked, face still beaming.

Beulah shook her head.

"It means married in Hebrew. I gave it to you in preparation for this day, when you would choose to become one with this Community and commit yourself for life. I'm so proud of you!"

Her mother sprang around to a crock pot on the counter, lifting the lid and poking at the food with a wooden spoon.

"Chloe and Helen are coming over for dinner. They should be here soon. Go on upstairs and get cleaned up. Chloe will be disappointed you're not wearing your new shoes, but we'll find them later."

Something rose through Beulah's chest, fighting to get out, but it died in her throat. She stood there, dazed.

After covering the crock pot, her mother turned back and gave her a shooing motion. "Go on, now. I expect you to be presentable for dinner."

Beulah turned and headed for the stairs. There were no answers coming, and the refuge she'd sought didn't exist.

With each step her pace quickened, until she ran up the stairs. The next thing she knew, she'd slammed the bathroom door. She fumbled with the handles on the nearest sink, turning the water on high.

Her stomach soured. She ran for the toilet, falling to her knees as she threw up the lid. She gagged into the water, stomach heaving over and over.

When she finally sat back, tears streamed down her face. She should get in the shower, but she didn't want to get up. She didn't want to have dinner tonight. Or see Chloe and Helen. Or her mother.

But she did want out of the dress. She stripped it off, eyes avoiding the bloodstain. She threw it in the trash.

Her mother's necklace thumped against her chest. She grabbed the chain and ripped it off, then flushed it down the toilet with her vomit.

The back of her neck stung. She reached back and felt a cut. Not a very long cut, nor deep. She wished it was. Wished that blood gushed from it.

She turned on the shower then, but she didn't get in. As she stood there, staring at the water hitting the porcelain tub and swirling down the drain, she imagined jumping in and shrinking until the water carried her through the holes in the drain cover, down the pipes to…she didn't know or care. What did it matter where she went?

Anywhere was better than here.

Chapter 23

A knock at the door awoke Brice.

"Brice, you have visitors." After a second knock, Mrs. Drew entered his room.

"What?" He blinked his eyes as he sat up. "Who? It's so early."

"It's nine." She went straight to his closet, removing jeans, a gray collared sweater, and a pair of tan shoes. "The FBI agents are here."

"Oh crap." He threw back the covers and sat up.

The clock displayed 9:02. He'd overslept.

"Why did you let me sleep so late?"

"You needed it." She handed him his jeans. "You're still recovering, and yesterday didn't help. This probably won't either."

"Where are they?" He pulled on his jeans, wishing he could have slept longer despite his complaint.

She grabbed a pair of socks from the dresser. "Waiting for you in the dining room. And I've got a plate of eggs and hash browns in the microwave for you."

He finished dressing and grabbed his cane. "Thank you," he told her as he headed toward his bathroom to relieve himself.

When he came back out, she was finishing making his bed. It was strange. She'd never done it for him before.

"Thanks for making the bed."

She nodded, then hurried down the hall to her room.

The special agents rose from the dining room table when Brice entered. Both wore suits, and one held a large silver travel mug. An iPad lay on the table.

"I'm Special Agent Aaren Dawson," the man with the travel mug said as he showed his badge. His eyes dropped to Brice's cane for a brief second.

"And I'm Special Agent Ricardo Amador." The second man showed his own badge as well. He looked tired, as if he'd been up all night.

"Sorry to make you wait," Brice said, wishing he didn't need the cane, but it was better than having Mrs. Drew walk him in here. "I had a rough day yesterday. It took a lot out of me and I overslept."

"No problem," Agent Dawson said. "Are you ready to talk?"

Brice gestured to the kitchen. "Would you mind if I grabbed a cup of coffee first?"

"Of course."

Brice retrieved a mug from the cabinet. "Would either of you like some?"

"I'm good." Agent Dawson raised his travel mug.

Brice shifted his focus to Agent Amador, who raised both hands palm out.

"Never drink the stuff," Agent Amador said.

"Never trust a man who doesn't drink coffee," Agent Dawson quipped.

Agent Amador smiled around pursed lips, as if he'd heard this from his partner many times before.

As Brice poured for himself, he felt a chill breeze hit him. The window over the kitchen sink was open. Mrs. Drew must've forgotten to close it after breakfast. She liked the flow of air while cooking, even in the winter.

For now, he left it and returned with his mug to the table, where he took his usual seat. Agent Dawson sat across from him in front of his iPad, while Agent Amador sat at the end of the table.

"I'd like to record this as part of the official record, if that's okay with you." Agent Dawson gestured to the iPad. "I've got a voice recorder program on here."

"Okay," Brice agreed, feeling weird about the recording, but refusing would seem suspicious, wouldn't it?

Agent Dawson leaned back in his chair and grabbed his coffee mug, though he didn't take a sip. "Do you know the name Garrett Elliott?"

Brice frowned. "No. That doesn't sound familiar." Was that the name of the man he'd seen yesterday?

"The name hasn't come up with Investigator Wright?" Agent Dawson asked.

"No." Should it have? Was Investigator Wright keeping things from him?

"Did you ever hear Mary mention the name?"

Brice coughed, feeling his face burning again. "I don't... I'm not sure what you were told about my case?" He let it hang in the air between them, not wanting to spell it out once more.

Agent Dawson did nothing to fill the space. He even took a sip from his coffee, waiting.

"My injuries... I can't... don't remember... Mary." Brice spent hours out of his day trying to remember her. To see her face in any other situation than the camera recording. His world revolved around her, which felt eerie when he had no memory of her.

"You don't know if she ever mentioned him?" Agent Amador asked.

"No." He didn't like the agents making him say it. Doing so made him feel defensive, like he was hiding something.

"How about Spencer Headley?" Agent Dawson asked.

"No."

"Elwin Pickering?"

Brice felt like the agents were driving him toward something, but he didn't know what. "No."

Agent Dawson pulled the iPad to himself, tapped on the screen, then showed Brice a profile pic of one man from the camera footage. The man in the image was the one that Brice had thought seemed to be the ringleader.

"Do you recognize him?"

"Yes." Another glimmer of hope surged through him, added to what Jaxon had given him yesterday. "He was in the camera footage I gave to Investigator Wright. He was here the day I was attacked. What's his name?"

"Do you remember him being here that day?"

Brice shook his head, grimacing. "No. I recognized him from the footage. I've studied it, trying to remember." Why were the agents hammering him on his memory? It was humiliating to not know. Didn't they realize this? "Who is he?"

This time Agent Dawson acknowledged his question. "That is Garrett Elliott."

Brice studied the picture again, affixing the name with the image. The man was a human trafficker, according to Jaxon.

Agent Dawson swiped a finger across the iPad to change to a different picture, this one of the older man who had removed the security cameras from his front and back porch.

"Do you recognize this man?"

"Yes. He was also in the footage. Don't you already know this from Investigator Wright? Or from my brother?"

The agent's face gave nothing away. "Neither of them was a victim. I needed your account firsthand for our case."

It felt a little like bureaucracy at work, but if it helped in finding Mary and the baby, as well as his attackers, then he would deal with it. "Yes, I recognize him. Who is he?"

"Spencer Headley."

"And these two are human traffickers?"

"I'm afraid I can't elaborate."

Brice squeezed his coffee mug a little tighter. "What about the other man? The one I saw yesterday."

"Are you referring to this man?" Agent Dawson swiped to a third picture.

This one gave Brice pause. Seeing the man from the store made him jittery. It brought back a wave of unease. He nodded in response.

"This is Elwin Pickering. We know the least about him at present, but we're hoping his connection in your case might give us some evidence that helps with our other case."

"What can I do?"

"Tell us about your encounter with him." Agent Amador leaned back in the chair as if they were having a casual conversation.

Brice recounted his visit to Dora's house to work on her truck and his trip out to O'Reilly's. During this part of the story, he remembered he still had the Segway. He'd have to ask Mrs. Drew to help him return it to Dora. He also had to call Nate about Dora's truck. Why hadn't he thought to call Nate before now? If he'd made Dora miss work today, he'd owe her big time.

"And what happened when you arrived at O'Reilly's?" Agent Amador prompted.

Brice realized he'd gone silent for no apparent reason. "Sorry. Lost track of where I was going."

"No problem, you're doing great," Agent Amador encouraged.

"I went into O'Reilly's to get a part for Dora's truck and I saw…" Brice grasped for the name.

"Elwin Pickering," Agent Amador prompted.

"Yes, Mr. Pickering went up to a register to check out."

"What did he buy?" Agent Dawson asked.

"I… I didn't hear. I pan… I turned away so he wouldn't see me."

Agent Amador leaned in, his expression concerned. "Did he recognize you?"

"I… I don't think so. He walked past me and out the store without a word."

"It seems like a big coincidence that he happened to be in the same auto parts store you had to go to for your job," Agent Dawson said.

Brice frowned. He hadn't considered the likelihood of running into the man.

"Was it possible he followed you?" Agent Dawson asked.

Brice dropped his gaze to the table. "I don't… I'm not sure. But he was already in the store when I got there." The possibility sent a shiver up his spine because that meant the man was spying on him. And had seen him at Dora's house. "Do you think Dora is in danger?" That sent a surge of fear through him. And guilt.

"I doubt it." Agent Amador shook his head. "If he's following you, we have to figure out why. What does he want with you?"

The agents looked expectant, as if Brice might have the answer. His first thought was that maybe the man was looking for an opportunity to finish the job he and the other men had started when they put him in the hospital. If the man kept tabs on him, was he safe here? Was Mrs. Drew safe?

"Could he come back?" Brice asked, his voice trembling. He hated the fear in his voice.

Agent Amador shook his head. "Investigator Wright posted a unit last night to watch your house after the incident. I guess he didn't tell you. I'd expect them to be here for a couple more nights."

Brice clenched his fists, trying not to show the relief he felt at that revelation. "Investigator Wright didn't track the man down yet?"

"I'm sorry, but I can't divulge that," Agent Amador replied, his expression apologetic.

"But if he had, no one would need to monitor the house."

"All I can say is you shouldn't worry for your safety. Local law enforcement is watching you."

The assurance didn't put Brice at ease. The man remained free. All three of his attackers were, and as long as they remained so, they posed a threat.

"What else do you need from me?" Brice asked.

Before Agent Dawson responded, his cell rang. He checked it, then rose from the chair. "Excuse me, I need to take this. Do you mind if I use your back porch?" He gestured for the door.

"Yeah, sure," Brice said.

The agent answered the phone as he strode to the back door and stepped outside.

Where were the local officers Investigator Wright had sent to watch the house? He assumed in a car somewhere out on the street, like in the movies. Would they be in a squad car or an unmarked vehicle to hide their presence? And would they see someone approaching from the back, as Elwin and his men had done before?

"Should I get new security cameras for the house?" Brice asked Agent Amador.

"I'm not a security consultant," Agent Amador answered. "But I'd say you should do what makes you feel secure."

Pain curled up in Brice's left leg from a cramp. He held up his coffee mug, standing as he did so to stretch out his leg. "I need to get a refill."

"Of course." Agent Amador slid back in his chair to make room.

As Brice entered the kitchen and approached the coffee pot, the heater clicked off. Agent Dawson's voice drifted in from the back porch.

"The investigator located the truck and is getting a search warrant for the property. He expects to be ready to go in by noon."

Brice grabbed the coffee pot and poured, taking care to make as little noise as possible. He hadn't ruined things yesterday. Investigator Wright *had* located the man after all.

"I'll stay for the initial questioning, then hop on a plane to Grand Junction."

Brice froze. What was in Grand Junction?

For a few seconds there was silence. He put the coffee pot back, then grabbed the sugar shaker and added a little to his coffee.

"With luck, this guy'll give us the leads we need to search the community."

More questions fired off in Brice's head. He started back for the table. He didn't want to be obvious, standing here listening at the window, but he took his time walking toward the table, making sure not to thud his cane on the floor.

Agent Amador had the iPad now and swiped repeatedly on the screen.

Brice reseated himself and leaned his cane against the edge of the table when the back door opened.

"Sorry about that." Agent Dawson passed by them and retook his seat.

"Last question." Agent Amador looked up from the iPad to study him. "Why you?"

Brice blinked. "I'm not sure…. What do you mean?"

"Why would the human traffickers come here?" Agent Amador pointed at Brice's chest. "Why your house?"

"I don't know." Brice thought he read skepticism on the agent's face. "I thought they knew Mary. Seemed like it from the video."

"What's her connection to the men?"

Brice shrugged. How could he answer that? Why did the agents think he'd know when he didn't even know her? "I've wondered myself, but I don't know."

"Because you don't remember?" Again, the skepticism in Agent Amador's voice.

"No. I don't." Brice put as much force into his voice as he could muster. He didn't understand why the agents wouldn't believe him.

Agent Dawson laid both hands on the table. "Okay, let's assume Mary knew the men, that they came for her. I see only two plausible scenarios." He tapped the table with his left hand. "One, she escaped from them and they found her."

That made sense to Brice. It would explain why she'd shared so little about her past and the attack on him. If he came home while the men were here, he would've tried to stop them. They would've had to put him in a coma before he'd let them take her.

"The problem is, how did they find her?" Agent Dawson asked. "And if she had escaped, why did your neighbor report she left alone, with no signs of duress?"

Brice shook his head. "I'm not… I don't know."

"Then there's the second scenario…." The agent trailed off, as if expecting Brice to fill in the rest.

Brice squirmed inside, unsure what Agent Dawson hinted at, but confident he wouldn't like it.

"Mary might've been their associate."

Not his Mary. She wasn't a human trafficker. Yet if she had been a victim, why had they let her go?

"So, I have to wonder," Agent Dawson resumed. "She lived here with you for a year. She kept you in the dark that whole time? Or maybe, just maybe you were an associate as well. Maybe you helped her and them?"

"No." Brice shook his head, staring down at the table as the familiar fire lit inside him. "I didn't. My brother's an agent."

"Wouldn't be the first person in law enforcement with family on the wrong side of it."

"They attacked me. Beat me nearly to death. Why, if I helped them?" The question left a foul taste on his tongue. He shouldn't have to defend himself.

Agent Dawson shrugged. "You had a falling out. Again, wouldn't be the first time in history."

"I didn't… I'm not…." Brice's thoughts scrambled. He gripped the table with both hands, squeezing.

Agent Amador leaned forward now, raising one hand in a calming manner. "It's okay, Mr. Dunn. Relax. We have to follow every trail, make sense of the evidence on hand."

"It's not my job to make sense of the evidence," Brice snapped as he raised his hands, balling them into fists. He pounded his fists on the table, knocking over his coffee cup. Coffee spilled all over the table, some of it spraying onto the iPad. Both agents sprang to their feet, Agent Dawson grabbing the iPad and stopping the recording, before cleaning the coffee off it with the sleeve of his suit.

"I don't know these men," Brice insisted. "I thought that was why you're here. To find them."

Mrs. Drew appeared in the doorway behind the agent, eyes wide. Her expression dampened his fury.

Don't blow up like last time. Don't blow up like last time.

He used his balled fists to lift himself to his feet. "It all goes back to those men," he barked. "Not me."

"Calm down, Brice." Mrs. Drew headed for the kitchen. "Breathe. I'll get some paper towels to clean up the spill."

He righted his mug, setting it aside and staring down at the spilt coffee. "I'm sorry. I'm still recovering. I have a hard time…."

"Don't worry about it," Agent Amador said, though his tone belied his words. "What you've been through is stressful. We'll show ourselves out. And I'm sure we'll be back in touch soon."

The moment the door closed behind the agents, Brice growled. Mrs. Drew returned with the paper towels and the trashcan.

"I'm not them." He half fell back into his chair. "I didn't hurt anyone. I'm the victim."

"Breathe," Mrs. Drew ordered as she wiped up the coffee. "Deep breaths. Focus only on that."

He almost snarled at her to leave him alone. What good would breathing do him? But he didn't want to lose control again, not with her. He took a deep breath, in and out. Another. A third.

"Good." She dropped a wad of soaked paper towels in the trashcan and grabbed extra off the roll. "Keep breathing. Let it out."

He did and the anger drained out of him with each exhalation. He looked at the coffee staining the placemats and cringed.

"Let me help." He reached for the paper towels, but Mrs. Drew placed a hand on his wrist to stop him.

"I'll take care of it. You need to rest. You may not realize this, but this is also part of your recovery." She got up and went to the kitchen.

He focused on his breathing as she directed, but his thoughts kept wandering back to his conversation with the two special agents. Were they right? Not about him. He was sure there was no way he'd assisted human traffickers. But would Mary? Had she kept it from him? He wanted to believe the first option Agent Dawson had brought up, that she'd escaped from them. She was a victim. It would've explained why she'd kept her past from him.

But she'd left here on her own the night the men had attacked him. Things didn't add up. Unless… she had escaped while the men were attacking him. Why hadn't he thought of that earlier? He would've defended her from those men. Maybe he'd kept them at bay long enough for her to escape? And they'd almost killed him for it.

"I need my phone," he said as Mrs. Drew returned with a rag and the trashcan to wipe up the coffee.

"What?" she asked.

"I need to talk to my brother."

Chapter 24

The afternoon passed without an update from anyone. Brice picked at the spinach lasagna that Mrs. Drew prepared for dinner, while repeatedly checking his phone to make sure he hadn't missed a call or text. Hadn't they found Elwin Pickering by now?

Or had the agents, suspicious of him, warned Investigator Wright against informing him of developments?

Brice had called Jaxon and filled him in on the agents' questions. To his relief, Jaxon responded with outrage and promised to handle things from his end. While he admitted they had questions about Mary, and he didn't sound convinced by Brice's theory about why she'd run away, he was adamant that no one would harass his brother with baseless accusations. He had also promised to call back with more details soon.

But he'd heard from only Dora. They'd exchanged a few texts about Nate completing the repairs on her truck. Brice had apologized for bailing on her, but she'd countered with how unfair she'd been to ask him in the first place during his recovery. That had stung a little. He hated her thinking him incapable of working, but he couldn't bring himself to elaborate on the actual reasons he hadn't finished the job. Instead, he promised to work hard on his recovery so that the next time she had an issue with the truck, he'd be ready to handle it.

Mrs. Drew ate in silence, first a salad, followed by a small portion of the lasagna. She skipped her normal attempts to engage him in small talk. Once she finished eating, she excused herself from the table and set about cleaning up the dishes. He wondered if his outburst that morning had scared her. Or if she'd overheard any of the discussion. If she believed him capable of assisting human traffickers.... He shook his head, dismissing the thought.

He had just handed his mostly uneaten plate of food to Mrs. Drew in the kitchen when his cell rang. He hurried back to find Investigator Wright's name on the caller ID.

Relieved at finally getting a call, Brice headed toward the living room to talk alone. "Hello?"

"Brice, it's Investigator Wright." His voice sounded drained, no hint of the excitement Brice would've expected if they'd caught Elwin.

"Did you catch him?"

Wright sighed. "No, Brice. We didn't. There's no sign of him. But we found several women living in the duplexes where we found the truck. They *worked* for Elwin."

"Did you find…?" He couldn't make himself finish the question.

"No. No Mary," Investigator Wright said, guessing the question. "Even showed her picture around. None of the women recognized her."

Brice's hope drained away like blood from an open wound. He slumped to the couch. "What now?"

"It's going to be a long night. We'll interview all the women. Maybe one knows where Elwin has gone. We'll also search the house and truck for evidence and further leads."

"But nothing right now leads to Mary or the men?"

"Not at present, but we've just gotten started."

Brice's hand ached from gripping the cane. He forced himself to set it aside, but curled the hand into a fist.

"I've got to go," Investigator Wright said. "But the reason I called was to warn you. I've got a patrol parked at your place. If you see or hear anything, get to them."

"Thanks," Brice said, right before the line went dead.

He nearly threw the phone across the room. The constant procession of leads that fell apart was too much. Even if Investigator Wright found something while interviewing the women, at this point it seemed like the odds were stacked against them.

"The news was bad?" Mrs. Drew stood in the doorway.

"They lost him," Brice managed. He turned his head away.

"It's not your fault, you know," she said.

He struck a thigh with his fist. "Isn't it, though? He got away because of me."

She approached and sat beside him on the couch. "Those men, they're predators. Men like that love violence. They live for it. They were likely raised with it. Accepting that Investigator Wright or the agents need to handle those men doesn't make you weak. The police are trained to take on those kinds of men."

"What am I supposed to do? What can I do? I couldn't follow that man. Or fix Dora's truck. You have to drive me around. I can barely dress myself. It's no wonder Mary left."

"You suffered horrible injuries." The exasperation in her voice was clear. "No one endures what you've suffered and shrugs it off like it was nothing. Your job is to recover. Push on with your exercises, write in your journal, and don't let what those men did to you be the defining moment in your life."

He snorted.

"There are many ways to be strong." She placed a hand on his fist, but he pulled away.

"I'm not strong by any measure. Not anymore. Not sure I ever was."

"Brice Dunn, I'm not your mother, but I'm pretty sure if she were here, she'd tell you to stop feeling sorry for yourself. If you're unhappy with where you are, do something about it." She stood and marched down the hallway to her room.

It surprised him how much she sounded like his mom. Was it a quality innate to all mothers?

Her words also had the effect of making him feel embarrassed about sitting there, moping. He grabbed his cane and rose, unsure what to do. They hadn't worked much on his exercises today, but he wasn't heading to her room to ask if she'd come out and help him. He sensed she needed a break for the night.

Mental exercises? He shook his head. His mind was a whirl from the day's events. He couldn't focus on a crossword. Instead, he milled about the room, trying to come up with something else to do. He debated trying again to write in his diary, but he couldn't bring himself to recount the day's events as his mother would've done. For her, it was a way to deal with and release what she'd been through during her day, good or bad. A ritual to prepare her for the day to come. For him, it would be reliving his mistakes, dwelling on them until they drove him crazy. He'd done enough of that already.

It was hard not to think about Elwin. The man was the best lead they had to Mary, and he'd escaped. Where would he go? To join his companions wherever they'd gone?

Jaxon had said the men were somehow tied to another investigation. And Agent Dawson had said something about grabbing a flight back out to Grand Junction. That was in Colorado.

Was that where Elwin and the men had gone?

During the call on the back porch that morning, Agent Dawson had also voiced hope for evidence that would let them investigate something. A fraternity? No, a community. Except he'd said it more like a name, like they were called the Community. Brice had never heard of them. What could he find out about them?

He headed toward the computer room, easing past Mrs. Drew's room to avoid disturbing her. Even if she heard him, he hoped she'd think he was headed to bed.

Only the rocking chair in her room broke the silence.

*****

The whirring of the computer made his breath catch. He muted the volume, feeling like a teenager staying up late playing video games after his mom had sent him to bed. Back in those days, he'd played in the dark with his door closed, so the light from the screen wouldn't give him away. He hadn't worn headphones and had kept the volume on zero, so he would hear if his mom passed by his room. He'd always paused the game anytime he heard the creak of footsteps, grabbing the remote, ready to turn off the TV if he thought she suspected anything.

It was ridiculous for him now, a grown man, to hide what he was doing from anyone, but he didn't want Mrs. Drew to hear him, or she might make him do exercises to stop him.

His first search for the Community turned up results on a television show. He vaguely remembered ads about it from a few years back, but had never watched it.

He added Grand Junction and Colorado to his search term. The second list of results started off with information about the local court system, with titles about courts in the Grand Junction community. Below that were links to a few foundations. The sites focused on raising money for their local communities. He doubted any of them had to do with the FBI's investigation.

Adding the name Elwin Pickering got him nowhere. What about the other men? Their faces floated in his mind, but he couldn't recall the names from the agents' interrogation. Another failure on his part. He couldn't depend on himself for anything, it seemed, physical or otherwise.

Two more pages of search results revealed nothing promising. What else could he use to help his search? He added human trafficking to the keywords. This time the results returned a list of news reports. The headlines and brief descriptions had terms like cult and extremists.

The first article detailed discovery of a teenage boy who had starved to death in an abandoned building near the Community compound outside Grand Junction. It had raised suspicions, but local authorities had found no signs of foul play, nor could they tie him to the Community. The next two articles rehashed the story with most of the same quotes from the local sheriff.

Another article, an investigative piece, described a half-dozen women found at different times over a two-year period, wandering a road between the Community and Grand Junction. None of the women recalled where they'd come from, or much of anything that had happened to them. All were reported missing about three months prior to their discovery. Each one had injuries consistent with sexual abuse. Again, despite rumors, local authorities had been unable to tie any of them to the Community.

He found a Reddit on the Community. Rumors insisted that Community members were rarely seen outside the compound. The Community appeared to be self-sufficient. Members might come into the city for basic medical supplies, or to buy alcohol, but they kept interactions to a minimum and never spoke about the Community or what went on inside the compound. Brice wasn't even sure whether the Community was an official name or a nickname from the locals.

Had this been where Mary had come from before she'd moved in with him? Was she an escapee? If so, had she gone back willingly, or not?

From what he gathered, local police had never entered the compound. If the men had coerced Mary into returning, the police wouldn't know. She might be a prisoner, and neither Investigator Wright nor Agent Dawson would ever be able to verify it.

Agent Dawson had hoped to get information from Elwin that would allow them to investigate the place, but that seemed over now.

Brice decided he could no longer wait and hope the FBI or Investigator Wright or anyone else found evidence against the Community. Many people had searched for evidence for quite a while now, without success. And judging from the news stories alone, it wasn't a good place for Mary or the baby.

No, he had to go there. If Mary had returned with their daughter against her will, he wouldn't leave them there. He wasn't sure what he could find that local authorities hadn't, but he had to try. He refused to stay here and resign them to their fate.

If they were inside the compound, he had to find out, and then devise a way to help them escape.

Chapter 25

The Greyhound bus stop shared a rather nondescript brick building with the Huntsville/Madison County Visitor Center off Church Street and Cleveland Ave, right across from the train tracks beside the Huntsville Depot Museum.

After purchasing his fare, Brice had gone outside to wait in the bus terminal. It surprised him how many people awaited bus rides at seven thirty in the evening but he guessed like him, they had no choice. His bus, scheduled to depart in twenty minutes, was the lone one for the day headed on a route toward Grand Junction. Thanks to the late departure, he was in for another poor night of sleep.

A cold winter wind gusted through the outdoor terminal, forcing everyone to hunker down in their coats. Brice pulled his Titans knit hat down to cover his ears.

To pass the time, he fiddled with the new prepaid cell phone he'd purchased that morning while Mrs. Drew picked up groceries. He forced himself to not look at anything in the web browser, rather than waste any of his limited data on the prepaid phone. With his unlimited data plan for his own cell, it had been a while since he'd worried about it. Not knowing how much he'd end up needing during this trip, he chose to deal with boredom for now.

A voice over a loudspeaker announced the seven-fifty to Nashville was now boarding, the first of several stops on his way to Colorado. Brice joined a dozen others heading toward the third bus.

He was the only one not struggling with luggage. He'd been too afraid that Mrs. Drew would catch him packing, or that the officers watching his house would see him sneak out the back with a suitcase or duffle. Instead, he traveled with the clothes on his back and head, and his new disposable cell phone. His old one lay buried in the bottom of a dresser drawer, the power off. And he'd have to buy extra clothes once he arrived in Grand Junction.

The positive of not having any luggage was that he got on the bus first, giving him his pick of the seats. He headed for the back to minimize the number of people who saw him. As he passed through the bus, he scolded himself for being ridiculous. It wasn't like someone would recognize him and report his whereabouts to Jaxon or Nate. That didn't stop him from choosing a seat at the rear. He placed the cane on the seat next to him, hoping that deterred others from trying to sit there.

He tried not to think about how worried his brother and boss would be by now—Mrs. Drew as well—at his disappearance. And he hoped he hadn't gotten the officers watching his house in too much trouble. After all, they were there to keep Elwin or the others from breaking in, not to stop him from sneaking out.

Brice would have to be careful out in Grand Junction. Without his phone, no one could track him. He had cleared his browser history on the computer and paid for his bus fare with cash. Even the Uber he'd taken to get here had dropped him off at the VBC a few blocks away, in case someone discovered he'd taken one, so that they wouldn't know where he'd gone from there.

Despite the precautions, it was only once the bus driver, an elderly gentleman who looked like he drove as a post-retirement job, had pulled the bus out onto Cleveland Avenue, that Brice relaxed. Up to then, he'd expected someone would find him and put a stop to the trip.

The bus was about half full. There wasn't a ton of leg room between the seats, but placing his cane on the seat beside him had worked. He had the row to himself. He stretched his legs out to keep them from cramping, hoping it stayed like this.

He still couldn't believe he was traveling out to Colorado on his own in search of Mary and the baby. For the first time since he'd awoken out of a coma, his heart sped up with excitement. It was crazy. He knew this. But it felt good to be doing something, no matter his limitations, or what he was up against, or the mistakes he'd made up to this point.

He was going to find his girls.

Chapter 26
(Twelve Years Past)

Beulah stood outside the truck stop at Palisade, watching truckers pull in from I-70, fill up their tanks, and head inside the restrooms before filling up on chips, beef jerky, sodas, or energy drinks.

She loitered outside the closed down restaurant next door, so as not to attract the notice of the gas station attendants. The two-story restaurant building reminded her of two house boats, one stacked upon the other. Stone lined much of the first story, with a chimney on the side closest to the highway, but portions of the first level and all the second had wood paneling. The second-story windows were boarded up, and it looked like the place hadn't been open for a few years. But it gave her a discreet spot from which to evaluate potential rides.

Most of the truckers she dismissed before they even went inside. Those with hard edges to them—clenched fists, scowls, excessive tattoos, such as the guy with a skull and another with a snake. She also wasn't taking a chance with anyone who exited the gas station carrying beer.

The sun was setting toward the giant mesa behind the gas station. She didn't want to be stranded here, and any trucker would be more wary of hitchhikers after dark.

A trucker with a gut shoving its way out between his shirt and pants came waddling up from the back where he'd parked his truck after getting diesel. His baby face, devoid of facial hair, with a few red spots that looked a lot like acne, caught her attention. He wore a yellow ball cap with a logo she didn't recognize, and an amused smile as if he'd been joking with someone a moment ago.

She walked to intercept him, pulling a small, cheap camera from her pocket; she'd swiped it in Grand Junction. When she was within a few steps of him, his eyes shot up to her, widening at the unexpected approach, before he realized she posed no threat.

She held out the camera, making sure he saw it, before speaking. "Would you mind taking a pic for me?"

"Not at all." He held out a hand for the camera, checking out her breasts in the process, eyes lingering a moment. He accepted the camera and gestured about the area. "Where would you like it?"

"Oh, I'd love to get the mesa in the background. It's beautiful." She feigned enthusiasm, as if it was the most wonderful thing she'd ever seen.

"Is it just you?" he asked, looking around as if expecting her to have a friend or parent.

"Just me. I'm on a trip to see my grandma in Kansas for the summer." Unsure how to pose for the picture, she clasped her hands behind her back and smiled wide.

He took a pic, then crouched a little and took a second, before offering her the camera back.

"Are you even old enough to drive?" he asked. This time his eyes did a complete pass over her from chest to calves and back.

Annoyance and revulsion made her hackles rise, but she controlled her face, keeping her smile. It was something she'd learned to do with the men of the Community over the last couple of years to keep them in a good mood. "I turned sixteen two months back."

"Ever driven a stick?" he asked, then burst out laughing as if he'd told the funniest joke in the world.

She didn't know how to drive a manual, nor why that would be funny, but she was regretting taking a chance on him. Despite his rather harmless look, she read his eyes. The way he looked at her was one reason she'd run away from the Community. She wanted out of here, but not enough for that. She'd keep an eye out for someone else. If a better opportunity didn't present itself, she could always break into the old restaurant, find a spot to sleep for the night, then come up with another option tomorrow. Perhaps she'd hike down the interstate for a while.

"Thanks for the pics," she said, keeping her smile warm and friendly. "I should get going."

"Hold on," he protested, spreading his arms wide to block her from slipping past. "I was planning to grab some dinner inside. They have decent sandwiches and stuff. Would you like to join me?"

"I can't. I've a ways to go tonight. I should get back on the road." She tried to step around him.

"Ah, come on." He moved with her, keeping up his arms as a loose barrier. "You can spare thirty minutes, can't ya? I'll let you see the inside of my truck afterward if you like? Have you ever been inside a big rig?"

She dropped her eyes to the ground, moving sideways toward the abandoned restaurant and hoping he wouldn't follow. "I'm sorry. I should get going."

His expression darkened. "Fine. Be that way bitch. Next time take your own damn pic. It's called a selfie, you dumb cunt."

Without another word, she picked up her pace, but kept a wary eye on him. He didn't bother to follow. Instead, he waved his arm as if to say forget her then, and headed on into the gas station.

She picked up her pace, deciding she'd better be out of sight before he returned. She hurried around behind the restaurant, relieved not to find any cars or people.

Another empty one-story building, with a sign advertising peaches on one corner, stood angled toward oncoming traffic from the south. Cigarette butts and crushed beer cans littered the parking lot. An occasional soda can broke the monotony. Weeds poked up through the cracks in the asphalt, which only made the area appear more destitute.

One of the restaurant windows she passed had a gaping hole in the boarding that covered it, the window completely shattered. The damage didn't appear recent, but she'd have to take care if she stayed the night inside. If anyone remained, they might not appreciate the intrusion.

Traipsing back around the front of the restaurant, bringing the highway to the west back into view, her pulse quickened. An old black pickup pulled into the Exxon parking lot. She darted behind a stand of pines that grew in a flowerbed to hide herself. She recognized the truck.

It belonged to Garrett.

She peeked around the pines, then shuffled forward alongside the front of the restaurant to the corner. The truck sat parked in front of the gas station. Arden, Garrett, and her mother walked inside. What were they doing here? How had they found her? She had told no one where she was going or even that she was running away. Sure, they would've missed her by now, but to have guessed which way she'd be traveling? There were too many directions for them to search, yet here they were.

The trucker with the baby face strolled back toward his truck holding something wrapped in aluminum foil in one hand and a two liter of cola in the other. Her stomach bubbled uncomfortably at the thought of approaching him again, but the leer and jokes, even a little something more, would be better than remaining here a moment longer.

Backtracking around the restaurant, she ran, desperate to get away before Arden or her mother saw her. She only slowed when she neared the trucker so that she wouldn't alarm him.

"What're you eating?" she asked.

The trucker frowned when he realized it was her and kept on toward his truck. The only one parked out back at present.

"I'm sorry about earlier. I was nervous. It's my first time traveling alone."

He grunted and didn't look her way.

"Would you still let me ride in your truck? Just a quick ride."

When he glanced at her, she returned her best wide-eyed, he'd be doing her a huge favor look.

At that, his entire face broadened into a grin that some might find charming. "Sure. I suppose I can do you the *favor*."

His eighteen-wheeler was red, but she didn't recognize the company logo on the side. He opened the passenger door to let her climb the couple steps up and into the cab. But she'd barely gotten seated before he slammed the door shut, as if afraid she might change her mind. Then he sauntered around to the driver's side as if someone had rolled out the red carpet for him.

Climbing into the driver's seat, he set the two liter and the aluminum-foil-wrapped food on the floor between their seats. An aroma of cheese and beans filled the cab as he started up the truck, shifted gears, and pulled forward.

Gauges covered the dash and a CB radio hung where the rearview mirror would be in a regular passenger vehicle.

"I'm Chaz, by the way."

"Beulah," she replied, not bothering to lie. She watched the gas station, terrified Arden or her mother would come out and see her. Slouching in the seat, she tried to look chill.

"This your first time in a semi?" Chaz asked as he passed by the gas station.

Her heart thudded in her chest as she eyed the front entrance. The truck remained parked in front, but there was no sign of Arden, Garrett, or her mother inside.

"Yes," she answered and turned to survey the back of the cab because it allowed her to duck out of sight.

A small bed extended from the back wall, with padding above it that made her think of the inside of a coffin. Her skin crawled at the thought of lying on that bed. She decided that if he pressed hard enough for a favor later, she'd find a better spot than back there.

Behind her seat was a mini fridge, as well as some storage compartments built into the wall. Mounted behind the driver's seat, with a closet beneath it, was a small TV angled toward the bed.

She wasn't sure what she'd expected from a big rig cab, but it wasn't this. She marveled at the space.

"You're welcome to go back and check it out," Chaz said as he pulled the truck out onto the highway. "The bed is more comfortable than you think."

She wasn't about to go back there and try it out. The last thing she wanted was to give him any concrete visuals to go with his imagination. Instead, she pretended to study the cab until they'd passed the last abandoned building, then settled back into her seat to study the road ahead.

"How far do you get on a tank of gas?" she asked, wondering how far he would go before stopping.

"I've got two hundred-gallon tanks on this baby." He tapped the dashboard as he spoke, then reached down to pick up his burrito from the floor. "I get around twelve hundred miles on flat roads. With all the mountains in Colorado, though, that drops a good bit."

"Where you headed?" she asked.

"Colorado Springs," he answered around a bite of burrito. "Then down to Texas."

Though she'd never been to Colorado Springs, it was much too close to the Community for her liking. Nevertheless, it might be as good a location as any to figure out what's next. And she didn't need him to decide she owed him too much.

"I can only spare fifteen minutes, before I'll need to get you back to your car," Chaz said. "I've got to reach the Springs tonight."

She bit her lip, hesitating because once she asked for a longer ride, he'd expect more from her. But she also didn't want him to drop her off a few miles down the road.

"I don't actually have a car," she said.

"You don't?" he frowned at her.

"No."

"Well, how were you planning to get to Kansas? That's a long walk." He took another bite that was large enough to puff his cheeks out like a squirrel gathering nuts for the winter.

"I was hoping you'd let me ride to Colorado Springs for a start."

His head swiveled to her. He broke into a big grin when he realized she was serious and slapped the top of the steering wheel. "Sure. I'd love the company. Gets lonely on the road."

Downing the last of his burrito, Chaz rolled down the window and tossed the wrapper outside. He grabbed the two liter from the floor and set it in his lap, before twisting at the cap. His hand paused as he stared out the driver's side mirror.

"What the hell!"

She tried to see what he was referring to, but the angle was wrong. She checked her mirror, but it showed only the landscape flying by behind them.

Over the rumbling engine, she heard a honking horn. He dropped the two liter and reached behind her seat, pulling out a shotgun she'd missed in her earlier search. He set it in his lap and resumed checking his mirror.

A chill seeped through her at sight of the gun. She'd seen plenty before, especially shotguns and hunting rifles in the Community. But he looked ready to use it, and if he opened fire on anyone, she didn't want to be here in the truck for it.

The honking grew louder and moved up near the driver's side door. Chaz flipped the bird at whoever it was. Beulah raised herself up enough to see.

Her breath caught in her throat. Garrett's truck. Arden leaned out the passenger seat, signaling for Chaz to pull over.

Beulah slumped back into her seat and hugged herself. She thought she might get sick. They'd found her. How had they known?

It didn't matter. They had and her escape was over. She hadn't even made it a day.

Chaz cussed out the window and even raised the shotgun where Arden and Garrett could see it. Beulah almost wished he'd shoot at them.

Instead, Garrett's truck pulled ahead and braked. Chaz dropped the shotgun into his lap and downshifted. "I don't know who these fuckers think they are." He guided the big rig over to the side of the road to avoid hitting the truck as he slowed.

"They're after me," she mumbled.

"What?" His head swiveled between her and the road.

"They're chasing me."

His eyes narrowed. "Why? They your parents?"

"Not my real ones. And they're abusive."

Garrett's truck moved off the road with them, like a cattle dog herding a run-away cow.

Huffing in frustration, Chaz pointed over his shoulder. "Hide back in the cab. I'll get rid of them."

Grateful for the unexpected support, she unbuckled herself and crawled into the back, crouching down on the ground beside the mini fridge. The truck slowed to a stop, the engine dying. She hated the silence. It underscored the end of her journey. She tried to tell herself this wasn't over. They didn't know for sure she was back here. They were guessing.

Chaz barely had the door open, climbing out of the cab, shotgun in hand, before he started cussing.

"What the hell you doing cutting me off? Who the hell are you?" He'd left the window open. She heard everything.

"I'm sorry to inconvenience you," Arden said smoothly "I'm helping this sweet lady here find her daughter."

"Have you seen my baby? Beulah? Beulah Clarke, honey? Are you in there?" Her mother's voice was high in pitch, with a bit of hysteria Beulah had never heard from her.

"I don't know who you're looking for, but I'm alone," Chaz said, but his tone had lost all heat. He sounded uncertain.

"This is her picture." Arden again. "She ran away this morning over a misunderstanding. We want to get her back safe."

A misunderstanding? She'd spent more time than she cared to remember in the sanctuary's basement 'caring for the men of the Community,' as her mother liked to put it. 'Doing her duty as a woman.' Everyone pitched in to the best of their ability for the good of them all. Beulah felt more like property passed around to meet the needs of others, while they ignored her own. Where was the misunderstanding in that?

"Please, if you've seen her, tell us. I just want my baby back." The pitifulness in her mother's voice made Beulah want to scream. How did she fake such concern?

"I'm sorry, ma'am. I—"

"Son," Arden cut Chaz off. "When we set off this morning, I put $200 in my wallet in case we needed anything while finding young Beulah Clarke. If you've seen her and can help us locate her, I'd be happy to pass this over to you for your help. We'd appreciate it."

Beulah clapped her hands over her mouth to stifle a cry, but tears blurred her vision.

"I didn't know she'd run away. She asked what it was like to ride in a semi, so I offered to give her a quick spin. A brief trip down the road is all."

"Where is she now?" her mother begged.

He didn't reply, but a second later, her mother appeared in the driver's window. "Baby. Baby, are you back there?" Her face was tear streaked. "Oh, thank heaven. Arden, she's here. We found her. We found my baby."

Beulah wiped the tears from her own eyes and rose to her feet. She didn't reply to her mother. Beyond her mother, Chaz slipped cash into his back pocket, the shotgun lowered at his side.

"It's okay, Beulah," Arden called. "Come on out, honey. It'll be, okay. We'll sort things out."

Beulah moved to the driver's seat and for a quick second, looked for the keys, wondering if she could start up the truck and shift gears well enough to get the truck down the road. She'd seen Arden drive his truck often enough. How hard could it be?

But Chaz hadn't left the keys in the ignition. Or anywhere in the truck as far as she saw. She opened the door and climbed down from the truck.

Arms wrapped around her, clutching tightly, and her mother kissed her. "Oh baby, I was so scared. Why did you run away? No matter. I'm glad we found you safe."

Beulah kept her eyes on the ground, not even looking at Chaz as her mother guided her over to Garrett's truck and opened the right rear passenger door.

Her mother raised her voice for Chaz to hear, as she said, "We'll get you home safe and sort this all out." She pushed Beulah into the backseat and shut the door behind her.

Garrett sat in the driver's seat and he didn't spare Beulah a glance when she climbed in. Instead, he studied Chaz and Arden, one hand clasped around a handgun resting on his knee.

As Beulah stared down at her hands in her lap, wondering what the consequences would be when they got back to the Community, her mother climbed in beside her. Arden took the front passenger seat. They sat there silent while Chaz pulled his truck out onto the highway and drove off.

"You ungrateful whore." Her mother's eyes blazed as the semi picked up speed. "After all I've done for you, you run away." She slapped Beulah hard. "You stabbed me in the back." She raised her hand again, but Arden halted her.

"Allison." He stared at her through the rearview mirror. Her mother huffed, but turned her attention out the window. Arden turned back to Beulah. All kindness, concern, and warmth had vanished from his face. "You broke your promise. To your mother. To me. To the Community."

Beulah recoiled, unable to speak. She couldn't think to argue or protest to defend herself.

"You took an oath, committing yourself as one of us." He paused, expression turning disappointed. "Today, you violated that oath. You decided you no longer wanted to live with us and contribute to your family."

"Ungrateful little—" Her mother began.

"Allison!" Arden's eyes darkened as he turned to her mother and waited to see if she'd hold her tongue. When she did, he focused back on Beulah.

"You don't have to stay. You don't have to be one of us, but you still owe a debt." He studied her for a moment, as if to gauge her reaction. Or maybe to see if she showed any remorse. She had none to give.

"I'm sending you out," Arden said. "There are other ways you can serve the Community. Other ways you can be of value until you choose to join us again, if that day ever comes." He turned forward and Garrett started up the truck.

As Garrett turned the truck around and headed back toward the Community, Beulah wondered what he meant. What else could they do with her outside of the Community? She didn't know anyone ever lived outside.

But she quickly discarded her musing. Whatever they had planned, it wasn't for her happiness. Or well-being.

Chapter 27

Brice's left knee cramped, so he gave up on sleep. Stretching the leg out into the aisle, he kneaded the muscles to either side of his kneecap. The right leg cramped as well, and he straightened it as much as the space allowed. The bus was more than an hour away from its next stop in Indiana; a bit out of the way, but that was the route before heading to St. Louis.

Most of the other passengers on the bus slept, but his exhaustion wasn't enough to overcome his discomfort. He wished he had thought to grab a couple of comics to pass the time, but that hadn't been on his mind yesterday. Getting to the bus, without anyone finding out and stopping him, had consumed his focus. That and debating what to do when he arrived in Grand Junction. How would he locate the Community?

He'd spent the first couple of hours on the bus obsessing over whom to talk to and where to go once he arrived. He'd jotted down a few ideas in his journal to help him remember. That was about as far as he got. Writing a list of things he needed to do, no problem. Chronicling his thoughts and feelings, his memories, seemed too mundane to warrant keeping a record in a journal. And those that seemed important enough, he didn't want to write where anyone could read them.

How had his mother done it? Not once or twice, but every day for years on end. At the end of each day, she had sat down and written as if it all poured out of her the way the ink flowed from the pen to the paper. She had opened herself up, making herself vulnerable. It made him shiver. At the same time, he longed for the days when he'd do the dishes, listening to music on the radio or an A&M basketball game, while his mother scribbled down her day.

He slipped his hand into a jacket pocket and pulled out one of her journals, not sure why he'd brought it, but wondering if he would remember the specifics of those moments based upon what she'd written.

He hadn't brought the first one he'd looked at, having no desire to rehash anything from their time in Michigan. Nor did he start with the first entry in this one, instead thumbing back the cover and letting the pages slide open to a spot in the middle.

The date was a few months after his mother's diagnosis. He almost closed the journal and put it back in his pocket, reluctant to intrude upon the darkest time in her life. The pain as she went to session after session for the treatments that had robbed a piece of her with every visit. And the despair as each treatment failed her.

Yet the words in the journal drew his eyes, as if his mother pulled him in, needing him to understand. And she demanded obedience, had always demanded it of him. The will of a mother determined to see her son a man. And to do right as she saw it, even after her time had passed.

April 18th

It's a hard day when your baby does something that makes you so proud your heart fills to the brim, yet simultaneously breaks. Brice came home from school this morning, I thought to drive me to my doctor's appointment, but with none of his books. I asked him where they were. I'd told him before he left that morning to check in with his teachers for the classes he'd miss and make sure he got assignments to complete. When I was first diagnosed and had no other means of getting to my appointments after the first few when I could drive myself, I'd met with his teachers and principal to ensure they would work with us. Help him keep up. I wasn't going to let my baby fall behind because of me.

Today he shrugged me off. Said don't worry about it. Now, I wasn't about to let my baby take that kind of attitude with me. It's not healthy for a boy to disrespect his mother. I told him to look me in the eye. He sighed, but complied. When I asked again, he'd replied that he'd quit.

At first, I stared, taken aback by the admission. Then my hand took up its position, conditioned by years of discipline, to slap Brice out the door to the car and back to school. Forget the doctor's appointment. We'd head to Johnson and I would undo whatever he'd done.

He didn't so much as flinch at my raised hand. He looked me in the eye, hands clenched at his side, not in anger but with resolve.

Before I could speak, he said, "Momma, I got a job."

Again, I was speechless, and this time he didn't wait for me to catch my bearings. He rushed on.

"Momma, we've no choice. You can't work. I'm gonna step up. Someone's got to pay the bills and it's gonna be me." His eyes dared me to argue, and while he was right that the treatments had laid me low of late, they hadn't stripped me of the strength to fight for my baby's future.

"Absolutely not. The doctor said my treatments will get easier so I can get back to work. Things'll be tight for a while, but I'll manage. I'm not letting you quit."

His posture weakened with concern. "Momma, you can't work. You—" He wanted to say more about my condition, but he hesitated. I could see the change in tactics before he even spoke.

"It's temporary. I can work and keep the bills paid, then finish school when you're better."

"No." I shook my head, wanting to sit down, but unwilling to show that bit of weakness. Yet, I found I couldn't muster the argument that I would work when we both knew that was a lie. It pained me that he saw it. I thought I'd hid things better than that.

"I'll call Jaxon," I countered. "Ask him to come home."

"You can't." Brice met my eyes squarely, even defiantly, for the first time in his life. "He got his orders. He's deployed to Afghanistan, remember?"

I stared at him in shock. I'd forgotten. My baby Jaxon headed to a war zone, and I'd forgotten. What kind of mother was I? Was this what was ahead of me?

Not yet. Not at all if I can help it.

I raised my chin to remind Brice who was the parent here. "We'll move into something smaller and sell this place. It's more than we need for the two of us."

He crossed his arms. The nerve of that boy crossing his arms at me!

Brice smiled at that note. That action must've infuriated her. She'd never allowed a smart mouth or dissension from either Jaxon or himself. God, how he missed her.

"This is our home," he said. "This is where we belong and where I want to be. If I have to work now to keep it, to keep you well, then that's the way it'll have to be for now."

For the first time in my life one of my sons had outflanked me. I didn't like it. Rather than belabor a losing argument further, I ordered him out the door. We were late for my appointment. And the doctor was none too pleased with my attitude during my treatment today.

I'm proud of my son. More than I can ever say. But at what price will he pay this sacrifice? Will it cost him a shot at something he really wants?

No! I won't allow it. I'm going to get better. I'll keep fighting, so I can get him back in school and make sure he follows his dreams as well.

Brice cleared his throat, almost chuckling to himself. He'd never felt so scared in his life as on that drive home from school after quitting. It had taken every bit of his courage to tell her the truth. At the time he'd debated seeing how long he could hide it from her. Attempt to clean up at the end of every workday at the shop, keep his textbooks, and make up his own homework to do.

But seeing her when he got home, the exhaustion that radiated off her; she'd already lost weight. Despite her best efforts with her hair, it was clearly thinning. Rather than lie, he'd told her the truth. He'd half expected her to kill him, bring him back to life, kill him a second time to make sure he got the point, then drag him back to school regardless of his arguments.

When she'd agreed, he'd felt on top of the world. Not because he'd beaten her, but because she'd accepted his help. Accepted him stepping up to do what had needed doing. Would she have still agreed if she'd known he never would go back to school?

He'd meant to go back when he'd quit that day. He'd meant the mechanic job to be temporary, something to endure for a short time to make sure they survived, then complete school later.

To his surprise, he had discovered a love of the work, of fixing engines. When momma had passed, Nate, Warren, and Lisa had become his family. Doing anything else was unimaginable.

When all this was over, once he'd found Mary and the baby, whatever happened, he hoped to return home and to the job.

He shivered, uncertain if the bus driver had the AC on too high, or if he was tired and used to being in his warm bed at this hour of the night. Either way, there was nothing to do about it for now. Instead, he stretched out the spine of the journal, letting the pages flip on their own to another spot. He liked the randomness of it.

July 27th

I'm here at the table today. Somehow. Brice picked up dinner on his way home from work. God gave my boy a little extra compassion when he made him.

I couldn't keep down more than a couple bites. Brice makes up for it though. No idea how that boy puts away so much food. His brother's the same way, as if the moment they finish chewing their food and swallow, it evaporates.

The little bit I eat evaporates as soon as I eat it, too. It certainly doesn't replenish my strength. I'm starting to forget what it even feels like to be strong.

Enough of that. Stop feeling sorry for yourself.

The one bright spot about dinner is hearing Brice talk about his day. It keeps me returning to the dinner table each night. He opens up now, the surliness gone. He tells me all about whatever project that he's working on and what he's doing to fix it. Not that I understand any of it, but it's a pleasure to hear him rattle on.

Nate seems fond of him. He trains him. Some days they stay an hour or two after the shop closes, not because Nate is keeping him there working extra, but because he's answering all my boy's questions. Brice never asked questions in school. His teachers used to complain at parent/teacher conferences that they couldn't get him to speak up about anything.

I still don't love that he quit school. I expect this will bother me more in a few weeks when other kids return to school. But at least this all seems like less of a sacrifice since he's happy. Every day he comes home with his shoulders raised instead of hunched. A smile brightens his face as he talks during dinner, rather than scarfing down his food

Brice wiped a tear away, closing the journal, unable to continue. Even in all her pain, body deteriorating, she'd focused her energy on him. His happiness, well-being, and future.

He'd thought more than once about his promise after her death. After they'd learned she was going to lose her battle, he'd expected her to remind him of his promise. Yet she never had. At the time he'd taken that as silent approval, her recognition that being a mechanic was his future. What he wanted. Or had she just chosen not to force him to lie to her?

Jaxon, on the other hand, had pushed him to go back to school, to quit the job, keep his promise, and work toward a real dream. Brice had sat back, not arguing, just accepting the criticism until Jaxon had to return to his post. Even after Jaxon had left the Army and joined the FBI years later, he'd kept at Brice to return to school.

Brice understood the criticism. Jaxon was trying to fill the void from the loss of their mother. He thought it was his duty to keep his little brother in line and on the path their mother had set out for them. It was how he coped.

Brice's eyes burned. He wanted to close them and try again to sleep, but they were reaching the outskirts of Evansville. In another fifteen or twenty minutes they'd arrive at the bus station for a brief stop. Once they were on the way to St. Louis, he'd try to get a few hours of rest before the sun came up. He'd rather not spend the full day in a dreary state, though he supposed it didn't matter a great deal. He'd be on the bus all day and through the night to early Wednesday morning.

Chapter 28

Brice arrived thirty minutes early to Coffee Outdoors for his meeting with Owen Fitzpatrick, a reporter from the Grand Junction Daily Sentinel. Despite the heavy coat, gloves, and knit hat he wore, the cold seeped into his bones during the hike over from the inn he'd stayed at the previous night. He hunched in on himself and blew warm air into his gloved hands. The whole Midwest had been in a cold spell for the last week, with daily highs in the teens for Grand Junction.

Anxious to get out of the cold, he hurried inside Coffee Outdoors, a brick-walled building that looked decades old. Tables constructed from large round bicycle wheels with clear plastic covers rested on bicycle frames reconfigured as table legs, around which people sat in a variety of camping chairs. From the walls hung bicycles, old tennis shoes and hiking boots, backpacks for long duration hikes, and several framed maps of biking trails in the area. More outdoors-related gear hung suspended from the ceiling.

The aroma of roasting coffee beans, with a hint of chocolate and caramel, infused the shop. Brice imagined campers, hikers, and mountain bikers stopped in for their caffeine fix before heading for the scenic trails of the Colorado National Monument. He had read up on some of that to pass time on the bus ride once he'd found everything he could on the Community.

No one in the shop gave him more than a casual glance or seemed likely to be Mr. Fitzpatrick, not that he'd expected the reporter to arrive early as well. On the ride out cross country, Brice had researched the Community and discovered Mr. Fitzpatrick had the byline for a series of critical articles exposing the Community, which were published in the Daily Sentinel. The first article covered a woman found wandering State Highway 141 near the Colorado–Utah border. She'd been severely malnourished and dehydrated. She'd told authorities she'd escaped from the Community where she'd endured years of drugging and abuse at the hands of the cult's leaders. Before providing the Community's location or any evidence, however, she'd died in what authorities ruled a suicide.

In follow-up articles, Mr. Fitzpatrick had reported that a couple other anonymous sources described the Community as a religious cult, which treated its women as property. Despite rumors of planned investigations, the articles had ceased, with the last coming more than a year prior. Nevertheless, it served as the best source of information that Brice had, so he'd contacted Owen that morning, and the reporter had agreed to a meeting.

Brice approached the counter. A young man, with a runner's physique, cleaned the counter with a towel.

The kid looked up at him as he approached. "What can I get you?"

"I need a minute," Brice replied.

The shop's coffee blends were on display on a series of chalkboards on the back wall, ordered by light, medium, and dark roasts, with locations from which the beans originated. With names like Boma Highland and Peabury Robusta, Brice guessed Mrs. Drew would love the place. If things went well, he'd stop back by to purchase a couple bags for her before he headed home.

He settled on a Borneo Rubia with a little cream, foregoing any shots or flavor additions. He wanted something hot and simple to warm him up. Then he chose a table with a red camping chair he hoped he could raise himself out of later without embarrassing himself.

While he waited for Owen to arrive, he sipped his coffee, enjoying the warmth spreading through him. And the burn on his skin as it adjusted to the heated interior after the walk over from the inn.

He'd planned to contact the reporter when he'd arrived in Grand Junction yesterday, but after three nights of minimal sleep, he'd checked into the inn and lain down for a short nap, and he'd slept the rest of the day. It had been late by the time he'd awakened, so he'd gone to a nearby grocery store for a meal, an SD card, and the cold weather apparel, before crashing again last night.

He didn't have to wait long. Mr. Fitzpatrick arrived ten minutes later. His appearance matched the picture on the Grand Junction Sentinel news website. He looked to be in his mid-twenties and fashion conscious, wearing a heavy black coat, gloves, earmuffs, and a silver tie. He sported a thick beard and slicked his hair back on top, but kept it almost shaved on the sides. A backpack hung over one shoulder.

Cane in hand, Brice stood, relieved that he managed it almost fluidly. His left knee still ached from his fall the other day, which the long bus ride hadn't helped, but it was improving.

Mr. Fitzpatrick caught Brice studying him and approached, offering a hand. "Mr. Dunn?"

Brice set his coffee on the table and shook the reporter's hand. "That's me. Nice to meet you, Mr. Fitzpatrick."

"Owen, please." He set his backpack in a chair on the opposite side of the table, then gestured to the front counter. "I'm going to grab a cup before we get started. Need anything?"

"I'm good." Brice raised his own coffee. "Thanks." Then he sat and waited for Owen to return with a coffee and a scone covered with a strawberry glaze.

"You have information for me on the Community?" Owen asked, as he removed a laptop from the backpack. He also grabbed a cell phone and placed it on the table between them.

Recording their conversation without permission wasn't legal, was it? Brice didn't like the idea of being taped, but he was reluctant to ask Owen about it, for fear of sounding suspicious.

"Umm, a little, though I was hoping you might help me out," Brice replied.

"Help you out? How?" Owen frowned.

Brice took a deep breath, nervous to talk now that the moment had arrived. He wished they were alone in the coffee shop, so that no one would overhear them. "My girlfriend, Mary Smith. Men from the Community attacked us in our home in Alabama. She escaped, but I fear they caught her and brought her here."

While he didn't know any of that for certain, he'd spent a good bit of time thinking about it on the bus ride and it seemed to make the most sense. She'd left on her own the night of the attack. She'd escaped those men. Why hadn't she contacted him to let him know she was safe? Unless she hadn't gotten away like he'd thought. The men must've tracked her down again. And the Community was the only connection he had to her. He had to hope they'd brought her here.

"Why haven't you contacted the police?"

"I have," Brice replied, feeling defensive. "I worked with the police in Huntsville, but they've turned up nothing on her. Nor anything tangible on the Community."

Owen snorted. "I'm not surprised."

Brice removed the SD card from his pocket and set it in the middle of the table beside the phone.

"What's that?" Owen asked, staring at the SD card, but not reaching for it.

"Videos of the men that attacked me. And of Mary, my girlfriend." He'd logged into the online storage site for his camera videos using the business office computer at the inn.

Owen tapped on the side of his black laptop and a slot opened up.

"The footage came from cameras on my front and back porch. Caught the men approaching my house. That's also how we identified and connected them to the Community."

Owen inserted the SD card into his laptop and typed away on the keyboard. "If you've got that, what's the problem? Why aren't the authorities going after them?"

"The videos don't show the attack itself, just the men approaching the house from the back. My neighbor told police that Mary left on her own. He never saw them."

"The men are persons of interest to the police, but not actual suspects then," Owen finished.

Brice stared down at his coffee, unable to respond. He couldn't bring himself to agree that the men weren't suspects, even if Owen only meant from the laws' perspective.

"What am I looking at here?" Owen asked, staring at his screen.

"There're two videos. The one labeled back porch camera is the one you want." Brice wished the reporter would turn his laptop where they both could see, but he seemed too engrossed. "It starts at twelve am, but they don't arrive until after four that afternoon."

"No audio?"

Brice grimaced. "No."

For the next ten minutes, they sat in silence, Owen watching the videos. The reporter didn't give any visual cues of his reaction to what he was seeing.

"Who are these three men?" Owen asked finally, turning the laptop screen toward Brice.

"The one on the left is Elwin Pickering. Have you heard of him?"

Owen shook his head. "Nope."

Brice told the reporter about his encounter with Pickering, what Investigator Wright found when they located his place, and that Elwin had escaped.

"This her?" Owen asked, interrupting. "The blonde on the video. Is she your girlfriend? The one you're looking for?"

"Yes."

"And the other two men?"

"I don't know. FBI agents told me, but I forgot."

Owen's eyes shot up and he arched an eyebrow. "The FBI's involved in your case?"

"Yes, once police confirmed the men's identities. They tie back to a case the FBI is working on the Community."

"Didn't know there was much activity on their end these days," Owen grumbled.

"Yeah, what happened?" Brice asked, feeling it was time to press for information. "I read your articles. You had witnesses of what was happening in the Community, but no details on an investigation."

"There wasn't one." Owen resumed typing on the computer.

"Why not?" If there were witnesses, what else did the police need?"

"My sources quit cooperating. They wouldn't talk with local law enforcement."

Brice frowned. "Why not?"

"The death of the woman from my article."

"The one who committed suicide?"

Owen snorted. "She didn't commit suicide."

Brice hesitated, confused. "But your article said—"

"Yeah, well that's not what happened," Owen snapped.

Several people at other tables turned to look at them.

"But that's what the police believed. What the evidence showed." Owen scowled, leaning back in his chair. "So that's what I had to write, because the Sentinel prints the news, not what I believe."

Brice guessed it was an old argument for Owen. Most likely with his boss.

"After that, your sources stopped cooperating?" Brice asked.

Owen flexed his jaw in anger. "They told me if they didn't, they'd end up like her."

Brice didn't blame them, though from Owen's expression, he did.

For the next few minutes, they sat silent, Owen still working something on the computer. Brice debated what to ask next.

"The woman from your article, you wrote she bore signs of abuse. What happened to her?" A big part of him didn't want to ask. He already worried about Mary and the baby and what the Community might do to them. Yet he also felt it was the key to understanding Mary. Why she would steal someone's identity. Why she'd been unwilling to talk about her past.

"When they found her, she was near starved to death, emaciated, and drugged to the point that she hadn't known where she was or how she'd gotten there. Only reason I knew she was from the Community was a tattoo of a vine with thorns above her left ankle."

Owen stared past Brice as he spoke.

"After a couple days she started to remember the abuse, being drugged and chained to altars for sexual ceremonies. What I didn't realize was that they still kept tabs on her. Once she started speaking, they got to her before I recorded her story."

Owen gestured to his phone on the table between them. "That's why I'm recording this conversation. After that mistake, I promised myself I'd always record any discussions with sources to ensure I had real evidence to take to the police, instead of hearsay."

Brice's voice caught in his throat at the confirmation that Owen was recording their conversation, but hearing why, he let it alone. What did it hurt? Just because it made him uncomfortable wasn't a good reason.

"I'll turn it off if you request it. I can't record this against your will."

"It's fine," Brice answered, though he knew nothing he said would help the police with the investigation.

"I don't know this woman, your Mary. You think she's in the Community?"

Brice shrugged. "Not sure, but these guys, they're tied to it, so I'm guessing if they caught up with her, then that's where she's at."

"Not much to go on."

"If there was much to go on, I wouldn't be here."

"Fair point." Owen pursed his lips. "I'll tell you what, if you believe she's in the Community with your child, you need to get them out. Whatever you have to do."

"How?" Brice's pulse quickened. "I don't know how to find it."

"That I figured out." Owen stood up and moved to the chair beside Brice, rotating his laptop as he did so. "The Community's in a valley southwest of Piñon Mesa, not too far north of State Highway 141."

Owen pulled up a map on his computer and zoomed in on an area. The map had Grand Junction, the Colorado National Monument, Glade Park, and Piñon Mesa HP. The place Owen pointed to was a decent bit west of the HP area, and down closer to Highway 141 around North Fork West Creek.

"Is it hard to find?" Brice asked.

Owen shook his head. "I can give you a specific mile marker on 141 and some other landmarks to guide you, but what will you do? If she's there, they won't hand her over because you came calling."

Brice played with his now empty coffee cup, tearing at a loose piece of the lid. "Not sure. I was hoping you'd know something. Perhaps have some other lead for me, or at least have some way of finding out if Mary is even there."

Owen pursed his lips. After a few seconds, he said, "Let me call you later. I'll reach out to those sources with these videos. It's a long shot that they'll help, but you never know."

"Great," Brice said, trying not to let himself get too hopeful.

Owen stood and returned the laptop to his backpack and retrieved his phone. He extended his other to shake. "It was nice to meet you."

"And you." Brice shook his hand. "You'll get back with me soon?"

"Today." Owen slipped his backpack over his shoulder.

"Thanks."

Owen nodded and left.

Brice tossed his coffee cup in the trash and debated what to do. He didn't want to mill about in his hotel while waiting on Owen to get back with him, and he didn't relish getting back out in this weather.

One more cup of coffee, then he'd find a local map to use when the time came to head to the Community.

Was he really going out there? In coming to Grand Junction, he'd hoped to find evidence to hand over to Investigator Wright or Agent Dawson. But based on what Owen had told him, the Community was thorough in protecting itself.

It didn't matter though. He would do whatever it took—one way or another—to locate Mary and the baby.

Chapter 29

Brice headed back to Coffee Outdoors after dinner that evening, this time in an Uber. Owen hadn't called until an hour ago, leaving Brice to pace his hotel room for most of the day, except for a brief period where he'd slept after returning to his room with a map. After waking to find no missed calls or messages from the reporter, his good mood had dissipated, and it had gotten worse as the hours of silence stretched on. He'd been in the middle of eating a burger and fries—takeout from a restaurant near the inn—when Owen called and asked if they could meet up that evening.

Despite the sub-freezing temperatures and darkness, people crowded around every table in Coffee Outdoors, while many others milled about. As Brice exited the Uber and limped toward the door, his left knee aching a little more in the cold, he searched for Owen, but he couldn't single him out in the crowd.

There was a buzz when Brice entered. Everyone seemed engaged in energetic conversations that reverberated off his skull. He found it difficult to take more than a step or two at a time, especially with the cane, before having to pause or pivot. The only thing that kept him from retreating outside was that the path had closed behind him.

A young man (nineteen or twenty) backed into him, chortling. The man glanced at Brice before returning to his conversation. Brice's head pounded and the room seemed to rock.

This was a bad idea. His chest tightened. He gulped for air, but each breath didn't seem enough. He needed to sit, but there were no open seats. And it was much too hot in here, as if the shop had set the thermostat to eighty.

A hand clamped on his arm and Brice bristled, jerking his arm away.

"Brice." It was Owen. Instead of business attire, he wore an active winter coat over a brown sweater, jeans, and tennis shoes.

"I've got a spot for us along the edge of the room." Owen turned and waved for Brice to follow him as he headed for a spot near the back of the shop.

It also meant they had to pass through the center of the room. Fortunately, Owen cut a wide path through that Brice followed. Within minutes they stood over a waist-high table against a wall. It lacked chairs, but being on the edge of the crowd, rather than in the middle, lessened Brice's unease a bit.

"I got you a decaf." Owen gestured to one of the two cups on the table, then he grabbed the other. "Not sure about you, but I prefer not to have caffeine this late at night."

"As cold as it is outside, I'll take anything," Brice answered, though as hot as it felt in here in the crowd, he might regret that in a moment.

"Yeah, I expect you're not used to temps like this back in Alabama."

"Not this cold, no. If it gets this cold, it's not for long."

For a moment they drank their coffee in silence as if they were two buddies hanging out for the evening. Owen casually scanned the crowd. When he turned back, his expression had sobered.

"Why didn't you tell me your girl was *from* the Community?"

Brice's stomach fluttered. "She is?"

Owen wrinkled his nose. "Don't lie to me. I'll walk out right now."

Brice set down his coffee, then held up his free hand in a hold-on gesture. "I thought she might be. After all, why would these men attack two random people in their homes? But I didn't know. She didn't talk about her past."

He paused, debating how much he wanted to reveal right now. His words thus far hadn't swayed Owen to his side. If he wanted the reporters continued help, he needed to be completely honest.

"Another thing I didn't tell you this morning, but you being a reporter, you may know now. That attack left me in a coma for ten days, which caused some amnesia. I don't actually remember Mary."

This gave Owen pause and seemed to lessen some of his anger. "You traveled halfway across the country in search of a woman you don't even remember?"

"And a baby," Brice added. "One that might be mine." He almost told Owen about his dreams of the baby, then stopped. It would sound crazy. He also felt protective of the dreams, as if by keeping them to himself, he kept the baby safe. A ridiculous notion, but he kept the secret.

"I can believe that," Owen said, but there was still a reserve to him. Something that let Brice know the reporter didn't trust him, though he wasn't sure why.

He needed to slow things down. Get everything on the table and then figure this out. "You said Mary is from the Community. What did you mean?"

Owen studied him for a few seconds, before nodding once. "Her real name is Beulah Clarke. She's twenty-eight. Grew up in the Community."

Brice pressed his lips together and ground his teeth. Grew up in the Community? Not a prisoner, but one of them. The knowledge brought him back to the question of whether she'd attacked him or allowed the men to do so; encouraged them even. He'd wanted to believe the men attacked them, not him.

The name, Beulah Clarke, didn't seem to fit the woman he'd seen on his camera footage. He'd already accepted that Mary wasn't her real name, but she'd become rooted in his mind as Mary. To confirm that wasn't her identity left him feeling like he chased an apparition.

"Her mother's name is Allison Clarke, who is rumored to be close to Arden Haywood, the leader of the Community. She's a genuine believer in Arden and ruthless with anyone who gets out of line."

Brice dropped his eyes to the table, unable to return Owen's gaze at this addition. It didn't paint an innocent picture of Mary. Now he understood why Owen had suspicions about him. How could he not when Brice had lived with her for going on a year? In fact, he wondered himself what his brain held locked away. What had he lost from his time with her that he might not be so proud of?

"The interesting thing is Beulah seems to have fallen out of favor some time ago in the Community," Owen said. "She has a few arrests for prostitution down in Florida."

Hot saliva filled Brice's mouth, which he swallowed. He drank his coffee in the hopes it might settle his stomach, but wished for something stronger.

Investigator Wright had found prostitutes back in Huntsville who were controlled by Elwin Pickering. The FBI suspected more widespread involvement from the Community in prostitution. But why would they use their own as prostitutes? Why would Mary's mother agree to her own daughter's abuse rather than exploit her connection to the Community's leader to protect her?

Brice wouldn't get those answers from Owen, but the questions also begged another. Women were forced into prostitution, either against their will or in desperation. Why would a woman forced into that life later help the place that caused it?

"There's one other detail I've been wondering about." Owen set down his cell phone between them and it took everything Brice had to remain there. He wanted to turn away. He didn't want to hear anymore. "One of my sources said Beulah recruited her."

Brice shook his head and kept on, as if unable to stop. No, he wanted to say. No!

"It's not a surprise," Owen said. "Women in those situations become dependent on the men in charge. They're often coerced into extreme harm. But I wonder, did Beulah ever try to recruit you?"

"What? No?" Brice felt himself swaying. He tightened his grip on his cane, using it to center himself. "I don't—"

"Remember?" Owen supplied.

"Know her past," Brice corrected. "Not now, but I don't believe I ever did."

Was that true though? Or just what he wanted to believe?

"*Right*," Owen replied. "All the last year gone; Beulah and anything tied to her. How convenient."

There it was, the accusation, just like with the FBI agents. Once more a flame ignited in Brice's head. The burning made him want to lash out, and the crowd noise didn't help. It crashed against him and made him want to fight, like a cornered animal desperate to survive.

"Come with me, I want you to meet someone." Owen grabbed his phone and turned toward the rear exit of the shop. "One of my sources."

The move was so far out of left field that Brice stared at him a moment. Meet one of his sources? Why?

But the chance to speak with someone from the Community—a survivor—propelled him forward. If one of Owen's sources knew

Mary, the person could answer some of his questions. Or if not, maybe the person knew how to find Mary.

He needed to know his relationship and standing with her. After all, his entire world revolved around her now, and he needed to know why.

And if it should.

Owen opened the back door and stood aside for Brice to go first. The door led out to a rear parking lot. Brice halted. Why was Owen's source waiting out here? Why hadn't Owen invited the person inside?

A hand gripped his shoulder hard and shoved him through the door. He stumbled. The moment he was outside, bright lights clicked on, shining in his face, blinding him. He froze, blinking. He sensed others, but saw only vague outlines behind the lights.

"Brice Dunn, you know Beulah Clarke under the identity Mary Smith," a voice stated. It was feminine and strong, a voice that Brice associated with lawyers.

He tried to retreat into the coffee shop, but Owen's hand between his shoulder blades halted him. Owen closed the door then slipped off to the side, leaving Brice alone. He tried to shade his eyes, but it didn't help.

"For the last year, you lived with Beulah Clarke at your home, in a physical relationship." The statement was cold, accusatory.

"Beulah Clarke is a member of the Community, a cult with ties to human and sex trafficking." Someone new said this, off to his right. "Do you deny it?"

"I. No." Brice realized too late that he'd answered wrong. "I mean—"

"What's your connection to the Community? How long have you been involved?" These questions came from the left.

His heart hammered in his chest. He gasped, finding it hard to breathe. "I'm not. I've never."

"You lived with Beulah Clarke for a year. Do you expect us to believe she never discussed the Community with you?" It was the woman again, her tone incredulous, as if he were weaving some elaborate lie.

His chest hurt and he backed into the rear door of the coffee shop. He turned, tripping over his cane. He banged into the door and grabbed the handle. The door was locked. His hands shook.

"Brice Dunn, do you deny involvement with Elwin Pickering, a known human trafficker?"

Involvement? What did they mean involvement?

"How do you explain the pictures of you with Mary and Elwin recently found during a police raid of Elwin's home in Alabama?

Pictures? What pictures? His chest throbbed. Was it about to burst open? Wright hadn't mentioned pictures of him.

"Brice Dunn, brother of Jaxon Dunn, an FBI agent, have you requested your brother's help in covering up for the Community? Is this why no authorities have acted to end the cult?"

Brice banged against the coffee shop door. Who were these people? Why had Owen brought him out here for this? And if he didn't give them the answers they wanted, what then?

"A cult with ties to human trafficking—to the slave trade— operating within the U.S. with corrupt federal government knowledge. Brice Dunn, do you deny this? Do you deny your involvement with the Community? Do you deny your brother's and the FBI's knowledge of the Community and their failure to stop it?"

"This is crazy," Brice gasped. He stumbled along the rear of the coffee shop. He had to get away from them. Had to run.

"What is your relationship with Arden Haywood, leader of the Community?"

"Were you involved in human trafficking with Beulah Clarke?"

His breath came out in wheezes, as he fought to maintain his balance. He feared they would start attacking him, angered by what they believed he'd done. How had this happened? Why did they think he had all these ties to the Community? Or that he would ever ask his brother to cover up something this monstrous?

The angry questions continued until he rounded the corner of the coffee shop. None of them followed him, content to humiliate him until he fled.

He didn't know where to go. What had Owen and those others wanted from him? A confession? Why?

Looking over his shoulder, he spotted a figure leaning out from behind the coffee shop, video camera in hand aimed at him. They'd taped the whole thing. He limped down the street to get as far away as he could on foot.

Chapter 30
(Eleven Years Past)

Beulah and Fernanda sat on a low wall behind an old mall, smoking and waiting for customers to finish their dinners, have a few drinks, and get lonely. Beulah hadn't eaten since lunch, but the cigarette dulled her appetite. Kendall might have something for her at the end of the night, if she earned enough.

The setting sun, touching the horizon, cast both girls' shadows a long way down the sidewalk. Customers would be along soon, and that sent her anxiety spiking.

"Fernanda, you got any pills?" she asked, holding her hand out.

The nineteen-year-old immigrant from Tlaxcala, Mexico always had something on her. Fernanda was the preferred girl for Kendall's dealers, and they tipped her a little extra out of their supplies.

Fernanda reached down her shirt, removed a small Altoids tin from between her breasts, and handed it over, before taking another drag from her cigarette. Beulah opened the tin, sifting through the various pills for an Oxy, which she popped in her mouth and swallowed. She handed the rest back to Fernanda, who deposited them back down her shirt.

Beulah wondered how Fernanda kept the tin there, since she didn't wear a bra to work. Neither of them did. Customers didn't like them. And Fernanda didn't have bigger than c-cups, but Beulah never asked. All she cared was that Fernanda had them. Something to dull her emotions and make the evenings bearable.

"Is that an undercover?" Fernanda asked, pointing out a maroon Charger idling down the road.

Rather than look, Beulah swung her legs over the back wall and dropped to a crouch. It was best to hide before the cop spotted them, if it was an undercover.

But Fernanda remained atop the wall, now cackling. "Girl, you should see yo face." Fernanda gave her a mock gasp, hand to her chest, then resumed laughing.

Beulah rose to her feet, hands on the walls, searching for the car. It was already turning left at an intersection. "It's not funny. Last time I got arrested they kept me locked up all day. When they finally let me go, I barely had time to change clothes before my shift."

Fernanda only laughed harder at this. Despite herself, Beulah grinned as well. It was the only time of their day they felt free, alone out here behind the mall, or a strip club, before the customers rolled in. Beulah could almost pretend they were two girlfriends hanging out.

Almost.

The first dick pulled around behind the mall in an old blue convertible, top down. Reality set in. The unbuttoned Hawaiian shirt he wore over a wife-beater hung loose on him. His hooked nose was sharp and his longish hair inefficiently covered a receding hairline.

Beulah eyed Fernanda to see which one of them was taking the first customer. Fernanda took one more drag from her cigarette and tossed it behind the wall. She hopped to the ground, stepping forward to the curb. Beulah exhaled, relieved to have a little more time for the Oxy to kick in, though she hated it came at Fernanda's expense.

All too often, things came at Fernanda's expense. Of the girls in Kendall's care, Fernanda was the only illegal, which had surprised Beulah when she arrived. If asked before that, she would've assumed the opposite, that a majority of the girls in their situation were foreigners.

Whenever something came up the other girls didn't want to do, they'd demand Fernanda take their place. If she refused, they'd threaten to report her to Immigration, so she'd get deported.

At first Beulah had defended Fernanda, insisting the other girls handle their business themselves. She had stopped when she realized it only led the girls to mistreat Fernanda even worse sometime later.

Kendall wasn't any better. He threatened Fernanda with deportation whenever he felt she hadn't earned enough, despite her always earning more than anyone else.

The convertible stopped in front of Fernanda and she rested her arms on the door, making sure he got a good look at the twins.

"Looking for a drinking companion?" she asked, voice almost a purr. Beulah believed Fernanda's ability to control her voice was what earned her the most money. That and her exotic look.

The man grinned, ogling her breasts a moment, then his eyes flicked to Beulah. "I was hoping for a double shot."

Beulah's stomach plummeted. It wasn't unusual for a customer to request two girls, but it was rare that one could afford both. If a man did have the money, he always insisted that the girls work on each other first, to get him hot. She had avoided such encounters with Fernanda, and she didn't want to start now. Their friendship, small as it was, was the one good thing she had in her life. It wouldn't survive if they had to probe each other in such a crude manner and in such company. She'd never be able to sit here again and pretend they were just girlfriends chilling.

Fernanda quoted the price for two girls, and the man blinked. She then slid over to block his view and promised he would have the time of his life with her. Beulah didn't hear his response, but a second later, Fernanda opened the passenger door and climbed in. They drove off.

Beulah tossed her butt and lit up a fresh cigarette. She had a momentary reprieve.

It was Kendall in his old gray minivan who appeared next. Their man wore a shabby black suit that was one size too small, a fact accentuated by his severe beer gut. He grinned at her as if he had a winning scratch ticket.

He pulled up to the curb in front of her. "Get in."

"Why?" she asked, though she did as ordered. It was strange for him to pull her off the street, because that was money out of his pocket.

"I've got someone I want you to talk to." He pulled out of the parking lot onto Palm Drive and headed west.

"Special customer?" she asked. That would explain things.

He winked at her, giving her that winning grin again.

She wished she had volunteered to go in Fernanda's place. Or had grabbed a second Oxy. Kendall's special customers always had an arrangement with him. Usually because they possessed something he wanted, and the girls paid for him to get it. Pretty much anything the special customer desired was on the table, *and* they got extra time.

The van stereo played a CD with children's songs on it. Kendall had put the CD on while driving his two sons around, and it had gotten stuck in the player. Then the antenna had broken off, so no radio. It was the kids' CD or nothing, and Kendall preferred the former. Some of the girls speculated that it hinted at his personal tastes, which made Beulah's skin crawl.

They drove past a homeless shelter with a line of people sitting on the sidewalk out front. Beulah had stayed there for a single night not long after the Community had sent her here; her second attempt at running away. She'd slept on the floor in a corner because all the beds or cots were taken, but at least no one had demanded anything of her.

The next day Kendall had shown up, dragged her out of the place, and given her a beating that had left her bruised enough everywhere but her face so that all she could do to earn for him was to give blowjobs for the next three days. After that, she'd given up on running.

Kendall pulled off underneath an overpass. Homeless people lived down here beneath a giant cross graffitied on one of the overpass support beams. For a half second Beulah panicked, thinking Kendall was getting rid of her. But that made no sense. She wasn't the top earner for him, but she wasn't the worst either. She earned her keep.

Pointing out the windshield, Kendall said, "See that blonde over there?"

A girl or a woman—Beulah wasn't sure from here—sat on her own beside an old dumpster. She wore a plain gray long-sleeved shirt and green sweats, with her hair tied in a haphazard ponytail. She thumbed through a tattered old book.

"That's your special customer?" Beulah asked, puzzled. "What could she have to pay with?"

Kendall shook his head, eyes gleaming. "I don't want you to do anything with her. I want you to invite her to come stay with us."

Her face burned as she realized what he was asking. She focused her attention back on the girl. What had forced her out here on the street? Whatever her story, it couldn't be worse than what awaited her if she came back with Kendall.

"What if she doesn't want to come?" Beulah asked.

He cupped her chin and turned her to face him, his eyes now serious. His grip tightened until her jaw ached. "Convince her," he said through gritted teeth.

When he let her go, she opened the door and slid out of the minivan. The moment she'd closed the door, he backed away, turned the van around, and drove off. She was on her own to get the girl back to the house. And she was pretty sure what would happen to her if she failed.

For the next twenty minutes she loitered around the area, eyeing everyone, but none of them gave her more than a cursory glance, too consumed with their own troubles.

From a distance, Beulah studied the girl and her book. The girl looked a few years older than her. Beulah tried to spy the title of the book, but the angle was wrong.

Idling toward the girl, she took it slow. When she was within a few feet of the girl, she said, "What'cha reading?"

The girl's eyes rose to her for a second, her body tensing with alarm, then returned to her book. Beulah waited a few seconds to see if the girl would answer, but she said nothing.

"I used to read," Beulah ventured. "Back when I had access to books. My favorite was Slaughterhouse Five." That was a lie, but one of her customers had told her about it once on their ride to and from the hotel, talking to her like they were old friends. She'd guessed he was lonely.

Beulah sat down, leaning against the dumpster, leaving a few feet between them.

"A Wrinkle in Time," the girl said.

"What?"

"The book I'm reading. It's called A Wrinkle in Time," the girl answered without looking up from the pages. "It's about a girl who goes in search of her missing father."

"Does she find him?" Beulah asked. There was a time when she used to wonder about her father. Dreamed of him coming to take her away from the Community and her mother. She'd never considered going to look for him, not that her mother had ever told her his identity, or anything about him.

When she'd been very young, she'd imagined at different points that each of the men in the Community was her father. That was before she'd grown old enough to realize she didn't want any of them to be him. After that she'd lost all interest in who he was. What did it matter? He was never coming for her.

"Yes," the girl whispered. She hadn't learned not to care.

"Guess stuff like that can happen in books, since they're not real."

Again, the girl didn't respond. She seemed to shrink in on herself.

"Look, I'm sorry," Beulah said, realizing her misstep. "I guess I gave up on mine a long time ago."

The girl wiped tears from her eyes.

Wanting to change the subject, Beulah asked, "Do you have any food?" She didn't want any at the moment, not with the Oxy still in full effect, but it seemed like something one might ask in this situation.

"No," the girl replied.

Beulah hesitated, knowing she needed to invite the girl back. Food was probably the simplest solution to get the girl to come, but Beulah didn't want to do it. The girl would never thank her for it. But if she returned alone… she pictured Kendall's balled fists. With those he thrashed any girl who displeased him.

"I know a place where we can get something to eat," Beulah forced herself to say, hating herself even as the words spilled from her lips.

Now the girl looked up. There was hunger in her eyes, but also wariness. "Where? The shelter?"

Yes, Beulah wanted to say. The shelter. That's where the girl should go. "No. I've got a place. I live with a few other girls. We look after each other."

Tears filled the girl's eyes. She clearly wanted to come, but there was also hesitation. She at least knew enough to be wary of things that sounded too good to be true.

Listen to those instincts, Beulah wanted to tell her. Don't come with me. Run. Run far away. Instead, she said, "We don't have much. The place is small, but you seem like someone who would fit in."

"Why—?" The girl paused, eyes dropping once more to her book. She squeezed it in both hands. "Why would you want to help me?"

"Because it's in my best interest," Beulah replied. "The more girls we have helping each other out, the better we all do."

Walk away. Get up and walk away, Beulah cried to herself. Don't do this. Please. She doesn't deserve this.

Kendall would fuck her up if she didn't. She'd end up spending the next week in his bed when not working. She shuddered, knowing what that would be like. He didn't like no plain Jane.

"Are you sure?" the girl asked. "What if your friends don't like me?"

Beulah forced herself to smile even as she wished she could climb up onto the overpass and throw herself off. Let Kendall come find her then.

"Don't be ridiculous," Beulah said. "They'll love you."

She wanted to cry, to sob. Instead, she climbed to her feet, motioning for the girl to follow. "Trust me."

When the other girl rose, a cautious smile on her lips, Beulah longed to take all the pills in Fernanda's tin.

Then she led the girl toward the house.

Chapter 31

Brice caught a public transit bus. For the next ten minutes, he sat at the back of the bus, taking deep breaths to calm himself. He'd gotten away. No one had followed him onboard. Only a few passengers rode the bus, and they all looked tired and disinterested.

But what if Owen's people had followed him? They might've let him think he'd lost them. No one had hopped on the bus behind him, but they could have someone following in a car. They believed he had ties to the Community and might suspect he would lead them to more proof.

The picture they claimed Investigator Wright had found with him and Elwin, was it real?

Pain flared up in his chest again. He found it hard to breathe. His mind cycled through the horrors of Owen's people shouting at him, as well as the possibilities of another encounter with them.

Why did everyone seem ready to blame him? He was the victim.

He needed to get off the bus. It had already passed the street leading to his inn, but he didn't want to jump off at a random destination. He didn't want to be alone on foot if they were following.

If he found another bus with a stop close enough to this one, he could hop from one to another and lose any followers. Maybe do it a few times to be safe.

He looked around the interior of the bus and spotted a sign with a GVT logo and letters underneath it that he couldn't read. Rising to his feet, he stumbled a quarter of the way up the bus to the sign. It was difficult to use his cane in the tight space between seats, so he grasped the straps hanging from the overhead bars with his free hand to help.

An old lady several seats up eyed him, face stiff and wary. He gave her a smile, but she turned her head as if afraid smiling back might seem like an invitation for conversation. Just as well. He didn't want to talk any more than she did.

The words under the logo were Grand Valley Transit. He surveyed the rest of the bus, looking for a map with routes, but spotted nothing.

He returned to his seat and fished his phone from his pocket and ran a search for the bus line. After a ten-second load, the Grand Valley Transit site showed at the top of the search list. He clicked the link and after a couple of seconds of searching, found the various bus route schedules.

A map showed each of the eleven routes offered by GVT. He rode the bus for route one. Four different routes intersected with it—routes two, three, five, and nine. And route four (or was that seven? The color designations were similar) was only a short walk from an upcoming stop.

Since route two intersected this route first, he expanded the map to find out where they crossed paths, which turned out to be North Twelfth Street and Patterson Road. To his dismay, the route stopped running at 8:35 pm. It was now more than an hour past.

He tried route three and discovered it had stopped running at 8:05 pm. Route five and nine were the same. He started clicking the links for all the routes and they all ended at either 8:05 pm or 8:35 pm, all except route one, which ran until 12:05 am.

Had Owen set their meeting time for nine because he knew all the other buses had stopped running? Except Owen hadn't known his means of travel. For all Owen knew, he had a rental car. No, he was just unlucky.

At least this one would carry him all the way to the downtown transfer station if he wanted. Yes. That's what he'd do. There'd be enough going on, even at that hour, that he could slip away unseen.

He set his phone in his lap and leaned back, taking a deep breath. While he might've gotten away from Owen and the rest, their questions troubled him. What had Mary told him? What had he known about her past, or the Community, before the attack?

She hadn't recruited him. He didn't believe it. Only a person with a very corrupt soul could assist with the slavery and forced prostitution of others. The prospect horrified him. That sort of corruption couldn't be wiped away by the loss of memories, he felt sure.

But he'd also lived with her for a year or close to it. How much had she revealed to him during that time? Had she kept him in the dark? Lied to him?

At his core, all he wanted was to find Mary and the baby. To ensure their safety and fix things between them, if possible. Yet each plausible answer he thought of for what had happened between them meant something different for their future. He brooded over the possibilities until the bus pulled into the downtown transfer station.

It didn't provide the cover Brice had hoped it would. The area was a roundabout with a series of eight covered benches in the middle and bus parking spots in front of each. No other buses were in the station, nor were there passengers waiting for a ride. He was the only one left onboard.

The driver, an elderly gentleman with white hair and beard, pulled into a spot, parked, and rose to his feet. He glanced at Brice, but when Brice made no move to rise, the driver pointed toward the brick building next door.

"I'm headed for a restroom break," he said. "I'll be back in fifteen minutes."

Brice nodded. The driver departed. As soon as he was out of sight, Brice clambered to his feet, legs and hips a little stiff from sitting, and moved to a window to look for anyone who might have followed him. There were a couple of vehicles out on the road, but they soon passed on out of sight. There were no parked cars anywhere nearby.

He moved over to the opposite side of the bus, but couldn't spot anyone in a car or walking. If he got off the bus here, he could slip away undetected, but he didn't want to wander alone in downtown Grand Junction at night. Nor could he walk all the way back to his hotel; the temperature outside was twenty-four degrees. Instead, he settled himself back into his original seat to wait on the driver.

Why had Owen invited him out to the coffee shop to grill him over his supposed connections to the Community? And in such a hostile manner. Had his group hoped to scare him enough to get him to crack and reveal something they could use against the Community? They'd scared him certainly, but he had nothing to offer. And the speed with which they'd hurled questions and accusations at him had given him no time to answer. What had been their end game? He didn't understand. They hadn't followed him, so they must've gotten whatever they'd wanted. What had that been?

He puzzled over it for a few minutes before giving up. He failed to come up with a rational answer, if there was one. Did Owen and his friends hate the Community so much, and him by extension since they believed him connected, that the whole attack was a cathartic moment for them?

Whatever the answer, he was on his own once more, no closer to locating the Community, let alone Mary and the baby.

"Where are you headed?" The bus driver had returned, coffee in hand.

Brice hesitated, not wanting to reveal where he was going, but refusing to answer would draw further scrutiny. It was unlikely that the man had any connections to Owen and his people.

"Mesa Inn."

The driver nodded. "Up by the Country Club. You'll want to get off at stop twenty-one. Horizon Drive north of G Road."

"Okay. Thanks."

"It'll take some time to get up there, we've several stops along the way, but this time of night we're unlikely to have more than a few passengers, so it shouldn't be too bad."

"Don't rush on my account," Brice said.

The driver smiled and took a sip of his coffee, before taking his seat at the helm. A couple of minutes later, they pulled out of the transfer station and onto South Avenue, and headed west a block, before turning north onto 5th Street.

Exhausted, Brice longed for something to take his mind off Owen and his people. Mary and the baby, too. He needed a reprieve.

He pulled his mother's journal out of his hip pocket, unsure why he'd brought it with him, except that as he'd been leaving the hotel earlier, he couldn't stand to leave it behind. Since leaving home, he'd had it on himself at all times.

He thumbed through the journal to an entry a month before her death.

For years I've worried about Brice one day meeting the right girl. I've fretted over it even more of late knowing my time is almost up and I won't be here to look after him. Then I surprised him at work for lunch today and find out he's already met the perfect girl, he just doesn't know it yet.

She's one of his customers. Dora. Beautiful girl.

Brice read the entry twice, completely taken aback. Dora? He had never thought, never considered. Maybe considered in his wildest fantasies, but she had always been out of his league. He'd known that. And she'd shown no hint of interest. Had she? His mother must've been mistaken. The hopeful musings of a mother knowing she hadn't much time left.

Tears welled up in his eyes as he remembered that final month. This entry had been no more than a week before her admittance to the hospital for good. He'd been in such denial then, sure a miracle was forthcoming. Faced with it all, he'd still believed things would take a turn for the better and she'd recover. That day had never come.

Nor had any days with Dora.

He wondered what his mother would've written about Mary if she'd had the chance to meet her. She wouldn't have loved that they lived together unwed, especially with Mary pregnant.

If his mother were still alive, would any of his life with Mary have happened? If she'd lived, would he still be at home, oblivious to any this? Or was it possible she'd be here with him? The two of them in danger.

A flare of guilt made his stomach clench, before logic pushed it away. His mother had died. He couldn't have endangered her because she was gone. Only Mary and the baby weren't gone for good, although at the moment it felt like it. Like the crying baby in his dreams back in the hospital, Mary and the baby were out there, but no matter where he searched, they remained out of sight. And reach.

"You can do this. You'll find them," he mumbled, trying to psych himself up. But he couldn't silence the nagging doubt. He'd tried and failed to protect them once. Even if he found them, what would make this time any different? What could he do to free them from the Community?

And if he somehow succeeded, where would they go? Where could he keep them safe?

Chapter 32

Brice groaned as he awoke, his head pounding and his mouth as parched as a long-dry lakebed. He glanced at the clock. Almost ten a.m.

A few more hours of sleep, then he'd get up.

It had been close to eleven when the bus dropped him off at a stop a block from the inn. Despite not seeing any of Owen's people since fleeing Outdoors Coffee, Brice had still panicked at getting off the bus. He'd watched every car on the road as he'd walked. Instead of hurrying to the inn, he'd proceeded past it to a side road, followed it around, and come back at the inn from behind.

Once inside, he'd taken precautions to ensure no one saw him enter his room. On his first pass by his room, an older woman with a red suitcase had been walking behind him. He'd continued to a restroom and hidden inside for ten minutes, before returning to his room. Even then he'd lain awake in bed, agonizing over what Owen's people had wanted with their verbal assault, or how to locate the Community and what to do if he found it. The sun had leaked in under the curtains before exhaustion overtook his racing mind.

It was back now.

Pushing back the covers, he sat up, his left leg stiff and sore. He had to do his exercises this morning.

After he got out of the bathroom.

As he relieved himself, he debated what his next steps should be. While Owen had given him a general idea of the Community's location, he was in no shape to head out there. Nor was this the time of year to wander around the mountainous countryside hoping to stumble across the place.

Owen hadn't given him anything else with which to locate Mary, or to hand over to Investigator Wright or the FBI agents to further their investigations. He wanted to talk to Jaxon, ask his advice, but his brother would only seek to stop him. Even calling Jaxon would give away his location.

Brice put a Keurig pod in the coffee maker, needing the caffeine. Was there any way to convince his brother to help? They were close, and their mother had always told them that family came first before anything else. But Jaxon would believe he was doing what was best for his younger brother by giving him nothing. By insisting he let the FBI do their jobs. Yet Brice knew he couldn't sit back, wait, and hope. He had to do something.

For Mary.

For the baby.

For himself.

While the coffee streamed down into his mug, he picked up the map off the table. State Highway 141 started south of Grand Junction where it branched off from State Highway 50, running southwest above the Dominguez-Escalante National Conservation area until it crossed the Dolores River around an area called Gateway. From there it rotated to the southeast. He'd circled the area where North Fork West Creek intersected with Highway 141, remembering Owen mentioning that landmark. Still, he needed to narrow it further. It would be great if he could type "The Community" into Google Maps and get directions.

Frustrated, he logged into his email account, planning to at least send Jaxon a message to reassure his brother that he was all right without giving himself away. More than a hundred unread emails filled his inbox, a majority of the top ones all from Jaxon with demanding subject lines.

What are you doing?!

Call Me!

Where are you?!

The top email made him freeze up.

Who were those guys??? Call me immediately! This is an emergency! Please!

What guys? Had something happened back home?

He opened the email.

What are you doing in Grand Junction? Who were those guys interrogating you? You need to call me as soon as you get this. Please. You've no idea the trouble you're in. This is everywhere.

I'll be on a plane there by nine. I'll arrive in Grand Junction mid-afternoon. Let me know where you are. I have to bring you in before something worse happens.

Jaxon

How had his brother known he was in Grand Junction? And the question about people interrogating him. He must know about Owen and his people, but how had his brother heard about them?

Owen was a reporter. He must've put something out on the news. Had they filmed the whole thing? If they had, why had that alarmed Jaxon so much? They were only accusations. He had done nothing wrong.

Amidst several other urgent emails from Jaxon was one from Nate. Brice pulled it up.

Brice,

Please, if you read this, call me. Call your brother. Call Lisa. Let someone know where you are and that you're safe.

I don't know who those people are that made those allegations against you online. I know they're wrong, but it has us fearing for your well-being. Please, don't get yourself hurt.

Your brother can help you. We can help you. Please call.

Nate

Nate's phone number, Lisa's, and the shop's were all listed at the end, as if Brice didn't know them already. He closed his email, his stomach churning.

What had Owen posted about him?

He dropped the phone on the bed, hands shaking. He needed to know, but he also couldn't bear to look. Instead, he grabbed his mug and sipped his coffee. He cradled the mug in both hands, trying to settle his heart despite the injection of caffeine.

Half the mug was gone before he built up the courage to set his coffee aside and retrieve his phone. Then he logged into his Facebook profile. The first thing that popped up was a post from someone named Put These Scumbags Away on his profile. The post was a video that he recognized from the night before standing out back behind the coffee shop.

Lowering the volume on his phone, he activated the video. The fear and horror from last night burst through him, as if through a breaking dam, as he watched the accusations hurled at him onscreen. The lights that had blinded him clearly illuminated him in the video so that anyone watching it could identify him. Suspect number one in a police lineup.

Huddled against the back door of the coffee shop, he looked close to crumbling under the barrage of allegations. His hands fumbled for the door handle. The video ended with him stumbling down the alley.

Brice's legs weakened. He slumped to the floor at the foot of the bed. This was on his page where everyone could see it. He wasn't very active on social media, but he sometimes shared mechanic-related stuff. Over the years he'd connected with many of his customers, other mechanics around town, and some acquaintances from school.

A block of text followed the video, which he read.

Brice Dunn, the man shown in the video, spent the past year living with Beulah Clarke, a known member of the Community. He also associated with other members of the cult (picture below). After disappearing under suspicious circumstances from the couple's residence in Alabama, Brice has turned up in the Community's backyard.

The cult runs human and sex trafficking rings across many states in our country, yet authorities have done nothing to stop it. Law enforcement has made no arrests of any significance. The Community continues to operate unimpeded from their compound near Glade Park, southwest of the Colorado National Monument.

Why, you ask?

Further research revealed that Brice Dunn has a brother, Jaxon Dunn, who is an FBI agent in Chicago, Illinois. While our group has no direct evidence that Jaxon Dunn is in any way involved with the Community, it is our members' opinions that this direct link between the cult and the FBI, through Brice Dunn and Beulah Clarke, explains the lack of action against these known human traffickers.

We urge any right-thinking American, disgusted by these atrocities against women and children, to stand up with us and demand answers. Demand that the Community members be tried for their crimes. And if corrupt government personnel are aiding in these despicable crimes, demand they be held accountable.

For those connected to Brice Dunn, is this someone you want as a friend and neighbor? A sexual pervert who preys on the defenseless. We wouldn't want him living next to us!

The end of the post showed a picture of Brice sitting with Mary and Elwin Pickering around a wooden table at a restaurant, each with a beer in hand.

Brice dropped the phone and crawled on hands and knees toward the trashcan. He threw up in it, heaving until he'd emptied his guts. He rolled onto his back, tears running down the sides of his face.

Jaxon had read this. Nate, too. He guessed Lisa and Warren as well. Had Dora? How many others? How many would believe it?

Anymore, it seemed all too many people believed any accusations against anyone. And why wouldn't they? That picture of him with Mary and Elwin was damning. He *had* known the man.

His whole body shook. He could never go home again. His neighbors had shunned him for what they believed he'd done to Mary. What would they do now? No matter what happened, how many would ever believe he was innocent?

And Jaxon. What would happen to him? Would this ruin his career? Brice wasn't sure how he could ever face his older brother again if that happened. All he'd been trying to do was find Mary and the baby to ensure their safety. Help them if possible. How had it ended up like this?

A rage ignited inside him. This was Owen's fault. And those with him. They had slandered him. Libeled him? They had attempted to destroy his life because they believed he was part of the Community.

He hurled the trashcan at the lamp on the table, knocking it to the floor. The lampshade bounced away while the trashcan thumped against the window, leaving it and part of the wall covered with his puke.

Owen had to pay. The man's friends had to pay. Brice lurched to his feet, grabbed the coffee maker, and threw it against a wall. It broke with a crunch. Yells of shock came from adjoining rooms, but they did nothing to calm him. He swept the spare mug and coffee holder off the table, enjoying the sound as the coffee mug shattered against the bathroom door.

He took a step toward the TV, but slipped on the mess on the floor and went down hard. Pain flared through his entire left side, and his vision blurred. He lay there panting, a wetness on his cheek and neck that his nostrils identified as his own bile. He rolled away from it, trying not to get sick again.

The fall and pain had ripped away his anger, leaving only desperation. Jaxon was right. He needed his brother's help. He was in over his head.

His phone lay halfway under his bed, and he grabbed it. He entered his brother's number and called. The phone went to voicemail. His brother was in flight.

Brice felt a little relief at his inability to reach Jaxon right now. He didn't want to hear Jaxon's concern which, though well-meaning, would underscore his screwups. After that, Jaxon would tell him, with complete calm and authority, how they would fix his mess. His failures. His incompetence.

Brice closed the phone app and the Facebook post popped back up on screen. His anger grew again as he read until he reached one line in the post.

... continues to operate... Glade Park.

These people knew the Community's location.

He clicked on the name of the group, which brought up their profile. Cycling through the feed, he found other outraged posts concerning the Community. Posts leveling accusations against an Arden Haywood, the cult's leader. The group had posted and re-posted all of Owen's articles from the Sentinel.

Eventually he found what he wanted—a map with the Community's location marked on it. Along with the map, the group demanded that others help them cast this cult out. Root out the evil from next door.

That was where he needed to go. A spot southwest of Glade Park near a Piñon Mesa. There was a nearby river, the North Fork West Creek.

There were also pictures of the Community. Old fashioned homes built inside a wall of aluminum fencing crowned with chicken wire. The size of it surprised him.

A knock at his door jolted Brice.

Chapter 33

"Mr. Dunn?"

Brice crawled to where his cane had fallen between the bed and end table, then used it and the mattress to climb to his feet, remaining as quiet as possible. Pain flared through his left leg, and he stifled a cry. Had Owen's people found him?

Another knock. "Mr. Dunn, this is Bill Jenkins, the day manager. Are you okay, Mr. Dunn?"

Brice debated pretending to not be here, but everyone on the floor had heard him breaking stuff moments before.

"Mr. Dunn, I have hotel security with me. There are concerns about your well-being. If you don't answer, we'll have to come in."

With vomit covering the floor, Brice decided he didn't want anyone coming in at the moment if he could avoid it.

"I'll be right there."

He first made his way to the bathroom, gritting his teeth against the pain. Grabbing a hand towel from a rack, he wiped away the vomit from his neck and cheek, then dabbed at what was on his shirt to clean it as much as possible.

"Mr. Dunn?"

Tossing the towel into the tub, he went to the door and opened it partway, blocking the view. "Sorry, I'm here."

Two men stood in the hallway, one in a black suit with a red and silver tie. His name tag had Manager on it. Right behind him was a large man who resembled a club bouncer. He could probably crush the walkie talkie in his hand.

The manager opened his mouth to speak when his eyes widened. "Are... are you, okay?"

Brice could tell the manager recognized him. Had to be from the posts Owen's people shared on him. He hadn't anticipated how widespread it would be. Would everyone in Grand Junction recognize him now?

He feigned ignorance.

"I'm fine. I fell." He reached down and patted his left leg. "I'm still recovering from a knee injury and lost my balance. Knocked over the coffee pot. Then when I was trying to get back to my feet, I knocked the lamp off the table, too. I'm sorry."

"Oh." The manager eyed the knee and Brice's cane. The man looked ready to bolt. "Are you okay? Do you need an ambulance?" he asked, his discomfort warring with his training.

"No, I just need to rest," Brice replied. "I was going to lie back down, but I'll pay for the lamp and coffee pot. Let me know how much."

"Yes, well, let me send someone to clean it up for you." The manager took a step to the left, making room for the security guy, who remained disinterested. He clearly didn't recognize or consider Brice a threat.

"Thank you. I'd appreciate it," Brice agreed, knowing they were both trying to get this conversation over. The manager would promptly go contact the authorities, so it was time for him to leave.

"I'll handle it right away." The manager headed down the hall.

Brice closed the door. He grabbed his coat, knitted hat, and gloves from the chair, slipping them on before grabbing his phone, charger, his mother's journal, and the map, which he tucked into pockets in his pants and coat. The rest of his luggage he'd have to leave.

He opened the door and peeked outside. There was no one in the hallway, so he eased the door shut and headed to the rear exit he'd found last night.

The parking lot was empty as he made his way through the cars out to the street, then headed west. It wasn't a busy street, but there was a good flow of cars. The cold temperatures, which made him hunch in on himself, meant the sidewalks were largely deserted. He kept his eyes down as he walked, hoping no one driving by noticed him.

It was only once he'd gotten a couple of blocks away that he slipped into an enclosed bus stop. He sat on the bench and unfolded his map. He then fished out his cell phone, which still had the

Facebook post pulled up with the Community compound marked on a map.

He found the corresponding spot on his map, then he realized he didn't have a pen or anything to mark it. Nor was he sure knowing its location on the map would help him when he got to the area on Highway 141. He needed a better way to narrow his search.

He pulled up a new web browser on his phone and searched for Google Earth, wishing he had a laptop instead of a smartphone screen. A globe and search bar appeared onscreen. He typed in Grand Junction, Colorado in the search bar and the image of the globe zoomed in until it focused on a satellite view of western Colorado with an outline of the city in the middle. He scrolled right, but had to zoom in a fair amount to locate Highway 141. From there he followed the highway until he came upon North Fork West Creek. The river snaked up between mountains or foothills, he wasn't sure which.

There were no signs of human habitation along the river. He returned to 141 and branched out, looking at the surrounding areas.

A bus pulled up to the stop and he boarded, not caring where it headed, as long as it carried him farther from the inn. He paid the fare, keeping his head bowed, then made his way to the back of the bus. A handful of people were onboard, but none appeared the least bit interested in him. He sighed in relief as it pulled away from the stop.

It took an hour of searching, the last thirty minutes on a bench at the downtown transfer station, but he located the compound in a gorge west of the river.

The compound held more than thirty buildings inside a fenced enclosure. There appeared to be a front entrance on the south side and a second entrance on the east. A dirt road led down from the compound to Highway 141. Brice took a screen capture of 141, hoping to match the image with the scenery when he got there.

Was he really going to go to the Community? What was he going to do when he got there? The answers were yes, and he'd figure something out when he got there. He didn't know what else to do.

But first, he was going to follow through on sending his brother an email. He owed him at least that much before whatever lay ahead.

When he pulled his email back up, he spotted two new ones. The first was from an unknown person with a subject line about his court date. He ignored it.

The second was from Dora. He opened hers and read.

He wondered what texts she was talking about, but it didn't matter right now. He closed her email and pulled up the one about his court date. That was coming up soon, wasn't it?

The formal email reminded him he was due in court on February 21st, in a few weeks. Would he be back home by then? Would he ever go back? He didn't know what would happen if he missed court, but the possibility made his gut bubble.

It was ridiculous to worry about a court date with everything going on, but he couldn't help it. He didn't relish being on the wrong side of the law even for the smallest infraction. That was confirmation that the Community hadn't recruited him, right? No matter what Owen, his people, or anyone else thought.

Would they believe that when he was making plans to head straight to the Community compound?

He guessed they'd view his efforts as confirmation of his guilt or at least complicity, but that didn't bother him. Whatever they wanted to do to him was okay as long as he got to Mary and the baby first and helped them get safely away.

Chapter 34
(Fifteen Years Past)

Allison approached the altar where her daughter lay naked and unconscious, her golden dress poking out from beneath her. The others filed out of the room.

Wine warmed her belly and made her giddy. She wanted to hug her daughter and tell her how great she had done. How proud she was that Beulah had taken her place among the women of the Community.

Her satisfaction was muted when Arden pulled back on his red robe and, leaning against a corner of the altar, slipped his feet back into black shoes. She enjoyed seeing him naked—his powerful muscles and the rugged beard sticking out beneath his golden mask.

From her dress she removed a syringe, which she lay beside the wine mugs on the stand beside the altar. It was time for the last step to complete the ceremony. The final surrender to the Community, although few knew about it.

Allison grabbed her daughter's shoulders and rolled her onto her side. The yellow alpine buttercup in her hair had a few bent petals which Allison did her best to smooth out. She lifted her daughter's braids and draped them off the top of the altar, exposing the back of her neck.

"Would you like me to handle the injection?" Arden asked. He stepped behind her and rested his hands on her shoulders.

It took all her control not to lean into him, but she knew she couldn't take such liberties. He had to invite her.

She shook her head. "It's my duty and I'm proud to fulfill it."

The syringe in one hand, she pinched the skin right below the hairline, pulling it back from Beulah's neck. Then she inserted the needle into the taut skin and squeezed to insert the microchip. Beulah moaned, but didn't stir.

Thanks to the chip, the Community could locate Beulah anywhere, a safety precaution in case anyone got lost.

Or endangered the Community.

"I trust she satisfied you?" Allison asked as she slipped the syringe back into her dress.

Arden reached out and placed a hand on one of Beulah's legs near the knee and squeezed. "She's a credit to her gender." He grabbed Allison's wrist with his other hand. "And to her mother."

A shiver ran up Allison's arm at his touch.

"I was a little surprised that it was Beulah's thirteenth birthday," he said. "I had thought I remembered celebrating her eleventh last year."

Allison shook her head. "Time flies for us. Babies become children who then turn into grown adults while us parents are still getting used to the fact that they can walk."

Arden sighed. "Too true. Still, I wouldn't have blamed you if you'd waited a year or two. Given her a little extra childhood."

She frowned, clenching her fists. "I wouldn't want people to think I receive special treatment. Beulah either. We all have our duties to the Community, and no daughter of mine will shirk hers."

A single finger trailed up her spine. She clenched her hands all the tighter, until her nails cut into the palms of her hands, to keep herself in check. Oh, how she wished to use those nails in other, glorious ways.

"I commend your fortitude," he whispered in her ear, sending a thrill through her.

To her disappointment, his hands slipped away from her.

"You are welcome to head home to complete preparations for your evening's festivities. I'm sure you've planned a celebration for Beulah. I can finish up here."

"Would it be too much to presume you might join us?" she asked, her breath catching in her throat.

"Not for dinner, but I hope to see you later."

As she departed the chamber, her knees barely kept her upright.

Chapter 35

The Community compound was a pretty town, but for the barbed wiring that topped the tall brick wall that surrounded it. Built in a valley between two snow-capped mountains in Piñon Mesa, the small cottages resembled an 18th century town. For all the cult's faults, their compound wasn't one of them. It made Brice wonder at the Community's origins. Had they started off as something simpler, perhaps relatable, before a corrupt leader infected them?

Smoke filled the air from dozens of chimneys. Brice wished he could be in one of those houses beside a fireplace at the moment. The crisp late afternoon air numbed his cheeks and nose. And his legs froze beneath his jeans.

Sunset remained a couple of hours away. He needed to figure out a way inside before it got dark, so he hiked the perimeter, hoping for a discreet entry point. He also hoped he'd hidden the rental economy car far enough off the dirt road to keep anyone from the compound from stumbling upon it.

The drive into the Colorado National Monument, then down through Glade Park to Piñon Mesa, had been uneventful; a thirty-mile drive that should've taken a little over an hour. Instead, it had taken him almost four. He'd driven ten miles below the speed limit and still felt like he was weaving like a drunk, though he stayed in his lane. He'd had to take regular breaks to rest his left leg, which kept stiffening up. At least the two-lane roads he'd taken most of the way here had been clear of snow and ice.

It was only when he'd gotten within the last few miles of the compound that he'd come across icy dirt roads that jolted the car, sending spikes up his leg, even at ten to fifteen miles per hour. At that point, he'd deemed it best to pull off and hide the car. He couldn't very well drive right up to the front gate and start asking for Mary, after all.

Keeping well back from the wall and making sure he had plenty of trees for cover, Brice slogged through light patches of snow, using the cane not only for balance, but to identify ice or rocks. An escape tonight in the dark would be treacherous, especially with a baby in tow. He hoped Mary would have ideas, but walking out the front gate in broad daylight probably wasn't one of them.

Jaxon's help would've been nice, but despite the accusations from Owen's people, Brice knew his brother would be bound by FBI rules and the law. He was a good agent. Brice wasn't so bound, not when the law allowed men, such as the Community leaders, to harm women and children. But he had no wish to put his brother in a compromising situation.

About forty-five minutes into his trek, as the sun neared the mountain to the west, Brice spotted an entry point in the Community wall—a five-foot gap blocked by a pair of concrete pillars. It provided plenty of space to walk through, but not much else.

A teenage boy sat on the ground right inside the pillars, half-keeping an eye out at the forest, but he spent as much time watching kids kick around a ball within the compound.

Brice couldn't sneak up on the boy and neutralize him like an action movie star, though he indulged in a few moments of wishful imagining. Nevertheless, this was likely to be as good an entry point as he'd find, so he gave his knee a rest and waited.

Sitting on a knee-high boulder, shielded by an elm, made him even more aware of the cold, especially with the fading daylight. He wished he had the car with him, so he could turn on the heat.

To distract himself, he debated what he should say to Mary. His memories of her still hadn't returned. Would they ever? Would seeing her trigger something, as it had with Nate?

And how would she respond to his appearance? He was here to help her escape. Would she see it that way? Or would she view him as another abuser like Elwin Pickering?

Now that he was here, Owen's group's accusations resurfaced. What if they were right about his connection to Elwin and the others? To the Community. To their trafficking of women and children. The mere possibility seemed insane to him, except for the picture

Investigator Wright had found. How to explain that? There was so much he had lost.

And in the event Mary confirmed his connection, he wasn't sure what he would do. There was no walking away and living a normal life with that knowledge. Or facing his brother or his friends with any shred of dignity. Such a revelation would break him. Break who he believed himself to be. Was there any coming back from that? Could any amount of repentance make up for such horrors?

Nate had defended him in the hospital when Investigator Wright had questioned him. Brice had to trust that Nate knew him as well as he believed. Trust that he had always been the man he remembered, the one his mother had raised. That he couldn't have changed so significantly in a single year.

He clung to that like a man clinging to a lifeline while trapped in quicksand.

The boy guarding the side entrance from the compound, unable to control himself, darted after a wild kick from the game. Brice watched him run, slow to process the opportunity before him.

Then realization struck like a slap to the back of the head. Pressing his cane against the boulder he rested on, he used it to propel himself to his feet. He pushed himself forward, ignoring the protest from his left leg. He kept to the trees. Once the boy had kicked the ball back to the others in the game, he lingered, watching.

Brice prayed—something he hadn't done in a long time—that the boy wouldn't turn back now. Let his boyish desires dominate his good sense. His missing this one intruder wouldn't lead to anyone's harm. At least Brice hoped it wouldn't. Especially not Mary's or the baby's.

All the kids were still absorbed in their game when he reached the break in the trees. He had no more cover now until he made it inside. But the kids remained so focused on their game that no one looked up as he reached the pillars, striding between them and ducking to the right behind a house. Bent over, he made his way along the back of the house, stooping below window level.

The house had an underground cellar. He approached the entrance and dropped beside it for partial cover. It seemed like a decent spot to hide until it got darker. He'd duck into the cellar if anyone came along.

Once the sun set and things quieted for the night, he'd search for Mary.

Chapter 36

Brice hid by the cellar until almost midnight, hunched in on himself and shivering. Every inch of exposed skin burned from the cold. He wanted to be inside with heat or beside a fire so badly that he had to keep telling himself that he had to wait for people to settle down for the night. If he got caught, it would blow any chance he had of rescuing Mary and the baby. A few hours suffering in the cold was a small price to pay for getting them away from here.

The boy who had guarded the side entrance to the compound had returned to his post not long after Brice had slipped inside, remaining there until a man took his place around nine p.m. Brice thought he could've overpowered the boy to get Mary and the baby out. Not so the man, who was likely more than willing to use the shotgun he carried.

Brice spent the rest of the time behind the cellar attempting to devise a plan for getting past the man, but everything he came up with seemed ridiculous.

At last, it was time to go find Mary. As he moved along the row of houses, he peeked through darkened, frosty windows. Each time, he felt like a stalker or pervert, especially when he saw someone sleeping inside.

Observing how many innocent women and children the cult possessed, it struck him that he was leaving them behind to suffer the fate he was here to rescue Mary and the baby from. He couldn't save them all, but that understanding didn't make him feel any better.

His guilt mixed with fear that someone would see him and raise the alarm, and they would hunt him down before he even located Mary. That seemed like the most likely outcome.

But he had come this far. He intended to check every single building in the compound until he either found them or felt certain she wasn't here.

Toward what he thought was the middle of the compound, the sound of a crying baby gave him pause. The bawling came from a house opposite him. He had planned to circle around to check it out after finishing up the houses on his current row.

A swath of light from a nearby house illuminated much of the ground between where he stood and the house with the crying baby. He didn't like crossing here and making himself obvious if anyone in the surrounding houses was awake, like the parent of the crying baby, up to soothe their child.

As he stood crouched in shadow, debating what to do, a familiar woman passed the open window in the general direction of the upset baby. It took him a moment to process that she was the woman from his home security cameras: Mary.

He stared, unable to move. There she was, after all this time. Not a picture or a video recording.

Her.

A fleeting glimpse, but enough to eliminate doubt.

He crossed toward the house, flinching as a porch light spotlighted him, before he realized what he'd done. It was too late to turn back, so he pressed forward. He felt like a prison escapee from those old movies when a strobe light hits them. He half expected sirens to break the silence.

Then he was out of the light and around the corner onto the front porch of Mary's house. He ducked behind two chairs and a small round table with blue-flowered plants in pots, then peeked in the front window. Simple furniture draped in darkness filled most of the room. Light from a nearby room stretched across the carpet, a shadow filling part of it. The shadow rotated right to left in a rocking motion.

The crying had stopped, but for a few light complaints.

He longed to see the baby. To talk to Mary. He had so many questions. So many hopes. Yet he remained there, paralyzed with indecision.

He had imagined her a prisoner that he would have to liberate. Finding her here in a home, as if she lived here… Owen *had said* she was a part of the Community. But Brice hadn't expected to find her here like this, living in a home like it was her own. If he guessed wrong, she might be the one to raise the alarm, and he would've risked himself for no reason.

Still, he refused to walk away without at least talking to her, which meant taking a chance. He hoped their life together during the previous year had been real. At least parts of it.

He stood, approached the front door, and knocked. His stomach did loops while he waited, part of him wanting to run for cover. This was all a mistake. He shouldn't have come.

The door opened. Mary's jaw dropped and her eyes widened. His thudding heart was the only part of him that moved. He didn't know what to say. Or do. As he stared, her familiarity didn't grow to memory.

"Brice?" She recovered first. "What're you doing here?"

"I'm. I'm not sure." Tears pushed to the surface, but he squeezed them back. "I came… I had to k—"

Her surprise shifted to alarm, which made his gut plummet. But she reached out, grabbed his arm, and pulled him into the house. She slammed the door shut behind him, locking it.

For a second, they stood studying each other, she in a night dress. He turned away, embarrassed.

"How did you get here?" she asked.

"I was worried about you… and the baby." He glanced toward the room with the light on, but couldn't make himself ask.

"Why?"

The question surprised him so much, his head snapped around to her. "What do you mean why? I didn't know why you left after… If you were okay. If the baby was okay."

She frowned. "You don't remember?"

His gaze dropped to the floor, afraid of what would come next. "Remember what?"

She stepped closer, studying his head, the scars. His hair had grown back to cover some of them, but enough remained. "How bad was it?"

"I lost a lot of time." Would he ever get it back, as he had with Nate?

She reached out her hand as if to touch the scars, but she hesitated, fingers hovering inches from his head. "I guess it makes sense after what they did to you."

"They?" The words gave him a tiny spark.

"Garrett, Spencer, and Elwin." Her expression turned grave. "I thought they'd killed you."

Was that why she'd left? She'd thought he was dead? "Why… why were they there?"

"My time was up." She rubbed both arms as if cold. "I got summoned back. The baby was almost due, and they'd come to escort me home."

He felt like he'd waded into a field of landmines and had to watch each step. "You're one of them?"

She laughed bitterly. "Born and raised. A cow set free in the pasture from time to time, then brought back in to be milked. Or to bear the next generation."

He exhaled. One foot down safely, but that didn't mean he was in the clear. The next question he didn't want to ask, but couldn't avoid. "What about me? What did I know?"

She gave him a confused look. "Everything."

"Everything?" Bile rose in his throat, and he swallowed it down, but his stomach had soured. Maybe he should be thankful his memories of the last year hadn't returned. Nothing of her seemed to be returning to him.

"I hid nothing from you," she replied. "I told you everything they've done to me."

"Was I…"

"Were you, what? Involved?" Her lip curled in a condescending smile. "They never would've trusted you. You're not strong enough."

His head dropped. He was both relieved, but also chagrined. "What they did to me, that was to shut me up because I knew too much?"

"And because of your brother. They didn't want you to go to him with what you knew when I disappeared."

"Why didn't we go to him? If I knew everything, why didn't I tell him? We would've protected you. Kept you safe from these people."

She laughed hard, making him feel like the butt of a joke. When her laughter subsided, she wiped tears from her eyes. "No one can keep me safe from them. There's nowhere I can hide. I was there with you because they allowed it. Until it was time for the baby; then they brought me back."

"Can I see her?" he asked, eyes drifting back to the hallway and the light.

"How did you know she's a girl?" Mary asked.

He shrugged, unable to explain it. To change the conversation, he gestured and took a step forward. "I'd like to see her."

"No." She slid to block his path and crossed her arms.

He halted, grimacing.

"She's not yours, and you shouldn't have come. If they find you, they'll kill you."

Direct hit. He'd taken one step too many in the minefield and blown his guts out. Despite that, he wouldn't give up. Not after everything he'd endured to get here.

"I didn't come just to see you or talk to you. I came to get you out of here. Help you escape."

She snorted and nodded at his cane. "You're no knight on a white horse."

Another direct hit.

"Even if you were, you're fifteen years too late."

Her scorn made him angry.

"I'm here," he said. "I can get you both out of here. Then I'll make sure they never find us. Wherever we have to go, it doesn't matter."

She shook her head. "You're right. It won't matter. They always find anyone who runs away, and they'll never let me take the baby." Her expression hardened. "Nor would I. She's my ticket out. She'll stay here in my place."

He gasped, unable to believe or accept what she'd said. "You…you'd give her up? To them?"

"I've done my time," she spat. "Paid my dues to the men of this Community. The only reason I agreed to have her was for her to take my place here so I could go back out. Get away from all this madness."

He wanted to cry for her, cry with her for all she must've endured. It had likely been worse than he imagined. There was no judging her for wanting to get away. But leaving her daughter behind?

"She's a baby. You can't—"

At this Mary cackled. It sent a shiver through him.

"If trading her means not having to lie on my back for one more man around here, yes, I'll do it." There was a maniacal spark in her eye. "I'd trade her or anyone else, just so it won't be me."

His stomach churned. He needed a trash can before he emptied his ruined guts all over the floor. He suddenly wondered if, even before his lost memories, he'd ever really known her at all.

"I've given up others," she continued. "Friends, even, to get away for a while."

He stumbled away from her toward a kitchen and from there to the sink. He turned on the faucet and drank from it, trying to settle his stomach. When he stood, she leaned over the island and picked up a small tin, which she opened, removing a couple of pills. She put them in her mouth and swallowed.

She waved the tin at him. "This came from one who took my place." Her eyes flattened, her face going slack. She took no pleasure nor suffered any horror from this. It was simple reality for her.

"I worked with other girls down in Florida. One day, Kendall informed us that one of us would return here, assuring us what a privilege it would be to serve the Community. From the way he kept eyeing me, I knew he meant me. They'd summoned me back." Her hands, resting on the counter, curved into claws around it. "But I couldn't come back. Wouldn't.

"There was one girl there, a couple of years older than me. An immigrant. I made her volunteer in my place. Threatened to have her deported back to Mexico if she refused." Mary looked up at him, a single unshed tear in one eye. "I was her only friend, and I sent her here. I sacrificed that friendship so it wouldn't be me. Now I'm going to trade for my freedom again. If you interfere, I'll hand you over, too."

He pointed at one of the scars on his head and crossed the kitchen to her. "Did you do this to me? Did I interfere? Did you try to have me killed?"

She stared up at him, unflinching.

"Am I like this now, broken, because of you?" he shouted, a bonfire blazing inside him.

"You were broken when I found you," she snapped. "My grateful, pathetic puppy. That's why I chose you. You served a purpose."

He grabbed her shoulders and shoved her backward. She tumbled to the ground, smacking her head against the floor and sliding against the wall. He charged forward, screaming.

"You used me. Stupid bitch. Stupid. Damn. Bitch."

She made to rise, but he shoved her back down. Why had she done that? She'd manipulated him, then tossed him away when she no longer needed him. Straddling her, he grabbed her neck, squeezing. She slapped at his arms, but he ignored them, tightening his grip. He ground his teeth, his whole body tightening like a spring-loaded coil. He wasn't broken. Nor weak. He wasn't someone to be used, beaten, and discarded.

She gasped, face reddening. From the other room the baby cried, snapping him back to the reality of what he was doing. He fell backward into the counter, the bonfire of rage extinguished in an instant, drowned by horror.

How could he? Even if just for a moment. She'd been right. He *was* broken.

Mary lurched to her feet, holding her neck and coughing. She stumbled to the back door and opened it, pointing out into the night. "Go."

He stared at her, at the premature lines on her face. The glassiness in her eyes. They held no apology or remorse, just weariness and resignation.

"Say another word and I'll scream."

He hobbled past her, his cane thudding on the linoleum, desperate to get away. He'd failed her and the baby. Failed himself. He was no hero. No rescuer. Not when he couldn't control himself, his anger. He couldn't trust himself.

Stepping out onto the back stoop, he stared out at the growing darkness as the door closed behind him.

Chapter 37

Brice stood immobile on Mary's back porch, no longer caring if anyone else in the Community discovered him. What did it matter where he went or what happened to him? He'd come out here and failed. Mary wasn't the person he'd imagined. Someone walking by right then and shooting him in the head would be a mercy.

His phone vibrated in his pocket and he frowned, pulling it out. No one had this number. When he checked, there were no missed calls or texts. He must've imagined the vibration.

Then he checked his emails. He'd received thirty new ones since that morning. He skimmed the list, a majority of which were from Jaxon with desperate subject lines.

Where are you?

Please call me!

Brice, damnit. Let me help you.

If he didn't leave now and the Community discovered and killed him, Jaxon might never know. And he'd blame himself for not getting to Grand Junction sooner. For not doing more to protect his little brother.

Brice couldn't let that happen. Whatever happened later, he had to at least make it back to Jaxon first. Let him know what he had discovered. And if he lost Mary for good, he would at least stop the Community from doing to her little girl what they had done to her.

And to other women and girls.

"Who are you?"

He half jumped, half spun in shock at the voice. The sudden, uncoordinated movement dropped him onto his butt on the concrete. A jolt lanced through his hip and leg that left his eyes watering. He gripped the cane in both hands as he rose.

"Easy." A woman approached with gloved hands raised. "I can help you get out."

He looked around for signs of anyone else. She was alone.

The woman possessed a warm, if timid, smile. He estimated she was about Mary's age. She wore a plain gray coat over a full-length dress, with boots on her feet. She seemed like a woman who made cookies for the school bake sale, rather than someone who risked herself to help an intruder escape.

"How do you know I need help?"

The woman laughed, light and friendly. "I know all the men here. You're not one of them."

He smiled in return, unable to help himself. "Why would you help me?"

"You're him. Aren't you?"

"Who?" he asked.

She beckoned him to follow as she crept down a row between the houses. "I dreamed for years that someone would break in for me, but I've never been that lucky."

The words stung like a rebuke.

Before he came up with a response, she moved along to the next house over, bent over at the waist. She paused at the front corner of the house and peered in both directions. He followed, wondering if he should accept her help. He had no doubt he'd get caught. She would only end up in trouble helping him. How long before Mary told someone he was here?

But he didn't get a chance to say anything to her before she headed right. He didn't risk calling after her.

As they passed a window, he glanced inside, expecting someone else to be up and spot them. It seemed too fortunate that the only other person to see him in here would be someone offering to help.

The woman led him between two houses to the next row. This time when she peeked out, she quickly lurched backward, pressing herself against the side of the house.

"What is it?" he mouthed to her.

She held up three fingers for an answer, then touched one to her lips. He motioned back the way they'd come, raising one eyebrow. She shook her head, before dropping to hands and knees. She eased forward, crawling and craning her neck to study whatever she'd seen before. His chest constricted as she searched. If they had to run, he would never make it.

He waited for a sign from her that it was time to run; in his case, hobble. Instead, she relaxed and pushed herself to her feet so effortlessly that he gritted his teeth in annoyance. It was because of the Community that he moved like a man twice his age.

But it wasn't because of *her*. If he lived past this evening, it would be thanks to her.

They continued to an open field, like a square, that left him feeling way too exposed. He didn't see anyone outside, though. Other than the three people the woman had seen earlier, it seemed everyone else remained locked inside. As cold as it was out, that made sense. Who would want to be out in the middle of the night with temperatures in the teens?

On the far side of the square, she led him up wide stone steps to what looked like a church. She opened the front door and beckoned him inside.

Why was she leading him to a church? He doubted the priests, or ministers, or whatever the Community called them, would give him asylum. Could this woman be that naïve? Had he made a big mistake trusting her?

Regardless, he knew he was pot committed, as Nate liked to say. He wasn't even sure how to find his way back to Mary's house, much less the side exit from the compound. And he'd be pressing his luck wandering through the place on his own, no matter the hour.

It was clear to him that the Community had invested a lot in the church. The half dozen wide stone steps led up to white Roman columns that adorned the front of the largest building in the village, though Brice had seen bigger churches in Alabama.

The pair of windows on the building's front had stained glass murals. In the dark, he couldn't discern the pattern. Did the Community follow some bastardized Christian sect? Or had its leaders made up some brand-new religion to control its members, as Scientologists had?

As he stepped into darkness, the woman pulled the door shut behind them. Unable to see the way forward, he waited for guidance. She fumbled with something to his right. He detected her outline, but that was it, so he grabbed his phone and activated the flashlight app. The phone had no service.

The woman held a match and matchbox, as she stood beside a narrow table with a few candles on it. She paused to look at his phone, then deposited the matchbox in the table drawer.

"We keep those for ceremonies, or if the power is out," she explained, before inclining her head at the phone. "But that works better for where we're going."

"Which is?"

"Underground."

They stood in an entrance hall. Ahead were a pair of wide-open doors leading to a darkened sanctuary with rows of pews. To the left of the doors, hanging on the walls, was an enormous painting of a man. The Community's leader? The man stood on the steps out front, dressed in a suit that resembled those worn by televangelists. Like politicians and lawyers, they crafted their images to convey a sense of competence and professionalism. To Brice, it often signaled artifice. Considering the Community's success despite its alleged criminal activities, Brice guessed the man wasn't someone to cross.

"This way."

The woman led the way to a sitting area with four chairs surrounding a wooden table. A pair of bookshelves held neat rows of books. Old-fashioned hardbacks without fancy covers. He suspected that if he checked them out, none would be as old as they appeared. The church leaders likely believed the impression of age added legitimacy to the place.

In the back wall was a heavy black door. The woman grabbed the large metal ring that served as a handle and pulled. The door creaked open to reveal an old stone staircase. Near the bottom, a couple of unlit torches hung from the walls. The place made him think of a crypt. Was there one beneath the church?

It also screamed trap. He wanted to get out of here, but despite feeling he could trust her, everything about this place conveyed deceit.

"You said you know who I am. How?" he asked, blocking the stairwell.

She glanced over her shoulder at the entrance, drawing his gaze with hers. There was no sign of pursuers.

"I'm a friend of Beulah's," she said.

He waited, despite his instincts screaming they didn't have time to waste here talking.

"When I saw you at Allison's house, when Beulah let you in, I guessed who you must've been. And I thought…." She trembled. "I thought if you'd come to take her away from here, maybe… perhaps you'd take me as well." Her gaze dropped to the floor as if expecting him to refuse. He guessed she'd heard 'no' her whole life, the men of the Community never caring what she wanted or needed. Yet that hadn't stopped her from offering to help without knowing if he would reciprocate.

"What's your name?" he asked.

"Helen."

He wanted to reach out and grab her chin and raise it—as heroes did in movies—before promising to deliver her to safety. But he was no hero, and he didn't dare touch her.

Instead, he stepped aside, pointing down the steps. "How do we get out of here?"

The question sounded timid in his ears, and the clear opposite of heroic. Her head rose anyway, eyes filled with such hope that it broke his heart. He hated the men of this place even more.

But he was thankful for her presence. She was the only thing holy in this chapel, an angel ushering him to safety.

Her smile returned. She pointed at his phone. "May I? To see our way."

He handed her the phone. She started down the steps, holding it out to light their way. Before following, he tugged the door shut behind them, to hide where they'd gone if someone checked the place.

As they descended, the air cooled and turned musty. At the bottom, they followed a long corridor, with more unlit torches lining the path. They passed a doorway leading to a dark room on their left, but Helen swept right past it, her pace picking up. She almost bounced on her feet. It took all he had to keep up with her, but he didn't complain. He didn't want to dampen her mood.

The corridor ended at a four-way intersection. Three simple dirt tunnels, all dark, except for the faint light from his phone.

His right hand ached, and he realized it was from gripping his cane too tight. "Where do these lead?"

She passed straight through the intersection without hesitation. "They're old mining tunnels. The compound's located over an old uranium mine."

The revelation made his skin crawl. Uranium? Were they exposed down here? Were they breathing in uranium? He debated retreating and searching for another way out, but she charged forward with his phone. He supposed the threat from the Community scared her worse than uranium poisoning.

What did uranium smell like? The tunnel was damp, the smell of mold heavy. Beyond that, he could only guess.

"Arden tapped into the tunnels to create a means of escape in case anyone ever attacked," she explained.

Or law enforcement surrounded them, he thought. How many members had instead used these tunnels for escape from the Community over the years? He supposed not many, or Arden would've made them harder to access.

"If you knew these were here and how to use them, how come you've never tried to escape yourself?"

"They'd find me. They find every woman who runs."

He frowned. "Mary said the same, but if that's true, why run now?"

"I never had anyone to help me. Your brother works for the FBI, right?"

A chill ran between his shoulder blades. How much *did* these people know about him? Mary must've learned a lot about him during their year together. Had she told it all to the Community leaders, or just to her friend?

"How do you know they don't escape?"

She didn't immediately respond as she passed under a support beam crossing overhead, one of many lining the tunnel for support. When she did answer, she didn't look back at him. "When a runaway is caught, and they're always caught, they're brought back as a warning to others. Then they're sent off to work. Or, sometimes, they're killed."

He promised himself he wouldn't let that be her fate. He'd get her to Jaxon and into FBI protection. If she shared these details with his brother, that must be enough to enable the FBI to raid the compound and free Mary, the baby, and all the other women and girls here.

Then he remembered Owen telling him about his own sources from the Community who had the evidence needed to take down the cult before they committed suicide. Or were murdered, as Owen believed. They'd thought themselves safe, yet the Community had gotten to them. What if Mary was right? What if he couldn't protect Helen no matter what he tried?

He pushed those questions down. He couldn't let his fears enable the Community to keep operating. And he wouldn't abandon Helen when she'd asked him for help.

A change in the air flow alerted him they were near the tunnel's exit. Bursts of fresh air that teased freedom. Until the tunnel ended at a plain cement wall that blocked the way forward.

"It's a dead end?" he asked, drawing up short.

Helen didn't slow. She walked straight up to the wall and turned right, disappearing, leaving him in darkness. He stumbled after her, reaching out with his free hand to feel his way, half afraid she had tricked him. How had she disappeared like that?

A few more cautious steps forward, then light appeared to the right from a narrow exit with an open metal gate. Helen stood, cheeks flushed, illuminated by the moon.

"We did it," she said, as he exited through the gate.

"You did it," he corrected, relieved she hadn't abandoned him.

The exit to the tunnel was on the backside of a hill with an almost straight stone face. Trees surrounded the area, making it difficult to determine their location.

"Helen, I'm ashamed of you," a voice said.

Helen gave a short, startled scream. A flashlight blinded Brice. He raised a hand to shield his eyes, blocking out enough light to discern four men stepping out of the trees. He gasped, struggling to breathe. It was like being back behind the coffee shop with Owen's people blinding him.

The flashlight transitioned from him back to Helen, allowing his eyes to adjust. The man in the middle had a full beard. He was tall and imposing. The moment Brice caught a bit of his features, he recognized the man from the church painting.

Chapter 38

The Community leader was tall, maybe six foot five, weighing two fifty or so. Instead of a suit like in the painting, he wore jeans with boots and a heavy beige coat. He resembled a rancher out of Yellowstone.

As he approached, there was a fluidness to his gait. A strength and confidence. The man in the picture could've been mistaken for someone who led from the rear. Gave out orders, but was soft and never got his hands dirty.

Not this man. This man handled business when the situation called for it. Brice knew that he was no match for the leader. Not now. Likely not even before his injuries.

For the moment, the leader ignored Brice, his focus on Helen. "We've discussed this, Helen. I thought you were making progress. I thought you understood that we all have burdens in life, but shouldering them together, as a community, makes them bearable." He turned off his flashlight.

Eyes wide, Helen retreated until she bumped up against the stone face of the hill.

"I wasn't running away, Arden. I promise. I'm committed to the Community. To you."

She raised Brice's phone and tapped rapidly on the screen. Arden rushed her. She screamed, turning her back to him to shield the phone. For a brief moment they struggled, before Arden wrestled it from her. He threw it against the stone wall, the glass shattering.

Helen screamed again, ducking. Tears filled her eyes as she cowered. Her trembling grew until she shook so hard that her next words came out as a stutter. "I… I'm… s… sorry."

Arden placed a hand on her shoulder. When he spoke again, his voice was tender. "I know. This was a momentary lapse in judgement. That's why Spencer will escort you back inside."

He backed away, making room for the old man from Brice's camera footage, who stepped forward. He had a leer on his face as he set a hand on her shoulder.

"Oh… and Helen," Arden began. She paused and turned back to him. "Actions come with consequences."

She screamed and tried to run, but Spencer wrapped his arms around her, pinning her to him.

"Stop." Brice moved to defend her, but the last two men charged, grabbing his arms and dragging him out of the way. He struggled to get free, but was no match for them.

Helen fared no better, Spencer hoisting her over his shoulder and carrying her back into the tunnel. Her screams became sobs before fading.

Arden turned his attention to Brice. "Who are you and what were you doing in our home?" He still had the flashlight. He held it like a club. Brice doubted the man would hesitate to beat him with it if needed.

"I came for Mary." Brice didn't see any point in lying. He didn't need to cover up for her, and whatever they had planned for him, he doubted anything he said or withheld would change it.

"Ah." Arden grinned. "You're the young man she lived with the last year."

Brice raised his chin, meeting the man's gaze.

"You came here for… what?" Arden cocked his head a little. "Answers? Revenge? Or did you expect to steal her away from her family?"

"Some family." Brice squeezed with his right hand before realizing he'd lost the cane when the men grabbed him.

"I think you've been misled," Arden said. "We are a simple community. We live and work together. Take care of each other. No more."

"Men from your *simple community* attacked me in my home." Brice felt heat rising in his chest. "Left me in a coma for ten days."

Arden sighed and placed a hand on his chest. "I didn't intend for that to happen. It never should have, and as leader, I take full responsibility."

Brice stared, angered, but no clever response came to him.

"This is Beulah's home," Arden continued. "Hers and Patty's."

Was that her name? The baby's? It sent a thrill through Brice to hear it.

"They belong here. It's what's best for them."

"What you've done to Mary isn't best for either of them," Brice said through gritted teeth.

Arden bared his own, waving the flashlight at Brice.

Brice flinched, expecting a strike, but the two men held him fast.

"How about I make you an offer, Mr. Dunn?" Arden gestured with the flashlight back toward the compound. "You want Beulah, I'm willing to give her to you."

Brice snorted, knowing it wouldn't be that easy. Arden wouldn't free Mary to get rid of him.

"You join the Community, become one of us, and you can marry Beulah. You can raise Patty and take care of them."

Taken aback, Brice didn't know how to respond. What was the man playing at? He couldn't be serious.

"As your wife, Beulah would be yours alone, subject to no other man. I'm sure she'd be grateful."

It was ridiculous, but Brice considered it. He'd be with Mary again. They'd have the baby. He could protect them from the rest of the Community. Then, from the inside, he could obtain evidence and leak it to his brother to bring them down.

Arden's smile broadened. He pointed to the men holding Brice up. "I'll even sweeten the deal. Garrett and Elwin here, the men who attacked you, I'll let you choose their punishment."

Brice glanced from side to side at the men who held him. He hadn't recognized them in the darkness. He tried to pull away, furious that they had their hands on him, but both gripped him.

They were stone-faced, neither protesting Arden's offer.

Brice clenched his fists and ground his teeth. He imagined dishing out to them a little of what they'd given him. After what he'd lost, it would thrill him to see them punished. Or to mete it out himself.

Helen drifted into his thoughts. She'd been terrified when Arden found her and ordered her hauled back inside against her will. She would suffer if he agreed to Arden's proposal. After what she'd risked to help him escape, to accept would be a betrayal.

Brice shook his head.

Arden's mouth tightened, eyes turning cold. "Mr. Dunn, consider carefully. I've offered your life back. And your family."

But Brice knew Mary wouldn't agree to this arrangement. She couldn't fight it, but it was another form of abuse. Nor would he sell out Helen and the other women in the Community. They all deserved freedom.

"No. I will never join you." He braced himself for whatever came next.

Arden nodded. "I would be a poor leader if I let an intruder escape. My people need to know they are safe, that I will protect them and their homes."

Brice raised his chin, refusing to be cowed no matter what came next. "I'm not the one they should be afraid of."

A blow to the side of his head sent him to the ground. Stunned, he couldn't move. Kicks to his sides and legs jolted him. He curled up, trying to protect himself. A strike to the jaw flipped him over onto his back. Blood filled his mouth. He choked, spitting it out. He covered his mouth with his arms, the pain in his lower jaw so great he wished to pass out.

Instead, more kicks to his ribs and legs left him thrashing, trying to ward them off. A kick to his groin immobilized him again. He couldn't breathe. He tried to beg them to stop. Please. No more. His flight instinct had kicked in, but his body failed to respond.

"That's enough!"

The attacks stopped, to his relief, but he remained in a heap on the ground, his whole body pulsing in pain. He gasped for air. Blood drained down his throat. He coughed it up.

Someone crouched beside him. He shielded his head with his arms.

"Mr. Dunn, we're going to leave you now," Arden said. "I don't approve of killing except in defense, so I'm letting you go. It won't be easy to hike out of here in your condition, but you have a chance.

"However, let me make one thing very clear. You are never welcome back in the Community. We will consider any return on your part an act of aggression. Remember that before you attempt to break in again."

Chapter 39

For a while, all Brice could do was focus on his breathing and endure the pain. His head pounded. Most of his body ached. His mouth still tasted of blood. He felt around with his tongue until he discovered his split upper lip. His face and hands burned from the cold. It was below freezing out here. If he didn't get up and find shelter soon, he'd freeze to death.

Would it hurt to freeze to death? Or would he just go to sleep at some point?

He wasn't sure he could muster the strength to rise. He hated to think his brother might never discover what happened to him, but it wasn't enough to overcome his pain and exhaustion. It was too easy to lie here and do nothing. Let it all go.

Would letting go be so bad? His pain would vanish. He'd already failed Mary and the baby. Helen, too. Considering the outcome, he wished he hadn't gone with Helen after all. He had no illusions that he would've gotten away on his own, but at least if he'd refused her help they wouldn't have caught her.

Please, don't let them hurt her, he thought.

Who was he kidding? The beating they'd given him paled to what they would do to her. What they'd done to her for years. And done to Mary. And would do to Patty, a perfect, precious baby, if no one intervened. If no one stepped up to stop the men here, she would grow up suffering the same abuses as her mother. As Helen, and all the women in the Community.

No! Someone had to stop it. Someone had to do more than make accusatory videos and post them on social media, or write newspaper articles. Men like Arden didn't care about that. He would scoff and keep right on doing what he pleased until someone came along and physically stopped him.

Brice rolled over and pushed himself to his hands and knees. He'd come here for Mary and Patty. Now he had to go a little further for Patty. Helen now, too.

He attempted to climb to his feet, but his stiff legs refused to cooperate. Where was his cane?

Searching the ground, he spotted his shattered cell phone. A little light in the top showed it had power. He scooped it up, intent on calling Jaxon, but when he pressed the power button the screen didn't light up. He stabbed at the cracked screen, trying to get it to activate. A broken edge of glass pricked his finger, drawing blood. He rubbed the blood on his pants, then raised the phone to his mouth.

"Call Jaxon Dunn."

He held the phone close to his ear, but there was no ring.

"Call Jaxon Dunn."

Still no ring.

He tossed the phone away, then searched around for his cane. It poked out from behind a tree trunk. He crawled toward it, ignoring the protests of his muscles and joints. He grabbed it and planted its heel in the frozen ground. Between the cane and the tree trunk, he hauled himself upright.

For the next thirty seconds all he could manage was to stand there balanced between the tree and his cane, breathing and trying to recover his strength. Once he'd recovered enough to think, he debated what to do.

He was out in the middle of nowhere. He'd seen no other close stops out on the highway during his drive. Based upon the map, to the west, the highway ran to the Utah border with no major stops. But who knew if there were any smaller stops that didn't warrant marking on a map?

He debated ignoring Arden's threat and sneaking back into the tunnel. Not far, but enough for shelter. He could gather wood and start a fire to keep warm, until the sun rose and he could see where he was going. It was his best option.

Shifting all his weight onto his cane, he trudged over to the stone face. It took him a few minutes to find the opening, but when he did, he cursed. The metal gate he'd seen earlier now sealed the entrance.

He grabbed it and tried to slide it open, but it wouldn't budge. Setting aside his cane, he pushed and tugged it with both hands. They'd locked it.

Groaning, he grabbed his cane and limped away. There had been two other tunnels from the compound, but his chances of stumbling upon them in the dark weren't good. And even if he found them, there was no guarantee Arden hadn't sealed those off, too. His only option was to hike out of here, which elicited an incredulous chuckle from his lips. He was in no condition to hike anywhere, but he had no choice.

He used the western side of the gorge to orient himself and headed south. It would be great if he got back to his car. He could get warm and drive to safety. Feeling around in his pockets for his keys, he discovered they were gone. He backtracked and scoured outside the tunnel entrance, as well as his best guess on where Garrett and Elwin had given him the second greatest beating of his life—the bastards.

There was no sign of the keys. That would cost him with the rental agency when he got back to Grand Junction. The thought made him grin. Of all the things he was dealing with, that wasn't high on the list.

With the car no longer of use to him, he focused on getting to Highway 141. From there he would try to hitch a ride with an early morning traveler. The possibility of getting warm again was the only thing he looked forward to. Well, that and getting checked out at a hospital. The skin around his right eye had swollen, making it hard to see. And every time the wind brushed his split lower lip, his eyes watered. His jaw throbbed. Nor could he hike far before his aching left hip and leg stiffened to the point he thought it would lock up. Each time, he had to halt to rest and massage it with his free hand.

The cold wasn't helping either. Every bit of exposed skin, and even much of it that wasn't, burned from the cold. His teeth chattered, which amped up the pain in his jaw, but he could do nothing about any of those things. Instead, he focused on taking step after step because that was his only choice.

The constant stops to rest meant the sun was peeking above the horizon by the time he reached Highway 141 and turned east toward Grand Junction. It was better to head in the direction he knew, rather than hope for the best the other way. He remembered passing some stops, though he couldn't remember how far away they were.

Chirping birds were all that accompanied him at that hour. He crossed to the south side of the highway, wanting the road between him and the compound. That way if someone from the compound came looking for him, he'd have more time to find cover. He recognized the ridiculousness of the feeling, because the highway offered no barriers, but it comforted him as if the road were a line in the sand, allowing him to be on the right side and the compound on the wrong.

Fifteen minutes down the highway, he passed a small dirt road that headed up a ridge and out of sight behind a foothill more than a mile away. He didn't remember seeing it on his drive to the compound, or on a map.

He shifted from foot to foot, debating whether to find out where it led. A chance to get warm would be nice, and his mouth tasted as dry as the dirt beneath his feet. But anyone living that close to the Community… if there was a home at the end of the road, could he trust them?

In his present state, would anyone he found trust him?

Once more, he decided it was better not to wander off into the unknown. Who knew how far it might go, or what he might find at the end of it? He was better off putting more distance between him and the compound.

The hum of a navy blue truck on the road behind him sent a surge of panic through him. Was it coming from the compound? Had Arden reconsidered letting him go?

A hefty tree trunk lay on the ground a short distance off the road. It offered suitable cover. He took a tentative step toward the trunk, then halted. This was a state highway, after all. The driver was likely a random traveler who might give him a ride.

And he wasn't sure how much farther he could make it on foot. He had to take a chance, or he'd die out here. Did it matter much if he died by freezing to death or at the hands of the Community?

Turning back to watch the truck approach, he shifted the cane to his left hand and raised his right thumb, extending his arm out. His heart pounded in his chest. What if he'd made a mistake? What if the truck was from the Community? It was too late to run for cover. The truck driver had seen him by now.

Except the truck kept barreling down the road, not slowing a bit as it reached him. Brice shook a fist in the air, shouting, as the truck raced past. For an answer, the driver honked his horn and gunned it.

Brice kicked dirt after the truck. It was a pointless gesture, but he couldn't stop himself. Why hadn't the man at least stopped to see if he needed help? Even a phone call would've been huge. But far too many barreled through life like that driver down the road, too focused on their own destination to care about the stranger in need they'd passed. It was what let these men do what they wanted to women and children. It was what let human trafficking exist. Everyone else was too busy to care. Too blinded by their own desires and hardships to acknowledge the pain and anguish of so many innocents destroyed because they lacked the ability to defend themselves.

Mary.

Helen.

Patty.

Countless other women and children crying out, their stories vanishing unmourned.

He'd seen them. He'd heard. He would tell their stories for them, hopefully stopping some from disappearing in the process.

Chapter 40

Before long, Brice's feet began complaining almost as much as his hip and knee. His split lip, aching jaw, and swollen right eye weren't much better. He needed to rest, but he feared that if he took a break, he might not get up again. Sitting would make it easier to dwell on his injuries.

Another side road appeared up ahead, this one paved. Once he reached it, he spotted a house hiding back a quarter mile into the trees— a brick rancher with a small clearing for a yard.

It was closer to the Community than he liked, but they couldn't possibly control everyone along the state highway. And he didn't know how much further he could go on without help.

No cars filled the driveway. No smoke rose from the chimney. The place appeared deserted. Even so, he ambled down the road. The place was in good shape, the gutters clean, the front porch swept.

No one appeared in the door or a window as he approached. He knocked on the front door, sensing the emptiness of the place, but not wanting to scare someone if he was wrong. No lights came on. No one answered. After a couple more knocks, he peeked in the closest window, but observed no one. He slowly circled the house. As he walked, he checked a couple bedroom windows and those of the kitchen, each time holding his breath and hoping he didn't scare the shit out of someone. He'd prefer not to get shot.

The home was furnished. It looked lived in, but the occupants did not appear to be home.

He tried the back door. Locked. No surprise there. The door had four glass panes in it. While he hated to break in, his strength was rapidly waning. He had to get warm. Perhaps tend to some of his injuries. And call for help.

With his cane, he bashed in the window closest to the door handle. His heart raced as he stood immobile, listening for signs of alarm. Only the memory of the shattering glass rang in his ears.

He cleared out the glass shards, reached in, and unlocked the door. As he slid the door open, he called out.

"Hello? Anyone here? I'm sorry I broke your window, but I need help. Is anyone here?"

He stepped over the broken glass and into the kitchen, then paused. "If anyone's here, I promise I'm not here to hurt you. I need help."

The kitchen looked a little old fashioned with white cabinets and appliances. A round wooden table to one side was marred with a couple of water stains and a handful of cuts. Wall-paper with a design of little purple flowers covered the walls.

He passed through it to the living room, then checked each of the three bedrooms and two bathrooms. In one bathroom mirror, he saw his closed and swollen right eye, and his bloody and busted lip. Was this what he'd looked like when the police had found him in a coma on his living room floor?

A small hand towel hung from a ring beside the sink. He grabbed the towel and let water run until it warmed. With it, he cleaned away the dried blood from his lip and a little from his scalp. Once he was relatively clean, he rinsed off the towel and returned it to the ring.

Feeling better, he exited the bathroom and raised the thermostat from a set temperature of sixty up to sixty-eight. Returning to the kitchen, he searched the cabinets until he found glasses. He got water from the sink. It was cold coming up from the pipes. The owners were lucky none had burst in these temperatures.

Nothing had ever tasted so good as the water as it washed down his throat. He gulped down a full glass and filled it a second time, but set it aside on the counter for later. His stomach roiled from the sudden influx of water, but also from hunger. The fridge had nothing but condiment bottles in the door. The freezer held a couple of bottles of rum and a box of frozen waffles.

A cordless home phone was mounted to the wall behind the kitchen table. It was time to call Jaxon. Brice retrieved the handset and dialed his brother's number.

"Hello, this is Agent Dunn," Jaxon answered, fatigue thick in his voice.

For a second, Brice hesitated, feeling like a little brother running to his big brother for help because things gotten had too hard. His coming here, thinking he could play hero, had been nothing more than delusions. His personal Clark Kent complex that every man seemed to share. What had it gotten him? Nearly killed again without helping anyone. In fact, he'd put Helen in greater danger because of his actions.

"Hello?" Jaxon repeated.

"It's me," Brice said.

"Brice, are you all right?" The relief in his brother's voice was clear.

"Yeah. I'm fine." Brice rubbed his brow with one hand. He should've checked the cabinets for aspirin.

"Where are you?"

"I saw them."

"Saw who?"

"Mary. The baby. They're with the Community."

"You're in the compound?"

"Was. I got out. Mary wouldn't come with me." Brice squeezed the phone at the admission, grateful his brother couldn't see his face—the guilt and shame on full display.

"Where are you now?"

"I found a place to rest several miles from the Community."

"Do they know where you are?" There was an edge in Jaxon's voice.

"No, I don't think so. But Mary, the baby…" His voice broke down.

"It's okay. We got your message. It was enough. We're going in."

"What message?" Brice frowned. Then a chill flushed through him. Arden had taken his phone. Had they set a trap? Except Arden hadn't taken it, he'd broken it. Brice slipped his hand into his pocket where he'd deposited the broken phone.

"Your text message with the audio file of your discussion with the woman," Jaxon answered. "Helen. That conversation provided probable cause. We're going in today."

Brice shook his head. He hadn't recorded his conversation with Helen. She'd had his phone.

Had she recorded it? They'd been underground in a tunnel. No way the phone had gotten any service under there. She'd also had the phone when they got out of the tunnel before Arden took it from her. Had she somehow recorded something and sent it out before Arden destroyed the phone? How had she known whom to call? He hadn't saved Jaxon's number in the cell phone.

Of course, *he* had called Jaxon on the phone. And Helen had been struggling to do something with the phone while Arden fought to take it from her. She must've sent the file to the number in the call list and hoped it helped.

Wonderful Helen! She might have saved him, Mary, and Patty… right before Arden's men had taken her back inside to punish her.

He groaned.

"What?" Jaxon asked. "What is it?"

Arden would question her. If she told him about the recorded message, he'd know what it meant. They were compromised. And Arden would either flee, set a trap, or both.

"Jaxon, listen," Brice said. "That woman I was with, the Community captured her. If their leader, Arden, learns about the conversation, then he'll expect you. He might set a trap."

Jaxon laughed at that. "I'll pass the intel along to the raid commander, but it won't matter. We've got multiple agencies teaming up for this takedown. We'll be ready."

Brice didn't share his brother's good humor. If Arden and his men set a trap, and the FBI was ready for a fight, the compound would turn into a war zone. Patty and Mary—and Helen and the rest of the women in the Community—would get caught up in it.

Innocent casualties.

"First, I need to come get you," Jaxon said. "Tell me—"

Brice waited a moment, wondering at his brother going silent. When Jaxon didn't resume, Brice frowned. "Jaxon? Jaxon, are you there?"

No response from his brother. Had they gotten disconnected? Brice hung up the phone, then clicked the button to make a call again, but the phone had no dial tone. Something had happened to the line.

It was far too quiet. He realized the fridge didn't hum. There was no clock on the oven. The power had gone out.

He tossed the phone on the table. What now? He had no way to let Jaxon know his location. He thought about the raid. The FBI would do their best to avoid innocent bloodshed. They would try to protect the women and children. But in a battle, one in which Arden's men would be well-armed, the agents' first priority would be to protect themselves and each other, and their second to take down any threats.

Who knew what Arden and his men might do if they felt the compound was falling? To ensure Patty and Mary's well-being, Brice needed to protect them himself.

He limped through the living room toward what he thought was the master bedroom. He'd give himself a few minutes to search for a weapon; then he'd make his way back to the Community.

And if Mary still wouldn't escape, then he'd take Patty. He would at least rescue her.

Chapter 41

Before leaving the house, Brice grabbed a heavy camo coat from the hall closet by the front door, along with a matching winter cap and thick gloves. He'd never worn camo gear in his life, but it would provide better protection against the cold. It would help him blend in on his way back to the compound as well.

In his coat pockets he placed a dozen shells for a shotgun he'd found in a closet in the home office. Upon finding it, he was thankful no one had been home to use it on him.

Jaxon had trained him in how to use a handgun, but he knew the basics of handling a shotgun. He hoped he wouldn't have to use it.

The shotgun came with a strap, so he tossed it over his shoulders to keep one hand free as he made for the back door. As he exited the house, he ignored his compulsion to clean up the glass fragments. He had to hurry to the compound. After this was over, he'd return the shotgun and pay for the broken window.

Rather than return to Highway 141, he set off through the woods, angling toward the road, but maintaining a safe distance from it. He didn't want anyone to spot him as they drove past.

The icy wind whipped his face as he trudged through the forest. The borrowed coat, gloves, and cap kept him warm enough, as long as he didn't have to spend another night outdoors without shelter.

A light snow began falling. It thickened over the next ten minutes, eliciting a curse from him. This was not what he needed. Snow piling up would slow him down and make it harder to backtrack to the compound tunnels. The snow might even strand him out here if he wasn't careful.

He picked up his pace, using the cane to test the ground in front of him. He wouldn't abandon Patty. Or Helen. No one else was on their side. Perhaps the FBI raid would change Mary's mind about leaving. If he made it in time.

"Please don't let conditions worsen."

A decent layer of snow already covered most of the landscape, so that he almost missed the turnoff from the highway to the compound. He proceeded a couple hundred yards past it before approaching the highway, keeping a careful eye out. How soon would the FBI arrive? Would they raid the place in a snowstorm, or was he the only one foolish enough to be out in this?

As he hobbled across the highway, he prayed that no vehicle would appear, and that his feet would not slip out from under him, as they threatened to do with every step.

For once, something went his way. He crossed the highway without issue. Once back in the forest, he sought cover behind a V-shaped pair of trees and searched for movement of any kind.

Even the animals had taken shelter.

The lone positive from the falling snow was that it soon covered up his tracks. Already his footsteps on the highway had faded. Another ten minutes and they'd be gone. Of course, this also meant that with each passing minute, his chances of finding the tunnel entrance dissipated. Even without the snow, which was growing thicker, it would've been difficult. The compound, yes. The tunnels? He'd have to hope he got lucky.

He pressed on, tucking his chin and mouth within the neck of his coat to ward against the cold. Everything looked white, covered by growing snowy mounds.

A couple of voices broke the silence.

"Think Helen betrayed us?"

"Arden says so."

Brice ducked behind the nearest tree, his breath catching in his throat. Had they seen him? Leaning against the tree for support, he dropped his cane and pulled the shotgun from his shoulders.

"Even if she did, what's going to happen in a storm like this?"

"You questioning Arden now?"

"No. No. Nothing like that. It's just… I heard the guy who broke in was here for Mary. Also, that Garrett, Elwin, and Spencer fucked up."

The pair passed by a short distance ahead, each with a rifle across one arm. They wore heavy white parkas, which explained why he hadn't spotted them. He was lucky he hadn't walked right into them.

"I don't care. I want to finish up our round and get back in by a fire."

If the first man had a response, Brice didn't catch it.

He followed them.

It was difficult to keep pace with the men while ensuring he had cover to duck behind if they turned back. He kept the shotgun in one hand, forcing him to rely a little extra on the cane for balance. Fortunately, the pair barely checked right or left as they trudged through the woods. They appeared more intent on finishing up than on making a thorough search of the area.

Were they supposed to be out here searching for him? He doubted Arden was worried about him wandering around out here. If Arden had any idea about Helen's messages to Jaxon, though, he would prepare the compound to defend itself. Or set a trap.

Brice's stomach churned. He had no way to warn his brother or anyone else. Not without a phone. His brother was right, though. The agents raiding the compound would take precautions. They'd be armed and have other means of protecting themselves. They'd also have plans, as well as training, for how to adapt to whatever resistance they faced. But Arden and his men knew the landscape.

A gust of wind kicked snow into his face, forcing him to shield his eyes with his gun hand. He halted, waiting for it to pass. When it eased enough to see the way forward again, the men had disappeared. In a panic, he slipped behind the nearest tree.

Had they noticed him following them?

It seemed unlikely, or they'd be shooting at him. Still, he remained hidden, searching and listening for the pair. They appeared to have vanished.

Once he felt reasonably sure they weren't lying in wait to ambush him, he pressed on toward where he'd last seen them, though with the wind and snow covering up their tracks, he couldn't be sure of his direction. He hoped they hadn't redirected, or he'd never find them.

There were no big rock outcroppings within view that might hold the entrance to a tunnel. As he neared the last place he thought they'd been, the ground rose to a ridge. On the far side, it sloped down into a bowl with a frozen-over pond at its heart.

If he hadn't already been so cold, the sight of the pond would've chilled him. The mere proximity of it made him want to run in the other direction. He couldn't peel his eyes away from its surface, his fear taking over, immersing him beneath the ice once more. Skin on fire. Lungs screaming. Mind in shock as instinct took over and the body fought to save itself.

He forced the fear aside, though it lingered at the edge of thought. He had a safe distance between himself and the ice. And he needed to find the men.

The ridge and slope offered no explanation for how he'd lost track of them, nor was there any sign of them on the ice or across it. They must've come this way.

Despite his fears, he eased down the slope. He had to sling the shotgun back over his shoulder and take it step by step. The last thing he wanted was to fall down and onto the ice. But once he'd neared the bottom of the hill and gotten close to the ice, his legs locked up.

Still no sign of the men. If he didn't figure out where they'd gone soon, he'd need to head back toward the compound and hope for the best.

With a growl, he turned around. Then he spotted it: A lean-to at the base of a tree halfway up the hill. There seemed to be a sizable gap beneath it. He'd walked right past it, within twenty feet, but had missed it.

Trying not to get too excited, he slogged up the hill, his feet sliding on the slick ground. He fell multiple times. Each fall sent a jolt of pain through his lower half, and his left knee ached. He pressed on, doubled over, using the cane and his free hand to trudge up the hill to the lean-to.

Beneath it was a pit, a good ten feet deep. A tunnel with an open gate led back into the hill. A thick rope, tied to one gnarled tree root, hung down into the pit.

He sat on the edge and dropped his cane into the pit. Grabbing the rope in both hands, he rolled onto his right hip, leaving him suspended halfway over the ledge.

"Don't let the rope break," he whispered under his breath.

He braced his feet against the pit wall as he lowered himself. It didn't help. The rope shifted, spinning him. He fought against it, but the rope shifted more, rotating him until his back hit the wall. He wrapped his legs around the rope to steady himself. His right shoulder smacked into the wall, almost dislodging him.

He gritted his teeth and kept descending, fighting the urge to let go and drop. If not for his left leg and hip, he would have. As it was, by the time he made it to the ground he felt like he'd wrestled a snake. His arms and legs felt like goo only held in place by his skin.

The dark tunnel awaited, but this time he didn't have his phone to light the way. Chastising himself for not looking for a flashlight back at the house, he retrieved his cane. He left the shotgun slung over his shoulder. He wanted it for protection, but in the darkness, he needed a hand free to feel his way forward.

The light from outside gave him enough to see a short distance in. It looked more or less like the tunnel he'd used to escape last night. But despite his eyes adjusting to the darkness, he didn't make it far before his vision became useless. He listened for any signs of someone down here with him. And he took light steps, not wanting to make the slightest noise that might give him away.

He imagined Arden posting men down here in the dark, waiting to ambush him. Or creating a trap for him to stumble upon. And it was still an old uranium mine. What were the odds the Community had taken the proper safety precautions with the place?

His instincts screamed to retreat. To give up this foolhardy hero act and let the FBI handle it. He was way out of his depth. That had been proven over and over since he'd come out here. But in the firefight that was sure to come, collateral damage was bound to happen.

And what would Arden do once the compound was about to fall?

Ignoring the tingles in his spine, Brice pressed forward, grateful to at least be out of the snow. The tunnel was still cold, but it wasn't as biting.

After what felt like an hour stumbling in the dark, he began worrying the FBI raid might happen while he was down here. Then, as he extended his left hand, the wall disappeared. He lurched forward. When he'd regained his balance, he reached back where he'd been a moment before and found the wall. He ran his hand forward to where the wall ended, turning a corner.

Now what? Should he follow the wall? He didn't think so. Turning left should take him away from the compound. Or would it? He wasn't sure if he trusted his sense of direction.

The three tunnels met in a four-way intersection. Based upon where he'd found the entrance to the tunnel, he would bet he stood in the left tunnel, where Helen had led him straight through the four-way before. He needed to go right. Unless this tunnel had more than one turn.

Biting his lip, he leaned against the wall. It was his anchor in the darkness. Once he moved past this point, it was all up to luck. What to do?

He had no other information to go on. Helen had told him there were three tunnels. He had to decide based upon the information at hand. It'd be foolish to make things more complex.

He shifted his cane to his left hand and eased off the wall, holding his breath. As he plodded forward, he reached out with his right hand for the opposite wall of the tunnel. He took another step forward. And another.

He was lost in a black abyss. He'd made a mistake and would never get to the compound. He'd die down here.

Shut up!

Three more steps. His right hand touched wood—a support beam. Exhaling in relief, he followed the wall until torchlight appeared ahead. A short distance farther, the dirt tunnel gave way to a stone wall. He'd reached the passageway under the sanctuary.

He'd made it!

Gunfire erupted overhead.

Chapter 42

Brice's cane clinked on the stone floor. A faint light flickered from a doorway up ahead on his right. The room hadn't been lit when he'd escaped with Helen. Were people hiding in there?

With the gun battle going on outside, anyone capable of fighting would most likely not be down here. Still, he pulled the shotgun from his shoulder and eased forward along the wall, allowing him to drop the cane and use the wall for support if he needed to defend himself. His heart kept rhythm with the sounds of assault rifles.

He took a deep breath and peeked inside the room. A single form lay prostrate on an altar in the middle of the room. A woman. Unconscious. Wrists tied to the sides of the altar above her head. Her dress, tossed haphazardly across her belly, left the rest of her exposed. Yellow and blue welts covered her legs and arms.

Was she alive or dead? He retrieved his cane and took a few hesitant steps in before he recognized Helen, her left eye swollen shut. Blood stained her chin and neck from a split lip.

"Helen. Helen, wake up." He leaned the shotgun and cane against the altar and maneuvered the simple gray dress to cover her torso and legs.

Her chest rose and fell, but she didn't stir. He worked at the knot on her closest wrist.

"Helen, it's me, Brice. Can you hear me?"

She didn't rouse as he freed her hand, so he placed it on her belly before shifting around the altar to free her other hand.

"Helen, I'm here. Wake up. Helen. Helen."

As he freed her other hand, she groaned. Her eyes bolted wide, flicking to him. She screamed and tried to roll away, her dress slipping off her. He grabbed her shoulder with his free hand to stop her from falling off the altar.

"It's okay, Helen. It's me, Brice. You're safe."

She batted at his hand, before recognizing him and collapsing onto her back. "Brice… you're here?" Tears appeared in her eyes, and he had to fight back his own.

To distract himself, he eyed the door. They were alone.

"What happened to you?" As he voiced the question, he guessed what she would say.

Instead, she sobbed, hands covering her face, her whole body shaking. He stood there, unsure how to comfort her or if he should even try. He should say something, but what would make any of this better? And touching even her shoulder felt inappropriate.

Then, seeming to register the sound of gunfire, her head shot up, eyes wide. "What is that? Are we under attack?"

"It's the FBI. They're raiding the place."

"You came back for me?" She asked, her tear-streaked expression both incredulous and grateful.

"Yes. And Patty. Mary, too, if I can convince her to escape."

She nodded and, seeming to notice her nakedness, sat up and grabbed her crumpled dress. She began to pull it on. "Yes. Go. Go get them."

"What about you?" He didn't want to leave her, though he averted his eyes. Balling his hands into fists, he berated himself for letting Arden and his men take her. He should've fought for her rather than watch them capture her. He'd failed her, same as Mary.

"I can't," she answered.

For a second, he feared she meant she wouldn't escape with him, that she was too afraid to risk Arden's wrath again. The bruises on her body showed how thoroughly they'd punished her.

"I'm in no shape to help you. I'll just slow you down," she clarified. "Get them and come back. I'll wait here."

Doubt tugged at him. A part of him feared if he left her now, he'd never see her again. Alive, anyway. But he couldn't ask her to risk the chaos outside to help him search for Patty and Mary. They were his responsibility, and he wouldn't abandon them, but they weren't hers. Yet if he left her here, wasn't he abandoning her? She might not remain safe down here.

"Go," she repeated, waving at him to leave. "I'm fine. Save your family."

He nodded, retrieving the shotgun and cane. His gut churned with guilt about leaving Helen behind, but Patty was helpless. If he didn't go get her, no one else would save her.

He sent up a silent prayer that Helen would be here when he returned. And followed it up with one that *he* would return, as he exited the room and struggled up the steps to the sanctuary. Only fear and adrenaline kept him moving forward.

*****

It took Brice throwing all his weight into the closed door to shove it open. Stumbling into the entrance hall, he found women and children hiding out. Several screamed, and a few of the women ushered young girls into the sanctuary, casting uneasy expressions at him.

"Who are you?" one woman demanded. Back straight, chin raised, she clenched her fists and shifted to a position that shielded the others. She was an older woman, with long auburn hair streaked with gray.

"I'm not here to hurt any of you." With the shotgun in his hands, none of them was likely to believe him. "I came to rescue Patty and Mary Smith. I can help any of you that want to get away, too."

The old woman's eyes narrowed. "I won't let you near my baby," she snarled, before risking a glance at the few women who hadn't hidden in the sanctuary. "Go. Get inside and close the door behind you. Lock it."

She turned back to him, arms extended, hands splayed so that they resembled claws. "You're the one who tried to steal my baby. Arden warned you not to come back."

She must be Mary's mother. He couldn't remember her name, but Owen had claimed she was close to the Community leader.

"I don't want any trouble, but the FBI is shutting this place down tonight." He pointed outside. "I'm here to make sure Mary and Patty stay safe. Protect them."

"The only one they need protection from is *you*." She lunged forward, but he raised the shotgun, dropping his cane as he did so to hold it upright. She halted a foot from the end of the barrel, glaring at him, looking like she'd love to rip his face off.

222

"Back away." He gestured at her with the shotgun. "I'm going for them, and there's nothing you can do about it. You get in that sanctuary with the others and lock yourself inside."

"No!"

"Lady," he began, taking a step forward, forcing her to retreat. "That baby and Mary are everything to me. I don't care if I have to shoot you, I'm going to find them and get them out of here. Take them somewhere safe. Now get inside."

He didn't know what he would do if she refused. He couldn't shoot her unless she forced him to defend himself, and she didn't possess a weapon he could see. But he also didn't have time to stand here arguing.

Fortunately, she couldn't read his thoughts on his face. Her own reddened, and she backed into the sanctuary. He didn't follow, afraid to walk without the help of the cane. She didn't need to know how vulnerable he was.

Her fists remained clenched, eyes trying to stab holes in him, as another fearful woman yanked the doors shut. He sighed in relief. He used the shotgun for support to kneel and retrieve the cane, before marching toward the front entrance.

He hadn't seen Mary among the women. After their encounter the previous night, he didn't think she'd hide out here. She'd likely seek shelter somewhere in her own house, safe from the others *within* the compound as much as from the FBI outside.

Easing the front door open, he glanced out. The snowfall had stopped, but the gunfire was louder. He wanted to cover his ears, retreat to Helen, and flee. A pounding filled his head. He cringed, hunching down, but forced himself to study the area. There was no one close by. The FBI hadn't breached the walls yet.

Was Jaxon outside risking his life, same as he was in here?

Brice pushed that worry aside and focused on getting to Patty. He didn't remember how Helen had led him here the previous night, but he knew the general direction.

He lurched down the steps, searching for anyone with a gun. Residents with rifles or shotguns raced through the snow along the perimeter, all too far away to harm him. Even so, he kept his head down as he crossed the now snow-covered square, struggling to push through to the nearest row of houses.

Through all the chaos from the attack, he sneaked past house after house, taking cover wherever he found it. When several men with assault rifles raced along the street ahead, he ducked behind the closest porch rails, clutching the shotgun.

Please don't let Jaxon or any of the other agents get shot.

He located Mary's house by the blue flowers on the front porch. This time, in the late afternoon daylight, the strobe light from the house across the way didn't flick on at his passage.

As he neared the front door, he caught crying from inside. He burst through the front door.

"Mary! Mary!" he shouted.

No one but the crying baby responded. Was Patty scared? Hurt?

"Mary?" Still no response, so he headed toward the first room on the left.

His first sight of Patty stopped him in his tracks. She lay in a crib, a chubby angel with little blonde wisps of hair, her face bright red from crying. She belted out her feelings like a singer at a song's climax. She wouldn't be one to trifle with someday, assuming she got the opportunity to grow into self-confidence, rather than having it beaten out of her every day of her childhood.

He stepped closer to the crib, setting the shotgun against it. How could he comfort her? One hand poked out of the top of a yellow swaddle wrapped around her. Beside her ear lay a little rubber pacifier with a pink elephant. He picked up the pacifier and held it close to her mouth. She opened wide and he inserted it. She clamped down, sucking, but squealed in displeasure a couple extra times.

"It's okay, Patty," he said. "It's me, your—" He paused, trying to figure out what he was to her. Mary had said he wasn't the father. He was nothing more than a stranger to her.

The realization twisted like a knife in his gut.

More gunfire reminded him he had greater things to worry about. Protecting her from harm remained his number one priority. After that, once he'd carried her to safety, he could figure out the rest.

"Mary! Mary, it's me, Brice. I came back for you and Patty."

Where had she gone? Was she hiding because of the gunfire? Why hadn't she taken Patty with her?

He picked Patty up, wrapping her in a blanket from the crib. He refused to leave her unguarded while he searched the house. She was so small, and looked so fragile in his hands, that he feared dropping her. The gunfire outside… he'd always known guns were dangerous, but as he stared down at her, the knowledge became visceral.

And terrifying.

He wanted to wrap her up, to be her shield in every sense of the word. He had to get her out of here. Every second they stayed, every gunshot, was a potential threat to her life, cycling up the odds against her.

He carried her down the hall to the next room. "Mary! Mary, you here?"

A simple bedroom held an unmade bed with pajamas discarded on the pillow. Dresser drawers hung open, clothes tucked half-hazard inside. Across the hall in the bathroom, towels lay strewn about while jars of lotions and makeup covered the counters.

"Mary, please, come with me," he pleaded. "I want to get you and Patty to safety."

The pacifier popped out of Patty's mouth and he dropped his cane to catch it. She cried. He slipped the pacifier back in her mouth. "It's okay, baby. It's okay." He rocked her side to side, balancing himself against the counter to keep from falling. After a moment she settled.

He retrieved his cane, which had hit the wall, slid into the doorframe, and stuck upright. Then he moved down the hall toward the kitchen.

"Mary!" She wasn't in the kitchen or the small pantry. "Mary!"

He didn't know where else to look. Where had she gone? Was she out fighting? Or had they tortured her the way they had Helen because of him? Was she also in need of rescue?

For several seconds he stood there, debating what to do. Wait a little longer and see if she returned? Search for her? He might search every house in the compound before he found her.

He should return to Helen. She might know where to find Mary, and she could take care of Patty while he searched.

"Mary, I'm getting Patty out of here," he said as he headed for the front door. "If you can hear me, please, come with me. I'll get you out of here, too."

He listened, hoping for some sign of her, but there was nothing but the battle outside. Time to go.

As he retraced his path to the sanctuary, gunmen appeared all around him, retreating, driven back from the walls, their backs to him as they exchanged fire with law enforcement. Still, their presence felt like a noose tightening around his and Patty's necks. He could accept the possibility of his own death, but he had to get Patty to safety.

He clutched her to his chest, covering as much of her as possible as he crossed the open field, fighting through the snow past his previous tracks, to the sanctuary.

"A little farther. Almost there."

He raced up the steps to the sanctuary with giddy relief. As he reached the front door, something struck the wall around his knees, sending shards in all directions. He ducked but didn't stop. He yanked the door open and rushed inside.

From behind, he heard, "Brice! You bastard!"

Chapter 43

Glass shattered. Through the now broken window Brice saw Mary racing through the snow, a handgun aimed at his head. He ducked out of the doorway to shield Patty.

A second gunshot was followed by a bullet, which struck the inner door of the sanctuary, eliciting screams from the women inside. Patty lost her pacifier and started bawling again, drowning out the women.

Gritting his teeth, Brice looked for somewhere to set Patty so that he could grab the shotgun and warn Mary off. Except that he didn't have it. Had he lost it during the run here? Then it hit him. He'd set it against the crib when he'd picked up Patty, and he'd left it there. They were defenseless.

"Brice, give me back my baby. I'll kill you!"

With Mary shooting first, he didn't try to reason with her. He charged toward the door leading underground. Even with the cane, his legs wobbled. He hurried through the still-open doorway and began stumbling down the stairs, praying he wouldn't miss a step, fall, and land on Patty.

As he lumbered down the last few steps, Helen emerged from the side room, a lit torch in hand. She'd found a jacket and boots. They hid her bruises, except for the ones to her face. The sight of them made him want to hand Arden and his men over to a torturer.

"We've got to go," he yelled.

Without responding, she turned and kept pace with him, lighting the way.

A third gunshot ricocheted off the floor behind him. "Brice, I want my baby," Mary screamed.

He jerked to the left, dropping the cane and narrowly avoiding a collision with a ducking Helen. She reached out a hand to make sure he was steady on his feet.

"Are you crazy?" he shouted over his shoulder. "You might kill the baby."

Without his cane, he focused on maintaining balance. He had to stay upright. They passed through the four-way, Helen leading him back through the same tunnel she'd chosen before.

"Wait. Arden locked the gate." He slowed to turn down a side tunnel. She grabbed his arm and dragged him forward without breaking stride.

"I have a key," she said. "Retrieved it while I waited for you."

"Oh, thank God."

Every strike of a foot on the ground sent jolts through his legs. His left side throbbed all the way to his rib cage. He couldn't maintain the pace much longer. If it came to it, he'd hand Patty off to Helen and try to slow Mary down. He doubted she would stop and listen before she shot him, but he'd figure out something to give Helen enough time to get Patty away.

They reached the end of the tunnel faster than he'd expected. Helen reached it first and went to work unlocking the gate. He stopped and glanced back. He couldn't spot Mary in the darkness, but he heard her steps closing in. She wasn't far.

"Let's go!"

Helen jerked the gate open and gestured for him to go first. Without hesitation, he darted through. Another gunshot rang out behind him, but he was outside.

The gate slammed shut.

He turned to find Helen on the other side.

"Helen, no! What are you doing?"

She had fallen into the gate, the torch dropping from her hands to the ground. She slid down the bars, one hand clapped to her neck. Blood spilled out between her fingers.

"Helen!" Bile rose in his throat. He stepped toward the gate. He had to save her life. Cover up the wound and stop the bleeding long enough to get someone from the FBI here to help.

Her eyes met his. She shook her head and tried to mouth 'Go' even as blood spilled down her lips and chin. She extended a finger through the bars, pointing. It was too late for her. He saw the truth in her eyes.

"I'm sorry," he said. Then he ran, tears rising that he had to blink back in order to see.

Though the snow had stopped falling, at least a foot of it covered the ground. He felt like he was running in slow motion as he tried to push through the snow. Mary would catch up with him in no time.

Shadows lengthened as the daylight faded. He didn't know which way to run. She'd see his tracks no matter which direction he took. There was no hiding. He only hoped to stay ahead of her and find help.

With any luck, having to drag Helen's body out of the way would slow Mary down. He felt a surge of guilt for wishing that Helen's death would help him, but he couldn't deny that he needed it.

His best bet for safety was to reach the FBI agents out front of the compound, so he followed roughly the same route he'd taken before. He had to stay far enough from the compound to not get shot by anyone inside, but close enough to reach the agents before Mary caught up with him.

The gunfire was more sporadic now. Would any agents remain out front, or had they all entered the compound?

Patty's crying had died down to mewling. Her skin had taken on a bluish hue. She hadn't quit breathing, but she was cold.

He hadn't wrapped her up for this weather. Furious with himself, he enveloped her with his arms, hoping his body heat would transfer to her. He'd give it all to her if he could.

"Hang on," he whispered. "A little farther."

He stumbled, but kept his feet, cursing himself for his weakness. If he fell now…if anything happened to her because of him….

Before he recognized the transition, the snow gave way to ice. He skidded, then his feet slipped out from under him. He landed on his right side, the pain making his vision pop as he slid over a sheet of ice. When he came to a stop, he lay several feet out onto a frozen pond. The one he'd come across earlier.

Panic flooded him. He lay there, rigid, unable to move.

He was twelve again. The ice cracked under him, dumping him into the icy water. Searing pain covered his body. He thrashed about, reaching for something to pull himself out. The overwhelming imperative to struggle to safety poured through him. Unable to breathe, he struggled to find a way through the ice.

Except that he could breathe. And his pain was different. He wasn't drowning beneath the ice. And he held something in his arms.

He opened his eyes. He was on top of the pond, not in it. A grown man with a baby girl to save. He struggled to his knees, sliding as he tried. Holding Patty made it more difficult. He had to get off the ice before it broke open. There'd be no one to save him this time. Or her.

A part of him screamed to drop her, that he couldn't save them both, and he had to get off this ice, whatever it took. He couldn't go under again.

He fought that urge—the weak, broken parts of himself—refusing to let Patty go. Somehow, he climbed to his feet as his instinct screamed to retreat. To get off the ice.

A gunshot from behind alerted him that Mary had found him. Retreating would only bring her closer.

He set out across the ice in a wobbly skate. He cradled Patty with his left arm, using his right to maintain balance. Right foot hit the ice, slid out. Left foot down, slid too far forward, forcing him to shift his weight to rebalance. Step. Weave. Step. Wobble. Step. Stumble.

He encircled Patty with his arms, terrified he was about to crash. A half step saved them from wiping out. He scanned the ice for weak points or cracks. Would it hold up under his weight?

A crack and plop rang out behind him. He sucked in air, his heart skipping a beat. They were a few steps from the far edge of the pond now. He exhaled in relief as he reached shore.

He turned and checked for Mary.

She wasn't there. Not on the ice. Not running around the pond. Just gone.

Was she circling around to get ahead of him?

A hand shot up out of a patch of open water in the middle of the pond. It scratched for a handhold, then sank back below the surface. She had fallen in, and there wasn't much time to save her.

He couldn't take Patty out on that ice to rescue Mary. Nor did he want to go back out on the ice where it had broken.

But he couldn't leave Mary to die. It was a horrific way to go. He might still be able to save mother and daughter.

He laid Patty in the snow, terrified of how cold she looked. She squirmed, still mewling. They needed to get out of the elements before they got frostbite. Or worse.

Sure that he was doing everything the wrong way, he rushed out onto the ice, even as his instinct screamed at him to stop, to go back. A quarter of the way out, he dropped to his hands and knees as he forced himself closer to the broken ice. His skin crawled. He shuddered, hoping it wouldn't break under him. Only an insane person would do this.

Forcing his fear down, he eased forward, arms outstretched to maintain balance. When he reached the edge of what he thought was safe, he lay flat on the ice. He plunged his hand into the water, inhaling from the cold, even through his glove. It took all his restraint not to yank his hand back, but he gritted his teeth and felt around. Deeper he reached, his arm going numb. Then he hit something thrashing. He gripped hard and yanked upward.

Mary's head surged out of the water. He had her jacket at the collar. An arm latched onto him, pulling. He panicked, afraid she'd pull him in with her. He lost his grip on her collar and she sank, but he seized her arm. As he pulled her head back out of the water, she coughed, arms waving wildly. He struggled to hold on.

He tried to grab her with his free hand, but missed. Again he reached, this time latching onto her hair. He tried to roll and pull her up, but only managed to shift her.

Her hands grasped his shoulders and for a second their eyes met. There was no terror in her eyes. Before he could think what else to do, she pushed off him. He lost his grip, and she sank beneath the ice.

"No!"

He stuck his hand into the water, but immediately yanked it back, his body taking over, his arm cradled to his chest. Lying there panting, he willed himself to try again, but his body refused to respond. His hand was so numb that he might've sworn it was gone.

That look in her eyes, right before she'd gone back under, had been resignation. Perhaps even a little relief.

He'd failed her again. How many times now? And this time his failure had cost Mary her life. He was pathetic. A poor excuse for a man.

Patty's cries pulled him from his mourning. He could still save her. Had to save her. But time was running out.

He rolled away from the broken ice, afraid to stand until he felt sure he was far enough from the hole. Then he crawled back to shore.

Patty had stopped crying. He surged to his feet and scooped her up. Holding her close, he felt life still in her, but it was faint. Was she weakening, or was he just growing numb from so much time out in the cold? Regardless, she needed warmth fast.

Unzipping the front of his coat, he pulled her inside and clutched her to his chest. He hoped his own body heat helped her. Not waiting to find out, he lumbered through the snow, angling for the compound. He didn't worry about who might see him at this point. He didn't care, not as long as he got Patty help.

Snow kicked up all around him. He felt like a shriveled self, buried deep within his body. Even his vision narrowed.

He pressed on. He didn't know how long, or even why anymore, just that he had to keep going.

"Brice."

Couldn't stop.

"Brice."

Ever.

"Brice!"

A face appeared before him, blocking his path. He slowed. His upper body toppled forward. As he did, an instinct shouted to twist, to land on his side, not his chest. He didn't feel the impact in the snow, but it covered up part of his face and one eye.

Someone hauled him to a sitting position. Jaxon knelt before him, arms outstretched. "I've got you, little brother. Don't worry."

Other men surrounded him. Hands lifted him up and carried him. Soon, he lay on the seat of a vehicle.

He blinked, feeling the pull of sleep. He wanted to fight it off. There was something he needed to do, but he didn't know what. And the pull was too strong.

Jaxon was here. Whatever it was, his brother would take care of it.

His eyes closed.

Chapter 44

Brice awoke to the sound of monitors. Cold pierced him to his bones. His head throbbed. He longed to sleep more. After lying there for a few minutes trying to drift off, he gave up. He opened his eyes and discovered a hospital room.

Again.

"You're making hospital stays a bad habit." Jaxon rose from a chair, then grabbed a cup with a straw and offered it to him.

Brice debated swatting the cup into his brother's fancy black button-down, but his thirst overpowered him. He raised his head and accepted the straw. The warm water needed ice, but it still soothed his throat and belly.

As he sipped, the memories hit him. Sneaking into the compound. Confronting Mary. Escaping with Helen. Arden and his men. Helen's battered body. Her death. Snow. Ice. Carrying Patty through it all, her little body turning blue from the cold.

"Patty… is she—"

"The baby? She's fine." Jaxon set aside the cup of water. "She's in infant care, but okay."

Brice slumped onto the pillow, relieved that he'd protected her. Whatever his injuries, he'd take the tradeoff.

A couple of nurses bustled into the room, shoving Jaxon out of the way. One studied a monitor behind Brice's head, while the other took the cup from Jaxon and added more water.

"How are you feeling, Mr. Dunn?" the first asked, her expression severe as if he'd done this to himself.

Had he? He remembered running through snow with Patty. Beyond that, details were a bit fuzzy.

"I'm alive."

She snorted. "You pulled through. That was a question for a bit."

He groaned. "Feels like it. My head aches. My left leg, too, from my hip to my ankle."

"How's your right hand?"

He raised it. Discolored purple and red splotches covered his hand. He moved his fingers. They all responded, if stiffly. "Okay, I think."

"You're lucky. There was some concern you'd lose it."

"It was coated in ice when we found you," Jaxon said. "We had to cut the glove off and wrap it well."

Mary. He'd failed her a final time. His eyes filled with tears.

"Mr. Dunn, are you okay?" The nurse asked, scrutinizing him. "Are you hurting? Do you need some pain relief?

He shook his head, then said, "Yes. It's not…." He turned to Jaxon. "Mary—"

"We didn't find her," his brother said. "She wasn't in the compound."

"She fell through the ice…" For a moment their eyes locked, before Brice closed his. The tears came.

"Is there anything you need?" the nurse asked.

"More water?" the second nurse offered.

He shook his head, wiping his eyes.

"We'll leave you alone for now, then. Dr. Andrews will check on you soon."

When they were alone, Jaxon placed a hand on Brice's forearm. "I'm sorry."

Brice didn't respond.

"I'll send agents out to recover the body."

Brice pulled his arm free from Jaxon and covered his eyes.

"I know this isn't the outcome you wanted, but you saved the baby," Jaxon said. "And the Community is no more. Most of the men are in custody, and those women who didn't resist are being helped."

"The leader? Arden?"

Jaxon grimaced. "He escaped out some underground tunnels. We brought in helicopter support, but so far, we haven't found him. Not sure who might've escaped with him."

Brice's gut clenched. This was all wrong. He shook his head. Arden couldn't be free. Not after everything he'd done. "Find him. The things he did to Mary, Helen, the other women in that place…he can't go free."

Jaxon held up a calming hand. "We'll get him. The evidence collection team is working the compound. They'll find something so we can track him down."

"You don't understand—"

"We'll get him." Jaxon squeezed the bed rails. "In the meantime, we've shut down the Community. Rescued a couple dozen women and children. With the evidence we've collected, we can free others in Alabama and likely additional locations across the country. One thing that will help us identify all the victims is the Community inserted GPS chips in all their women. Tracked them like cattle."

Brice's eyes widened in disbelief. "That…that's how they always found her."

"What?" Jaxon cocked his head.

A familiar burn ignited inside Brice. "Mary. She tried to run, many times, but they always found her. That's why she…." His chest filled up with pressure. "Why she…."

Brice found himself hoping that Owen and his mob would find Arden before the FBI could catch him. Given how they had harassed him for his *suspected* involvement, what more would they do to the actual cult leader?

But it was all too late for Mary. And Helen. They had deserved better.

Guilt washed through him once more at the thought of Helen. He'd gotten her killed to save the baby. If only he'd refused her help, she might still be alive. Though if he hadn't accepted, maybe it would be Patty who wouldn't be.

"What happens to Patty?" Brice asked. She would never have a chip inserted in her, or if the Community had already done so, he'd have it removed and destroyed. She would never suffer like her mother.

"The doctors are confident she'll recover fine. Her injuries were remarkably minor."

"But her mother is dead." Brice shook his head. "What happens to her?"

"She's not yours?"

He wanted to say yes. Who would argue? It would be the easiest way to protect her. Yet despite his good intentions, he didn't want their relationship built upon a lie. "No."

"I'm not sure, then."

Would he be able to adopt her? He didn't know the father, but he suspected it was someone from the Community, either dead or in custody. Regardless, Patty would be better off without her father.

It was up to him to step up. Brice didn't know the process for adoption, but no one would fight harder for her than he would.

Chapter 45

Jaxon's cell phone rang. Brice wondered if she would pick up. If she answered, how would he start the conversation? What would he say to her? Part of him hoped she wouldn't answer and he could leave a voicemail.

Was he in over his head, as Jaxon insisted? Should he let Patty go to a foster family, with guardians better equipped to raise her? The thought of letting her go, of never seeing her again, made him want to roll over and never get up from this hospital bed.

"Hello?" the familiar voice answered.

"Dora, it's Brice."

"Brice, how are you?" Dora exclaimed. "I've been so worried."

"Doing okay," he said, thrilled to hear the excitement in her voice. "I'm recovering in a hospital, but they're discharging me a little later today."

"A hospital?" Her voice rose an octave. "What happened?"

"It's a long story. I'll tell you later. Listen—" He paused. It was difficult to take this next step. "You're a lawyer, right? You work with kids who need help?"

"Yes, that's right."

It had been Lisa, Nate's office manager, who'd remembered her specialty. That revelation had given him the first glimmer of genuine hope.

"There's a baby, a little girl. She has no one. Her mother died." His voice caught a little. He knew Mary was dead. The FBI had recovered her body. Still, voicing it out loud stung. "She has no identified father. She's alone."

"Poor baby! What else can you tell me about her?" Dora asked.

"Her name's Patty." Brice started off small, with details about her, and expanded until he'd shared everything about his last month, and even what he knew prior to that.

Dora listened, only interjecting here and there with concerns for his well-being. Each time, he reassured her that his injuries weren't bad, that he would recover fine.

Jaxon stopped by once to check on him, but Brice waved him away.

After telling Dora everything, he found it easier to follow up with his request. "I want to make sure Patty never suffers the way Mary did. The way others do. I want to adopt her, and I need a lawyer. Will you help me?"

He wanted to ask her for more than that, knew he needed more help, but he wasn't ready to say it.

"Yes! Absolutely!" Dora launched into details about the process for a child with no parent or guardian, the steps they'd have to go through, the paperwork he'd need to sign.

He leaned back in the hospital bed, content to listen to her rattle off more than he'd ever expected to need to know about becoming a guardian for a child.

Of course, there was much more than the legal aspect to all of this. He had his recovery ahead of him. Therapy. And he didn't know a thing about parenting a child.

Nor could he do it alone, not with the anger that still simmered, flaring up without warning. He needed help, but he would get it. Whatever it took. He'd make sure that Patty never ended up in a situation like her mother's. She would have a better life than that.

He hoped Dora would help him build it.

Acknowledgments

I hope you enjoyed the Community. Thank you for giving it a shot! It was a lot of hard work, and I received invaluable feedback from a lot of people to get to this point.

Thank you to Andrew and Emily Wilson, Troy Farsoun, Kay Glover, Kirk Edwards, and Lisa Prince for their feedback on many technical details within the story. Thank you to Shirley Garrett for her invaluable insights on how to improve the quality of the writing. Thank you to my HLA writer's group for their great critiques at our meetings. Thanks to Lisa Prince again for editing the novel.

I'd like to thank 100covers for the terrific cover for the novel. And thank you to thank Dana Austin, Lee Judge, and Mel Howard for their feedback on drafts of the cover to get it just right.

About the Author:

Daniel Austin is a suspense and crime fiction author who lives in Huntsville, Alabama. Following the release of The Community, I will be starting on an FBI crime fiction series with Brice's brother Jaxon Dunn as the main character.

If you would like to learn more about the novels, visit:
Facebook Author Page:
https://www.facebook.com/DanielAustinAuthor

Thank you for reading my book! If you enjoyed it, please consider leaving a review wherever you purchased the book, or on your favorite book review site. Even just a few words would help others decide if the book is right for them.

Best regards and thank you in advance!

www.ingramcontent.com/pod-product-compliance
Lightning Source LLC
Chambersburg PA
CBHW070456200726
48293CB00007B/2236